DON'T STOP THE MUSIC

Martin,

Peace, Love & Tie-Dye.

Enjoy!

Written by

JOHN MICHAEL MCCARTY

Inspired by true events in celebration of the 50th anniversary of the Summer of Love.

J. M. McCarty

For more information regarding John McCarty's novels or to subscribe to his free online monthly newsletter, visit **http://www.johnmccarty.org**.

Cover design by Ron Friedland.

ISBN: 154853384X
ISBN 13: 9781548533847

"McCarty, with iconic landmarks in this historical fiction, keeps you hopping from The City to The River and asides."

Russian River Historical Society

"The author shapes a variety of plot lines, including memories of the Summer of Love and The Grateful Dead concert in Rio Nido. Read it for the history, save it for posterity."

Sonoma County Historical Society

"The author offers a fascinating peek into the minds and activities from another time period."

Windsor Times

"John McCarty writes with a descriptive flair that is easy on the eyes and tickles the nostalgic bone."

Russian River Times

"Great characters live in John McCarty's *Don't Stop the Music.* A must read."

Sonoma County Gazette

"The author can make the most jumbled scene seem like the norm along the Russian River, which, in fact, it often has been and often is. Fans of John McCarty will not be disappointed."

Sonoma West Times & News

"The author gives us characters and plots that seem beyond the pale but are actually rooted in history. A delightful read."

The Upbeat Times

The author wishes to express his gratitude to the following individuals and organizations: Diane Barth, Dave Camarillo, Ron Friedland, Pat Green, Jennings family, Bob Jones, Glen Leone, Patricia Morrison, John Schubert, California Historical Society, San Francisco Museum and Historical Society, Sonoma County Historical Society, Russian River Historical Society, Friends of Rio Nido.

"Turn on, tune in, drop out."
Timothy Leary

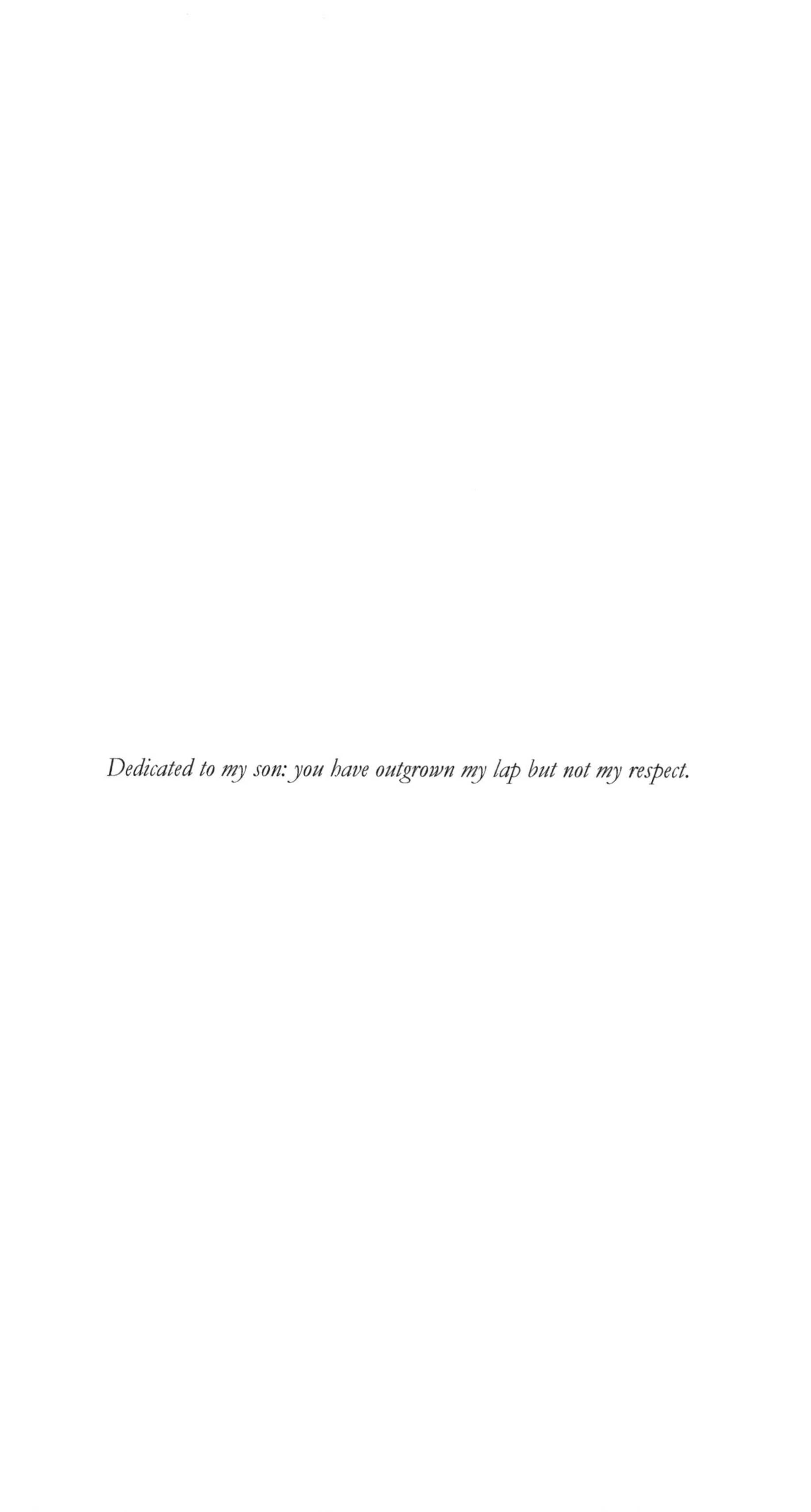

Dedicated to my son: you have outgrown my lap but not my respect.

Chapter 1

Jonah Berkowitz and Otis Wright pushed their way through the mob toward the Oakland Induction Center. Ten thousand protestors lined the streets. Police in riot gear marched five abreast, nightsticks at the ready. Garbage can lids clashed to the beat of battle as voices spilled over each other.

Words came to Otis from a six-wheel flatbed. "Hey, brother, you in the hat."

Otis was as black as the night with a tall, paper-thin physique. He peered over the canopy of heads, scanning the area.

"Over here," the stranger said from beneath a Peace and Freedom banner.

"Me?" Otis asked.

"Yeah, you, brother," the stranger said. "Don't do it. Walk away."

Otis raised his fist in a black salute, walking with the swagger of downtown funk. He turned sideways to his buddy and said, "Nice of 'em to say hello, don't you think?"

"Regular sweethearts," Jonah said in a sarcastic tone. A scar over his left eyebrow provided a sense of balance to his fair hair and baby blues.

"Good to see blacks and whites on the same side for a change," Otis said.

"Nothing like a war to bring people together."

A teenager lit a draft card on fire, raising it for all to see. Hundreds chanted anti-Vietnam slogans. Police cuffed several of the dissidents and dragged them off.

A photographer, wearing a CHRONICLE logo on the front of his windbreaker, was taking shots of the scene when Jonah tripped into him. "Sorry," Jonah said. "You okay?" and he placed his hand on the man's arm in apology.

"Fine. I'm fine," the photographer said as he tried to untangle himself from the stranger's hold.

"Positive?" Jonah asked with another pat as if to make sure that the guy was all right.

"Yes, yes," the photographer said in a hurry, anxious to get back to work.

"Do you know Hal Butler?" Jonah said as he continued to rub up against the guy within the crowded confines.

"Ah, don't think so."

"He writes a music column for the *San Francisco Chronicle*," Jonah said.

"Listen, buddy, I'd love to chat but…"

"Big ugly guy," Jonah persisted. "Has the kind of mug only a mutant could love." He repeated the man's name. "Hal Butler. I send him concert reviews from time to time."

"There's a riot ready to breakout here," the photographer said as he hiked up his shoulders with the obvious.

"Right…Well, good luck with those shots." Jonah smoothed out the man's jacket one last time before meandering away.

"Pathetic," Otis said to Jonah as they distanced themselves from the photographer.

"Just a little rusty is all," Jonah said.

"Rusty?" Otis retorted. "Shit, you slower than mud."

"The guy wouldn't stand still," Jonah said as a defense.

"What, you want him to pose for you?"

With a stare as cold as the cavernous structure he was guarding, an MP opened the door for Jonah and Otis before pointing with his baton at a demarcation underfoot. "Follow the white line."

At a manned station, another collected their valuables. Otis placed a money clip and a diamond stickpin into a manila envelope. Jonah repeated the process depositing a photo lens as well as three rolls of Kodak film.

Otis surveyed Jonah's haul. "Like I said, slow as mud."

"The day has just begun," Jonah answered.

The soldier told the pair to hold onto their I.D and step to the next stall. At a kiosk Jonah started to strip while Otis took his time, showing off.

"Can't nobody wear this better than me," Otis said as he removed his feathered fedora from atop his Afro.

"You look like a prancing peacock," Jonah said.

Otis eased off his burgundy cloak and matching pants. "These soldier boys never put eyes on a specimen such as this," Otis said as he waved a hand over his spindly, six-foot-three frame. "God's honest truth. It prob'ly scare the bejesus outta 'em."

"Not enough meat on those bones to satisfy a cockroach," Jonah said while standing there in his Jockey's and socks, waiting for the show to end. "You about through here, slick?"

"Wanna give these Marines an idea of what the future holds."

"Let 1967 be the year they honor you with a front row seat in 'Nam."

"Prob'ly only way you honkies find Charlie."

"Make sure you say hello to him for me."

"What you talkin' 'bout? You're goin', right?"

They had been inseparable, roaming the Fillmore and Haight-Ashbury Districts of San Francisco since they were old enough to hold their own. Their birth dates fell just hours apart on June 10, 1949. They had made a pact early on—*you and me, the world on its knee.* If they stuck together, they could conquer all. While the cliché was the stuff of innocence, it continued to beat to a steady rhythm as they entered adulthood.

The boys honored their eighteenth birthday by lighting up a reefer in a piss-soaked alley. It was a fitting arena at the time, both knowing that the good old U.S.A. would soon own their asses.

Jonah wondered if his tomorrow would be as bleak as that pungent alley or this place they call Oaktown, the third weirdest city in the nation behind Bezerkley and Frisco. Jonah's connection to Oaktown was secondhand as his employer resided here. Sonny Barger was the founding father of the Hells Angels, rebels known for their Harleys and Box Chevys, sipping whiskey and blowing purple clouds while running drugs. The game wasn't for sissies. Turf wars had started, the kill number piling up.

Viet-friggin'-nam? Jonah thought. It's got nothing over the Bay Area. Can eliminate just as many here. Why go all the way across the globe just to put a hole in somebody?

"Jonah?" Otis said from behind.

No response.

"Jonah, what you doin', dude?" Otis warned as he spied an MP staring them down. "The man's got you in his sights. He'll spoon you till mornin' light if you don't get a move on."

"Hey, Ebony and Ivory," the MP said to the duo, "move those cheeks on down the line."

"Didn't think you noticed," Jonah said as he came around.

"What?" the MP said with a scowl.

"My cheeks," Jonah repeated to the MP, "I didn't think you noticed."

"One of these days that smart-mouth of yours will be all mine, sonny," the MP said.

"Did you have a specific date in mind?" Jonah said. "I'd like to check my social calendar first."

"Man here is only doing his job," Otis said to his friend before turning back to the MP. "Ain't that right, general? Right as pain. Or rain. I get confused. Sometimes I can't even..."

"Look at these stripes," the MP interrupted as he pointed to the chevron insignia on his shoulder. "Do these look like brass bars to you, boy?"

"How should I know?" Otis said.

Jonah stepped in between the two, saying to the MP, "I'll tell you what you do have. You got my daddy's looks, and he isn't any blue-plate special, if you catch my drift."

A curvy woman in her pressed, white uniform called for the next batch to come forward. Jonah sauntered forward but not before nodding goodbye to the MP with an icy look.

"Which arm?" the nurse said, boredom in her delivery.

"Pardon?"

Not there for chitchat, she poked his arm with an air gun. A high-pressure jet of liquid penetrated his skin.

"What the hell?" Jonah said as he crunched up his face. He turned to register another complaint when a second nurse gave him a shot on his other arm. His sudden movement caused the air gun to tear a half-inch gap across his bicep. Blood oozed from the opening.

Jonah held back a yelp, wondering where the next blow would come from. With the assembly line backing up, the first nurse snatched the clipboard from him and initialed the forms.

"Don't you like me anymore?" Jonah said to her as he massaged his bicep.

From his blindside, the second nurse shot him again.

Fog washed over the Oakland Induction Center enveloping the building in gloom. Inside, shadows shifted under hanging bulbs.

The boys returned to the kiosk, put on their clothes and went to the last station where they received their wallets, car keys and other valuables.

"Gotta say," Otis interjected, "these dudes look sharp in their uniforms. Particularly like the ones with all the medals and doodads. Think I might want to get me some of that."

"The thing is, they earned those decorations in combat. I don't think they give them out as party favors."

"The brother would look pretty with all that lettuce on him. Catch some fine hooch, that's for sure." Otis spied Jonah's wandering look and said, "Hey, you listenin' to these pearls of wisdom I'm dishin' out here?"

Jonah's contemplation drifted to a desk-jockey. The woman was distracted with the flirtations of a younger co-worker. With her back turned to the line of exiting inductees, she accepted Otis's clipboard with her blind touch.

A scheme began to take shape inside Jonah's head. Without thinking it through to its inevitable conclusion, he replaced his physical exam papers with blank forms, passed the file to the clerk and skipped thru the checkout station.

"Whaddya wanna do now, soldier boy?" Otis said as the duo walked along the sidewalk. "Has a nice ring to it, don't it? *Soldier boy*. Could get used to that."

He spotted a Marine strutting in front of a string of young men waiting at the nearby train platform. Otis slapped his buddy on the chest to get his attention causing a ream of paper to escape from under Jonah's clothing.

"What's that?" Otis asked as he motioned to the scattered documents.

Jonah lunged at the forms as a breeze kicked up. "Shut your pie-hole and help."

Otis rattled on as he lent a hand, asking why his friend was in such a hurry to go to jail. "You best return these papers ASAP," Otis said, scooping up forms.

Jonah rushed to grab an airborne document when the Marine intercepted it.

"Thank you, sir," Jonah said as he snatched the form away. "Made a copy of my induction file," he said with a lie. "I plan on framing it...Proudest day of my life."

The officer shook his head and started to return to his duties when he felt a tug on his sleeve...and another.

"Excuse me, sir," Jonah said, "but my friend was wondering what you have to do to get those medals," and he fingered the decorations on the man's uniform.

"Son," the Marine said, "touch me again and you'll have one less tool to wipe your ass with. Understand?"

"Yes, sir," Jonah said. "Got it. You bet. No misunderstanding here. No, sir."

"Save it," the Marine said and walked away.

"What you tryin' to do?" Otis said to Jonah.

"Just making polite conversation."

"You on some kind of suicide mission?" Otis asked as the pair headed past a train depot. "Eager to spend some time in lockup, is that it?"

"What?" Jonah asked, his attention elsewhere.

"Why you wanna steal your file from those nice folks back at the Induction Center anyway?"

"Thought I'd buy myself a little time."

"What you want with time?" Otis asked. "Not like you can save it for a rainy day."

"Maybe, maybe not," Jonah said.

Otis's vision veered back toward the train depot where the Marine from earlier was chatting with a civilian. "The general shook that guy's hand. Military can't be all bad, not with that attitude."

Jonah studied the scene as the young man followed the Marine to a transport. "Your general probably just invited that kid to a four-year stint in the Marines."

"Thought that the all-you-can-be-boys were strictly volunteers."

"Ninety percent are. Ten percent are draftees," Jonah said. "Maybe you'll be one of the lucky ones."

"Yeah?" Otis said with a hopeful look.

"I can't think of a single reason why the Marines wouldn't want a man of your caliber."

"Can't argue with you there."

"Where else are they going to find a skinny-ass black man who can talk a blue streak all night long. Maybe you'll be their secret weapon—bore Charlie to death." Before Otis could counter, Jonah eyed the law. "We should split."

Thousands of protestors pressed against a wall of police. Banners reading STUDENTS FOR A DEMOCRATIC SOCIETY bobbed up and down to the rhythm of angry voices.

"Hey, hey, LBJ, how many kids have you killed today?
Hey, hey, LBJ, how many kids have you killed today?"

"Who's this LBJ guy?" Otis asked.

"Don't you read the newspapers?" Jonah asked, as he opened the driver-side door to his truck.

"Got no time, been busy helpin' momma at the pharmacy."

"Nice way to say drug outlet."

"Look who's talkin'," Otis said. "You be workin' for the Hells Angels in case you forgot."

"One, two, three, four—we don't want your fucking war!
One, two, three, four—we don't want your fucking war!"

"White boys seem upset," Otis said as he peered out the passenger window.

"Nothing but some U.C. Berkeley brats mouthing off on their daddy's dime," Jonah said.

Otis took in the turmoil behind them. The cops had formed a line between the crowd and a cluster of inductees. A sheriff's transport blared a warning as it approached the mass.

"Not good," Otis said. "Boys in blue don't take shit. Prob'ly gonna take those college punks to Santa Rita Prison, give 'em some pointers on their communication skills."

"Maybe they'll get acquainted with some of your relatives while they're there."

"Why you always want to put a negative spin on things? Not cool, dude."

Jonah turned on the ignition to let the motor warm up while he plucked an object from the pocket of his Pendleton. "Here," and he handed Otis a medal. "Consider it an early Valentine's Day present."

Otis widened his smile as he accepted the gift and placed it over his heart, admiring it. "Don't know what to say. Thanks, dude."

"Give us a kiss." Jonah leaned across the seat and puckered up.

Otis slapped the gesture away. "Ain't funny."

"Everything all right here?" an MP asked as he glanced inside the truck.

"Just fine, yes, sir," Otis said as he slid the medal under his pants.

"Move this crate outta here," the MP said as he slapped the door panel.

Jonah put the truck into gear and motored toward the exit where another cluster had gathered, but these protestors were not your preppy-types. Longhairs paraded in polyester bell-bottoms and love beads.

One held up his fingers in a peace sign as he walked toward the vehicle. "Hey, man," the hippie said to the passengers, "don't get sucked in by Uncle Sam. Forty-two thousand drafted a month, for what?"

"Well, gotta be a good reason, right?" Otis retorted. "For sendin' all those boys is what I'm tryin' to say. Don't want those gooks running the show over there. Know what I mean?"

"You're wrong, man," the hippie said. "Does killing twenty-five thousand civilians, women and children each and every goddamn year sound right to you? Does it, man?"

"Gotta do what you gotta do," Otis said.

The hippie held up a mustard-colored leaflet, saying, "Go to thy place and yee shall find salvation," the longhair said in a biblical voice before passing the flyer to Jonah.

He tossed the leaflet to the floor where it fell amidst a mound of Twinkie wrappers, an empty Slurpee cup and a half-eaten burger. "Sorry," Jonah said to the hippie, "but we're going to have to end this party. It's been swell," and he slid the vehicle back into gear.

A young girl perhaps fourteen, wearing granny glasses and a red Dashiki, held up a sign at the exit—MAKE LOVE NOT WAR.

"The streets will eat her alive," Otis said to Jonah as the truck cruised past and onto the main road.

"Not like us, right?" Otis said. "We *is* the streets. Born from, raised from. No denying."

Otis spotted the discarded meal on the floor and picked it up, saying, "What, you don't like the new Big-Mac? Feelin' like you're slummin' it? Burger not good enough for you, that it?"

"We come from the same neighborhood, jerkwad."

"Love...love...love the sauce," Otis said as he bit into the cold slab of meat. He began to wipe his mouth with a crumbled paper when its print caught his attention.

"What's this?" Otis said in garbled tone as fragments of food spilled from his lips.

Jonah ignored the rambling and felt for the military file tucked under his Pendleton as if to make sure that some mysterious specter hadn't pilfered it.

"You heard of Morningstar Ranch?" Otis asked as he read the flyer. "Some place up north accordin' to this…near Occidental." Otis held it closer to read a passage: "'…overflowing with tranquility and harmony where no one is refused entrance.' Sounds lame if you ask me."

"Let me see that," Jonah said. His vision shifted from the leaflet to the road and back again. Thoughts ran amuck inside his head as he stared out the window. With robotic-like motions, he tucked the mustard-colored flyer into his shirt pocket.

"You want some of this?" Otis asked as he offered a bite of the Big-Mac.

No response.

"Anyone home?" Otis said, spying the glazed look aboard Jonah.

No response.

"Hey, dude, where you at?"

Chapter 2

Sean Maloney was a product of the Mission District in San Francisco. He followed in the footsteps of his father and his father's father before him, becoming a policeman in the service of his community. That community had a narrow definition, which was fine with Sean since the Irish held a strong chokehold on the City. James McGinnis ran the powerful Redevelopment Agency, Thomas Cahill was chief of police while Jack Shelley occupied the mayor's office. All was as it should be. Until last year.

In March of 1966, law enforcement officials arrested 167 dissidents for blocking the entrance to the Sheraton Palace Hotel while picketing it for failure to hire blacks. The next month 180 civil rights demonstrators were hauled downtown for illegal sit-ins at Wessman Lincoln-Mercury and Cadillac dealerships along Van Ness Avenue's auto row. In August Charles Sullivan, Fillmore District's torchbearer, was shot dead. The case remained unsolved. Tensions spilled over. A three-day riot broke out. The National Guard was brought in to restore order, an order that was once defined by distinct boundaries where everyone stayed within their own piece of dirt.

Chief Cahill demoted Officer Maloney for using excessive force during the melee and bumped him down from lieutenant to sergeant. A corresponding reduction in medical and other benefits followed. Maloney thought he was being made a scapegoat to appease the cries of the community. His wife insisted that despite his reduced income, he should continue to pay the private tuition of their five children. The oldest was attending St. Ignatius

College Preparatory, which alone was setting Sergeant Maloney back some 550 clams a year. To make matters worse, Captain Cahill refused his transfer request from the Fillmore District. Word got around the precinct for everyone to get back in line.

⅄

A beat cop strolled north along Fillmore Street twirling his baton, whistling a tune. It was collections day.

Marion Sullivan's place posed as a diner by day and a dance club by night serving the best baby back ribs and jazz in the district. That wasn't difficult since it was only one of three such joints remaining, the Redevelopment Agency bulldozing the others.

In the backroom, John Handy took a break from rehearsal. He leaned forward with his eyes half shut to visualize the notes that streamed through his head. His brain was a receptacle for sound, still soaking up the trade at age thirty-four.

With the explosion of daylight from the doorway, Handy shielded his eyes and ordered the intruder to shut the door.

"Not likely," the visitor said.

The musicians squinted to better identify the inky cutout. The broad shoulders and baritone voice told all who was present.

"My mistake, officer," Handy said.

"Too bad about Coltrane," Sergeant Maloney said with a smirk.

Handy heard the insincerity in the cop's voice and wanted to challenge him. The musician remembered with fondness how he and Trane had played the circuit in New York, how they had reunited during the fifties and early sixties to play these backrooms of "Harlem West", as the Fillmore District came to be known. The sting of John Coltrane's death last month was still fresh.

Handy fell quiet, aware of what this Irishman was capable of.

"Why don't I leave you to your jungle music," Maloney said before tapping the brim of his hat in farewell.

There would be no thumping of heads today. No reason to ruin the good mood. He returned to the diner where the proprietor asked if everything was all right.

"Got to teach your boys a few manners is all," Maloney said.

"Is that what you came for," Marion Sullivan said, "to give a sermon on social behavior?"

Late on his round, Sergeant Maloney ignored the dig and said, "Let's have it."

Marion Sullivan reached under the register and handed over an envelope. Maloney counted the bills inside before nodding his approval.

"That's a nice little boy," Maloney said as he deposited the loot into a satchel.

Sullivan needed to keep open his illegal after-hours club in order to pay the inflated rent. When your landlord uses the city's "finest" to personally collect the fee, what choice did you have? It was a vicious circle—money came in, money went out. Very little remained in the pockets of business owners.

Maloney caught Sullivan's irreverent posturing, latched onto his collar and pulled him closer. "I know who killed your brother." Without waiting for a response, the sergeant released the proprietor and left.

Marion Sullivan stared at the exit long after the man in blue had left. Marion's brother, Charles, was beloved by all. He was the neighborhood's unofficial mayor as well as the top black music producer on the West Coast, the one who put the Harlem into the Fillmore.

Sergeant Maloney headed north to the New Chicago Barbershop at the corner of Ellis. This was one of the few places that had survived the wreaking ball of James McGinnis and his Redevelopment Agency.

"What you want now?" the barber said.

"End of the month," Maloney said.

"Already?" the barber said before sifting through the cash drawer with his wrinkled fingers. "You one blood thirsty mofo, ain't you?"

"Don't have all day."

The barber continued to scoop up twenties. "And that damn high-rise your friends downtown are fixing to build. Who can afford that?" and he handed over a hundred dollars. "Now, go on, get out of my shop."

In a strange way, Maloney admired the guy. He had gumption. More than he could say for the rest of the block. The policeman exited to the sidewalk where he eyed the activity from across the street. Men in black berets and leather jackets unloaded freight from a moving van into an empty storefront.

"Thought I closed that place last year," Maloney said to no one.

A familiar voice from behind came to him. "Black Panthers is shopping around, fixing to establish a West Bay chapter here in the City."

"Who?" Maloney asked the barber.

"Black Panthers. Started up in Oakland last year."

"They look like wannabes," Maloney said, dismissing the military-like attire with a grunt.

"They're going to hang your lily-white butt out to dry." The barber retreated inside, enjoying a good laugh.

The sergeant continued on his rounds, making his regular stops at the Booker T. Washington Hotel, the Birdcage Tavern, and Lee's Liquor Store until coming to a row of fallen Victorians. Some two thousand of the painted ladies had been demolished within the last seven years in the name of progress. The remains lay scattered in untidy heaps, leaving the area in squalor.

On the front steps of a surviving Queen Anne, a family of six waited as Maloney advanced toward them. "You folks can't loiter here," the policeman said.

"But it's our shift for the room," said a Negro with a gentle face. "Won't be but a few minutes. Two o'clock is coming up fast," and he showed the face of his wristwatch. "See."

"You getting smart with me?" Maloney said as he raised his baton. "Talk to me like that again, and you'll find yourself out in the cold for good, understand?"

"Yes, sir," and the Negro handed over his share of the rent before shepherding his family up the steps as another horde exited.

The shuffling of different families into the same apartment was not unusual. This particular unit provided shelter for four households, each taking different time slots to sleep indoors. Four families meant four times the rental fee, which was fine by the absentee landlord. To add misery to the disorder, the single room rental had no bathroom.

Maloney collected the usual fee from the exiting batch and warned them that they better not piss in the streets. "Use the toilets at the gas station…or else," the sergeant said.

Nearby in abandoned lots, kids played amidst the concrete rubble to see who could capture the biggest rodent. At the corner of O'Farrell, a man in a cropped Afro and aviator glasses scanned his territory.

Allan Theodore McCollum the Third, a.k.a. Papa Al, was an East Bay thug who had a reputation for getting things done. This was viewed as favorable when he applied for the community liaison position with the S.F. Redevelopment Agency. It also didn't hurt that he owned ten percent of the Fillmore.

"You want to make the exchange here?" Maloney asked, showing the satchel of cash to Papa Al.

Papa Al lowered it, looked around. "Not here. At the usual place, down at Berkowitz's."

"Fine by me."

"I thought that I would take advantage of my weekly trek across the bay to handle another matter," Papa Al said, letting the words hang in the air.

"Yeah?"

Papa Al motioned to a five-unit complex. "The people in 4D are three months lax on their rent."

"Well, they're never home when I come to..,"

"I don't entertain excuses," Papa Al interrupted. "I *entertain* business. Understand?"

"Yeah, but…,"

Papa Al held up a finger to his lips. "Quiet, my friend. Time is wasting away. Tick-tock, tick-tock."

Maloney laughed in his face, thinking the East Bay mobster was nothing more than a walking cliché. "Seriously, can't you come up with a better routine?"

"To live without cooperation shrivels the soul. We are all partners here. As a sign of my appreciation I will place a bonus on top of your usual cut."

"Well, that's more like it," Maloney said.

"I simply ask that you to do this one additional favor."

Maloney raised the palms of his hands. "What?"

"Remove the door to 4D."

"I don't understand."

"Yours is not to ask why."

With the promise of extra money for his kids' schooling, Maloney did as requested. It didn't take more than twenty minutes for the word to spread. Vultures descended upon the unsecured apartment in earnest, carting away furniture, TV's, clothes, food and a refrigerator.

A woman rushed out, clutching onto the arm of a would-be thief. The cop batted her to the ground after which she rose, crying she had nowhere else to take her babies, promising to have the rent by the end of the week. Mary Grace Davis was a good woman, recently widowed, with three children ranging in age from six months to eight years old.

Maloney brushed her aside. The sergeant understood the message that Papa Al was sending. Pay on time or else. The trick was to maintain just enough life in the neighborhood to fill the collection bag each month.

⅄

Berkowitz Pawnshop was centrally located to attract a diversified clientele. It was one block from the Geary Expressway with the Jewish and Japanese communities on the north side. A mere four blocks further was California Street where the wealthy of San Francisco planted themselves.

Jonah took a break from the front counter and picked a vinyl from its album jacket. He blew off the thirty-three before taking a closer look at the cover. At its center, a musician wore a top hat with a fireball framing him. Gold and blue encircled five other members of the band. Jonah squinted as he bent forward to read an encrypted phrase, the words shaped as if from some Egyptian tome: *In the land of the dark, the ship of the sun is driven by the Grateful Dead.* It was the group's first album, recorded just the spring before. The band didn't receive much airtime outside of San Francisco, but Jonah remained enamored with its fusion of psychedelic, blues and rock.

A diamond needle found a groove. "Beat It On Down the Line" pushed thru the speakers smoothing out the edges of his day. The music took him to a different place, a place where greed and hate didn't exist.

He let Jerry Garcia fill the background while he read the front page of the *San Francisco Chronicle.* In a photo a man was pictured speaking into a megaphone aboard a flatbed. The caption underneath read: "10,000 Protestors March Against the Draft". The article went on to say how the Peace and Freedom Party as well as the Students for a Democratic Society (SDS) had joined forces to demonstrate against the Oakland Induction Center. The police responded with nightsticks injuring twenty while arresting another ninety-seven who were hauled off to Santa Rita Prison.

Jonah lowered the newspaper when the front door swung open against a hanging bell. A Negro sauntered in wearing a burgundy cloak.

"What you think?" Otis said, puffing out his chest where a medal rested.

"Looks good on you," Jonah said.

"Think the ladies will like it?" Otis asked.

"They'll drop to their knees."

"Those whores up the block give discounts to war heroes, don't they?"

"The hero part comes *after* the fight, not before."

"Seems like a technicality," Otis said before another thought came to him. "You return your military file yet?"

"I figured I might sit on it for a while," Jonah said. "I need to pool my resources together."

"For what?"

"I'm not going with you…to Vietnam," Jonah said.

"Where you goin'?"

"Haven't got a clue," Jonah said before adding, "Someplace far from here, that much I know."

"You ain't got enough cash to pull that off," Otis said.

"My old man owes me three months back pay, plus my side job with Sonny and the Angels," Jonah said before adding, "Might pick up a quick buck at the Birdcage. Leola King says she could use some help with the promotion of the place."

"You think the boys at the FBI are gonna just sit back and wait till you build your little nest egg?" Perturbed, Otis paced the lobby. "Thought we was a team." He returned to the counter, staring down Jonah. "What happened to the pact—*you and me, the world on its knee*? Was that all bullshit, huh?"

Jonah gave his friend some space, letting him vent.

Otis motioned to the record player. Psychedelic rock continued to stoke the room. "Ain't you got no R & B 'round here? Some Percy Sledge or Aretha?"

"I thought you liked The Grateful Dead," Jonah said.

"Dude, get real."

"What's going on out here?" the proprietor interrupted as he approached from a backroom. Without expecting a response, he slid the needle off the vinyl. A sound like a witch dragging her nails across a glass pane reached Jonah. He rushed to inspect the record. Scratches defaced its once impeccable surface. Jonah placed the record back into its cover, turned and threw his father a scowl.

"What are you looking at?" Abraham Berkowitz said. At sixty years old he still possessed the same slight build as his bastard son but wore a hawk nose and a salt-and-pepper goatee.

"What did you bring back from Oakland?" old man Berkowitz said to his son.

"A photo lens and three rolls of Kodak film," Jonah answered.

"That's it," and he slapped his son across the face. "How do you expect me to keep the pawnshop open with that kind of effort?"

"The place can go down the crapper for all I care," Jonah said.

The old man turned his back to his son and sauntered to Otis. "What do we have here?" he said as he touched the medal on the boy's chest.

"Got it for Valentine's Day," Otis said with a sideways look to Jonah.

"It's September, you idiot," old man Berkowitz said.

No response.

"This is the Bronze Star," the old man said upon returning his inspection to the medal. "Awarded for meritorious service in the field of combat." He ripped the medal from Otis's cloak, saying, "You're a disgrace to our country," and he turned to include his son. "Both of you. Back in the day such medals were worn with honor, not mocked." He pursed his lips in disgust before stowing the medal into his pocket.

"Hey, that's mine," Otis said.

Old man Berkowitz ignored the complaint and squared up to his son. "You were suppose to have the card room ready over an hour ago."

"The front counter got busy."

Abraham slapped Jonah across the face. Again. "Wrong answer."

The boy clenched his teeth, balled his hand into a fist. He paused to cool down before retrieving his album and walking to the stockroom while his old man disappeared toward the rear of the building.

Within the confined space, Jonah swept can goods off a shelf, threw dirty clothes from a laundry bin, swearing. Otis followed, pressing down the air with his palms, gesturing to his friend to be quiet. Without a word, Otis pointed to the air duct above. Jonah took his meaning and nodded.

"I gotta get out of here," Jonah whispered.

"This time next month you won't have to worry 'bout your old man or nothin'," Otis said. "We'll be gettin' three squares a day, seein' the world and tastin' some of that Asian hooch."

Muffled voices sounded from above. The lads squeezed past the laundry bin and bent their ears toward a vent. For the boys, this was the best part of the pawnshop, listening in on the conversations in the backroom. Poker games occurred every Saturday night, most of the players being well connected throughout the City. James McGinnis of the Redevelopment Agency was a regular as well as Chief of Police Thomas Cahill

The bell rang from the lobby. The boys ceased their eavesdropping and went to the front desk where a disheveled man plopped a pocket watch upon the counter. Jonah opened the gold piece and read the engraving to himself: *to my dearest Mary Grace Davis / with love / granddad.*

"Where'd you get this?" Jonah insisted.

"How much?" The customer twitched and itched.

Jonah studied the heirloom in greater detail.

"C'mon, man," the customer said in an agitated tone.

"What now?" old man Berkowitz said to Jonah upon returning.

"This no-good is trying to pawn off the widow Davis's keepsake," Jonah said.

Berkowitz glimpsed at the item in question before turning to his son. "You know how this works. Pay the man."

"But..."

A thump on Jonah's head truncated any further discussion. With a frown, the boy withdrew a sawbuck from the register and laid it on the counter. The junkie fled with the cash, clanging the bell on the way out.

"If I have to come out here one more time," the old man said, "there'll be hell to pay," and then he noticed Otis and said, "You still here?"

"Ain't you gonna give me back my medal?"

Old man Berkowitz showed the back of his hand, saying, "You want a taste of this too?"

Otis mumbled something and left. Berkowitz put the watch, photo lens, and the Bronze Star into the floor safe. Jonah peeked over his father's shoulder, spotting stacks of money. Might be five grand in there, he thought.

Papa Al had been laundering money through businesses such as carwashes, strip clubs and massage parlors, which accepted large amounts of cash for their services. At Berkowitz's pawnshop it was easy enough to claim illicit earnings as legitimate. Simply add the transaction of a phantom watch or a non-existing photo lens to the daily ledger. This over-invoicing accommodated the in-flow of dirty money. Over time, the "ghost" sales had increased into a tidy sum, which in turn was used by Papa Al as collateral to secure property loans. If the Redevelopment Agency were to tear down one of his properties, there was an understanding that the purchase price would be inflated with an eventual kickback to certain downtown officials. These layers shielded Papa Al from any outside investigation that might come knocking on his door.

The old man spun the dial on the combination lock, rose and caught his son glancing at the floor safe. "Get back to work."

Jonah retreated to the storeroom feeling the heat from his father's glare.

Chapter 3

Near the corner of Turk and Fillmore, Jonah approached a batch of locals waiting in front of a private residence. He spotted the junkie from earlier at the pawnshop and brushed his shoulder, sending a message, but the guy didn't notice, too busy itching and scratching.

Piece of crap, Jonah thought before moving on. He avoided eye contact with a couple of heavies who were guarding the main entrance and slinked along the side to the rear. To avoid any face-to-face with momma Wright, he had to engage his biggest phobia—heights. As he climbed the fire escape, he clutched onto the railing, staring straight ahead.

Don't look down. Don't look down. He reached the third story, pried open a window and clamored in.

Jonah saw Otis slicing Mexican tar into bricks. "That shit shouldn't be allowed on the streets."

Otis never looked up from his task, saying, "You never complained before, not until that whore friend of yours kicked the can."

"Her name was Sara," Jonah said as he took a step toward Otis. "Call her a whore one more time, and I'll scrape the black right off you."

"Hey, lightin' up, dude. Didn't mean anything by it."

"She shouldn't have died like that," Jonah said.

"Got some bad dope is all. It happens."

"Your momma should get out of the trade."

"Can't. Why you think her place is still standin'? If she puts the nix on distributing Papa Al's product, the wrecking ball comes a visitin'."

Jonah knew there was truth in what his friend was saying. As the community liaison for the Redevelopment Agency, Papa Al held a lot of sway with downtown. The fact that he was a crooked landlord and a drug manufacturer were irrelevant.

"What do you get out of the deal?" Jonah asked.

"Roof and clean laundry."

"Food?" Jonah asked.

"Nah."

"That's some arrangement," Jonah said.

"Better than what you got. At least momma don't kick the shit outta me. Most times, anyways."

"Want to make some easy coin?" Jonah asked.

"Can't you see I'm busy here?" Otis said as he began cutting a second batch of heroin with quinine.

"I convinced Leola King to pay us twenty-five cents for every customer we brought into the Birdcage," Jonah continued.

"What, you gonna drag people off the streets one-by-one?" Otis said. "Thought you said you was in a hurry to build your getaway fund."

"We'll kidnap whole bus loads," Jonah said. "Tourists will be lined up all the way to Pacific Heights."

Otis pointed a finger at his friend. "That's what I'm talkin' 'bout. You got what they calls entrepreneurial skills."

"You want in on the action or not?"

"We'd make a hell of a team in 'Nam—you with your business flair, me with my good looks. I hear the black market is wide open over there. No tellin' how much scratch we'd bring back home. Feel me, dude?"

"The *Chronicle* says that McNamara resigned as Defense Secretary," Jonah said. "Three other top aides of Johnson's also quit. The whole thing is falling apart."

"Well, what we waitin' for? Better get goin' while there's somethin' left."

"You'll have to make your fortune without me," Jonah said.

"You're startin' to piss me off."

⅄

Jonah crossed the lane and backtracked north along Fillmore Street. A gold watch received his touch as he reached inside his pocket.

At 1336 he nodded to the men in the black berets, crossed Ellis and passed a string of Victorians leaning against each other. A gaunt looking lady sat outside with her three children on a discarded mattress, her head buried in her palms.

"Excuse me, Mrs. Davis," Jonah said in a soft tone.

A baby's hollow cry washed over the greeting. Two other tykes cowered against the woman.

"Mrs. Davis? Ma'am?" Jonah said as he patted her on the shoulder.

The woman caught the outline of the man and wiped the moistness from her cheek.

"I believe this is yours." Jonah dangled the heirloom from his fingers.

She studied the treasure, gazing back and forth between the holder and the watch. "What you want for it?"

"It's not mine to want." Jonah extended his hand further. "Take it."

With hesitation she started to reach for it then pulled back. In one final act of courage, she latched onto the gift and brought it to her bosom. The timepiece rested there for a moment before she opened the casing and read the inscription in silence: *to my dearest Mary Grace Davis / with love / granddad.* She smiled, knowing that a part of her past had found its way back to her.

Words stuck on the edge of her trembling lips. Unable to speak, she mouthed her gratitude before bowing her head to her crying infant.

Jonah drifted off knowing that the streets would revisit the woman. At the northern edge of the Fillmore District, he looked over the railing to the expressway below. The four-lane expansion was the first accomplishment of the Redevelopment Agency in dealing with the blighted area. Six years previous in '61, the underpass was completed to allow commuters to safely whiz thru the wasteland of the Fillmore and on to the Financial District. The project put an exclamation on segregation, erecting another wall between the prosperous and the Mrs. Davis's of the City.

A mechanical rumble brought Jonah out of his funk. He walked to the middle of the lane, stopped and put up his hands. Brakes pushed air from a motor coach as it came to a halt. Jonah withdrew his hand from the grill of the Greyhound and boarded.

"Jonah is my name and pleasure is my game," he said with a carnie-like smile to the driver. "Your fares look like they could use a bite to eat and a little music to lighten their souls."

"Mister," the driver said, "this is a tour bus."

Jonah snatched the microphone from its cradle and faced the passengers. "How about it folks, you in the mood for some tasty wings?"

"Give that to me," the driver said as he stole back the mic.

"Almost lunch time, right?" Jonah persisted. "The Birdcage serves up the best chicken baskets in the City not to mention some primo jazz."

The driver glanced down the street to where Jonah was gesturing. The man's vision stopped short of the restaurant when he spied women sitting on a stoop flashing some skin.

"No can do. The boss says the Fillmore is strictly off limits."

"Park the bus along Geary," Jonah suggested. He noticed the man's hesitation and said that the first drink was on the house. "C'mon, how about it?"

The driver glanced at the clock on the dashboard. "We're behind schedule. You're going to have to disembark."

"But…"

"Sorry, mister," and he released his foot from the brake.

Another gush of air told Jonah that it was time to leave. As the bus motored away, he retreated down the lane. At 1505 Fillmore Street he entered a cabaret where a pair of macaws greeted him from a gilded cage. Other species of fowl dangled from the ceiling. The lipstick-red walls encased a jukebox, a piano and a thirty-foot-long mahogany bar.

"I like the new stained glass windows," Jonah said to Leola King.

Not one for small talk, she said, "Where are those customers you promised me?"

"The driver was on a tight timetable," Jonah said.

"No customers, no pay," Leola said before returning to her tasks.

"I'll get the next one," Jonah said.

"Tour buses don't stop anymore," she said while collecting dirty baskets and silverware.

"I can make this work," Jonah said.

Leola stopped and turned to him. "Used to be a time when white folks couldn't get enough of the sound. Now it's just a lost memory, buried under the rubble where Bob City, Blue Mirror and other great jazz places once stood. Can't fight city hall, kid." She showed her back to him and headed for the kitchen.

"I need this, Miss King," Jonah called out.

"Ain't gonna happen," she said over her shoulder.

Jonah gazed at the glossy photos perched on the wall. Etta James, T-Bone Walker, Wes Montgomery, Benny Barth and others stared back. Jonah wondered where it had all gone. A whole genre of music simply upped and disappeared.

⅄

Ladies, made up from head to toe, called over a Negro in his matching burgundy cloak and pants. A toothy grin showed below his feathered fedora as he strutted up the stoop.

"You get paid by your momma, yet?" one of the girls asked.

"Tomorrow," Otis said.

"Well, you know where to deposit it, don't you, sweet pea?" and she tipped her cleavage forward.

"You is one naughty girl," Otis said as he wagged a finger at her.

"I try."

"God bless you," Otis said when another remembrance came to him. "You all give any kind of discount to generals? I'm gonna be a Marine."

"Never made love to no general before."

Jonah approached to pay his respects to the women before catching the cold stare of his friend. "So that's the way it's gonna be, huh?" Jonah said.

"Guess so," Otis said. He was still processing the idea that Jonah would not be joining him in Vietnam.

"Fine with me," Jonah said.

"Me too," Otis said.

"You get Miss King her customers?" one of the ladies interjected.

"I'm afraid it didn't work out."

"Hey, blue-eyes," another said, "you can have a job keeping my sheets warm. Whaddya say?"

"Cash?" Jonah asked with a smile.

"I'll take it out in trade," the woman countered before noticing the unsettledness in Jonah's step. "Where you off to?"

"Don't know," Jonah said. "Just need to go."

"Sit a spell," the woman said. "Haven't seen you since Sara passed away three months ago."

At the mention of the deceased woman, Jonah grew dispirited. "I miss her."

"We all do," the woman said. "I know you two had something special."

"She was like family," Jonah said.

"She certainly did fuss over you."

A nod.

"Maybe for the best," the woman said. "She was getting on in age. How old was she anyways, forty?"

"Thirty-eight," Jonah corrected.

"Might've had a couple a good years left in her."

"Well, I better get back to the pawnshop," Jonah said in an abbreviated tone. He turned to Otis and asked if he wanted to tag along.

"What you need me for?" Otis said. "'Sides, I got some negotiatin' to do here."

Jonah walked to the entrance of the pawnshop, but it was locked. He gave the midday closure little credence and opened the door with a twist of his key. Before he could turn on the lights, a leather strap slashed across his backside.

Chapter 4

Jonah was walking north on Fillmore Street when a black Caddy pulled alongside. The rear window buzzed down. Papa Al stuck his hand out, motioning for Jonah to get in. The teenager did as told while Sergeant Maloney exited from the driver's side to give the pair some privacy.

"It was a noble deed that you intended with the widow Davis," Papa Al said to Jonah.

"Sorry?"

"The pocket watch…returning her heirloom," Papa Al said. "Very touching indeed."

"I didn't…"

"Don't lie to me," Papa Al interrupted. "He who twists the truth loses all respect. With no respect he ceases to love. We need love in these godforsaken times. Wouldn't you agree?"

Jonah always thought it peculiar how men of violence and greed felt qualified to sermonize on such topics. Not wanting to anger the mobster, however, Jonah fell quiet.

"Your daddy was right in giving you that whipping last night," Papa Al said. "Karma is a bitch but it does level the playing field."

The mobster hand-brushed lint from his cashmere coat, taking his sweet time. "In my official capacity as community liaison, it is imperative that I have the respect of my constituents."

Constituents? Does this guy think he's running for mayor?

"If every resident of the Fillmore had a personal savior, there would be no need for rules. One could run amuck, knowing salvation was close at hand. The widow Davis failed to pay her rent and she must be made an example of."

Unable to remain silent, Jonah said, "She's got three little ones. What about them?"

"On certain occasions, it is necessary to make sacrifices for the good of the whole. The Fillmore is experiencing a renaissance. People with money will be stepping in. It is time to weed out the undesirables."

Jonah held back his anger, pissed off that such unethical types wheeled so much influence.

"Street credibility is the backbone of my business," Papa Al continued. "It is the driving force behind everything that happens in the district. Without it bedlam would reign supreme and that would very much displease not only future investors but downtown as well."

Papa Al turned sideways to Jonah. "I have a proposition for you."

"Oh yeah, what's that?"

"My sources tell me that you are thinking of bypassing your military obligation."

Jonah cocked his head, wondering how this creep came into possession of such information.

"Trust me when I say that I have no interest in politics. Kill gooks. Don't kill gooks. It matters little to me." Papa Al paused before adding, "Come work for me."

"As one of your drug pushers?"

"I'll set you up with your own distribution. No more penny-ante errands with Sonny and his Hells Angels. In addition, you will be given a new ID with instructions that you are off limits to the FBI or any other government agency that may come calling."

While Jonah had no intention of doing business with him, there was no reason to rile the guy at this point. "Let me sleep on it," Jonah said as he reached for the handle.

"Please do."

The teenager exited without shutting the door, sending as bold a message as he dared. Sergeant Maloney glared at him before returning to the Caddy. The vehicle made a U-turn and motored south on Fillmore Street while Jonah headed in the opposite direction.

⅄

A line snaked around the corner. Bearded young men with tie-dye headbands carried sleeping bags while girls swayed to the rhythm of silent notes in their heads.

"Keep the sidewalk clear," Bill Graham barked to the ticket holders. He surveyed the throng. Another sellout, but that could change with the wind. Downtown had the Fillmore Auditorium within its sights. In addition, neighborhood goons were preying on these suburban kids.

The music promoter spotted a team of blacks working the crowd. They had pinned a customer up against the wall, strong-arming him. Graham approached and told the punks to take a hike.

"How you know we don't have tickets, huh?" one of the youths said.

"Get lost." Bill Graham didn't need security to back up his demands. He was born tough.

At the entrance, a greeter passed out complimentary concert posters. Nearby, ice buckets brimmed with apples for the taking.

"I get the band posters. It's good promo," a familiar voice said from behind, "but what's with the apples? Seems kind of odd to me."

Graham turned around to Jonah, saying, "It's a private thing from long ago."

"I smell a story," Jonah said as he fished a tape recorder from his backpack. "Mind if I ask a couple of questions?" He pressed a button and held up a microphone.

He submitted weekly tidbits on the musical scene to Hal Hulbert of the *Chronicle*. The columnist would in turn surrender a press pass to Jonah that allowed the teenager free access to concerts. While he would have preferred money, the exchange nevertheless fed his hunger for rock 'n' roll.

"Not now," Graham said as they walked through billowing clouds of smoke.

Jonah put away the recorder and asked Graham if he had seen Otis.

"No," Graham said before seeing the concern on Jonah's face. "You're better off without him."

"You don't know that. He's had a tough life is all."

"Your choice."

A teenybopper with a sleepy look presented Jonah with a giant cardboard tube. He took a hit from the bong before catching up with Graham who was talking in a fast clip with the leader of the opening act.

"Where is everybody?" the music promoter asked, noticing the absence of two musicians.

"In jail," a shaggy haired Jerry Garcia said.

Jonah clicked his recorder back on.

"You want we should break 'em out?" Garcia said in a playful way.

A frazzled Graham spied Jonah with the microphone. "Turn that thing off."

"Only if you promise to tell the tale about the apples. Deal?"

"I don't have time for this," Graham said and he shot Jonah a glare.

"What will it be?" Jonah asked as he held a finger over the ON/OFF button.

In a hurry, Graham agreed before pivoting back to Garcia, saying, "What was it this time?"

"The Feds busted Weir and Pigpen with an ounce of weed."

"That's enough for a felony," Jonah added.

"They also impounded guitars, amps and shit," Garcia said.

"It might prove difficult to play music without instruments," Graham said.

"In the long run, we'll be okay," Garcia said. "Our attorney is used to these shakedowns. He put a special clause into our homeowner's policy to recoup such losses."

"Your attorney would be that Terrence Hallinan fellow, right?" Graham asked.

"He's young but tough. Represents a dozen other bands in the City as well."

"What about tonight?" Graham asked.

"Borrowed some equipment from Big Brother."

"We've never started late before," Graham reminded him.

"I got this. No need to panic."

The words resonated with Graham and he began to calm down. Garcia, while reckless and mischievous, was nevertheless the consummate professional, always showing up eight hours in advance to rehearse and check the sound system.

"Phil Lesh will pick up the slack on guitar," Garcia added. "Tom Constanten will sub in for Pigpen on the keyboards. No worries."

"I'm counting on it," Graham said.

"Here, have a taste," and the rocker held out a plastic cup of Kool-Aid.

Graham never knew if LSD had made its way into the house punch. He had experienced the unpleasant trip from laced sodas and wine bottles as well. Tonight was too important to take the chance, however, and he scurried off without accepting the offer.

Backstage, Graham noticed a familiar figure beside him. "You still here?"

"How about that story?" Jonah asked.

"You're a persistent little bugger, aren't you?"

"Got a deadline to meet." Since Jonah was not on the *Chronicle's* payroll, there was no official target date, but he liked hearing the sound of the words anyway.

Graham relented and began telling of his escape from Hitler's Germany during WWII. The Jewish kid had become detached from his family at age nine. Alone with no resources, he began a three hundred mile trek from Berlin to Lisbon. Fallen apples from orchard trees were his sole food source, continuing to nourish him on his ocean journey to New York.

"The free handout of apples from the ice bucket is my way of saying thank you to the powers that be," Graham said. "I'm always grateful for another day."

A melody reached backstage. "Damn," Graham exclaimed as he leaned an ear toward the sound. "They were supposed to wait for my introduction," and he rushed off.

Jonah clicked off his tape recorder and listened.

"Gonna wake up in the morning Lord / gonna pack my bags…"

The floor shook with the uncontained lust of flower power. Barefooted teenagers hopped and skipped, letting their painted faces sway to the stinging vibrations. At the conclusion of the number, whistles and claps and hoots streamed on stage from the four corners of the hall.

"Ladies and gentlemen," Graham said into a mic, "give it up one more time for The Grateful Dead."

The crowd went wild. Graham joined in the celebration and stepped from the stage to let the boys do their thing. The Dead took up their instruments, playing "Sitting on Top of the World" and "Don't Ease Me In" before Graham retook the spotlight.

The throng demanded more as the music producer's voice forced its way through the speakers. "We are proud to announce that tonight's proceeds will be donated to the Free Clinic." The Fillmore Auditorium had joined efforts with the Diggers in organizing the special benefit. The Diggers were anarchists who blended a desire for freedom with community consciousness. If we all shared with one another, there was no need to depend on the man downtown.

A professional type with a sober demeanor walked on stage and introduced himself to the masses. "My name is Dr. David Smith and I am proud to be associated with the Haight-Ashbury Free Clinic."

A humble sort, the good doctor would not brag about being the founder of the neighborhood medical facility. However, financial worries had surfaced hard and fast.

"My staff and I are overrun with medical problems that have accompanied the hundred thousand visitors to our beloved Haight during this past summer. Your generosity tonight will go a long way toward keeping us afloat. On a parting note, I implore everyone to wear condoms. Thank you."

While the doc was a popular figure, his homilies on "safe-sex" were countermand to the concept of uninhibited freedom. Polite applause followed Dr. Smith as he retraced his steps to the main floor. Graham retook the stage and introduced the main act as the crowd returned to its groove.

With her full-throttle voice, the lead singer of the Jefferson Airplane belted out "White Rabbit". She wasn't some glittering mermaid in her beehive hairdo or a counterfeit copy of Jackie Kennedy. This was the scornful and rebellious Grace Slick.

During "Somebody to Love", a snapshot of the band's mansion on Fulton Street came uninvited into Jonah's head. The three-story Colonial Revival, with its coal-black exterior, stood foreboding as the music faded to nothing behind him. An inexplicable melancholy settled upon Jonah and he went to the restroom.

He felt queasy. His palms grew clammy. He took the backpack and placed it in the washbasin. Stressed, he tilted forward, braced his elbows upon the carryall and peered at the image in the mirror.

"What the hell?" he said to the likeness before him. "What are you doing?" No way he should've stolen his military file from the Oakland Induction Center and he knew it.

A hippie fumbled into the bathroom and sped to the sink next to Jonah. A week's worth of pills and booze pushed upward in violence. The vomiting continued uncontained. Stunned, Jonah retrieved his backpack and withdrew a step. With a final purge, the retching waned.

"Man, that was some good shit," the hippie said.

"You sure about that?" Jonah asked before passing him a roll of paper towels.

The hippie explained that it was his last hoorah before reporting for basic training the next day. "Don't know if I'm ready. Know what I mean?" He tore a square from the roll, dampened it and started to clean the muck from his shirt. "What about you?"

"What about me?" Jonah replied.

"You going to 'Nam?"

Jonah fell quiet, not sure what to say.

"My best buddy came home in a body bag. Don't know, man." The hippie tossed the paper towels into the waist basket and left.

Jonah became despondent. He shouldered his backpack and retreated from the dance hall. Neon yellow cloaked the sidewalk in a netherworld-like glow. Candescent arrows ran down the brick façade of the auditorium to a street-level storefront. At 1:00 am, the line outside CHECKS CASHED HERE rivaled the activity from upstairs. Two different cultures occupied the same building that night, yet the distance between them could fill the universe.

Jonah sat on a bench and studied the neighborhood. A block down, the Booker T. Washington Hotel stood in marked contrast to a nearby billboard featuring a future image of the Fillmore Center High-rise. The wrecking ball was knocking on each and every door.

"That's one of the best sad-sack looks I've seen on anyone in sometime," Graham said as he approached.

"What's going to happen to the music?" Jonah asked.

"Hard to tell," Graham said.

"Maybe it's just as well Charles Sullivan didn't live to see this day," Jonah said.

"I miss him," Graham said. "He was the closest thing I had to a father."

Jonah lifted his expression, wanting more. "Mind if I tape this?"

Graham consented thinking that perhaps it was time to let the public know the truth. Jonah lifted the tape recorder from his backpack. He was about to push the "Record" button when he noticed that it was already on. Must have hit it accidentally in the restroom, he guessed. The tape continued to roll as he held the mic to Graham.

"Charles Sullivan put the Harlem into the district," the music promoter started. "Louis Armstrong, Duke Ellington, Count Basie, Billie Holliday—you name a prominent black musician and Sunday as to Wednesday, Sullivan was behind the artist, wiping his tears as if they were his own."

"I learned a lot from Charles," Graham continued. "When he thought I was ready, he turned over the lease on the auditorium to me. I owe him my start in the business."

"I remember reading something about his death in the *Sun-Reporter*," Jonah said. "There was a two-page spread on the incident, then nothing in the following days as if the whole thing was dropped down some well."

"Belva Davis was a reporter for the paper at the time and started digging around but was pulled off the story without any explanation. She was later told that there were powerful interests behind Charles Sullivan's demise."

"Was it a suicide like they said?"

"Off the record?" Graham said.

Jonah silenced his recorder.

"They found him in some alley pinned between his Chevy and a wire fence with a bullet through his heart," Graham said. "A snub-nosed .38 was found near his body. The lead detective was at a loss to explain why there were no fingerprints on the gun or no powder residue on Sullivan's hand. Even the coroner thought it unlikely that someone could shoot himself in the heart at that angle. It was murder all right. No doubt about it."

Graham let some stoners pass before adding, "I always thought that whoever did it was sending a message. Perhaps Charles was becoming too popular for his own health."

"Some say the same about you."

"I can take care of myself. Don't you worry about me," and he slapped Jonah on the back.

The kid winced.

"Did Abraham put the belt to you again?" Graham guessed.

"It's nothing."

Graham looked at the kid's discomfort thinking that perhaps some are better off without a father. While contemplating the merits of such an idea, he gazed onto the activity before him.

A cluster of blacks drifted down Fillmore while a band of hippies headed in the opposite direction toward Geary. Everyone knew where the Mason-Dixon Line stood. Across the way, a patrolman and a fancy-dressed Negro pranced the length of the block as if they owned it.

"There's trouble for you," Graham said to Jonah, nodding toward the pair.

Papa Al and Sergeant Maloney walked past the pawnshop and the Birdcage to the stoop of the brothel. Whores in their slit dresses and net stockings spun seductive poses.

"Maybe we should have a little fun with these yahoos," Graham said as he started to rise from the bench.

"Where're you going?" Jonah asked.

"Wait here," Graham said before retreating to the dance hall.

Jonah did as told, keeping an eye on the two reprobates who were enjoying a conversation with a couple of the hookers. Graham returned, went behind a vehicle and knelt to one knee. He fiddled with a camera before resting it on the hood of the car and clicking off a few shots.

Sergeant Maloney and Papa Al accompanied a pair of ladies inside, everyone arm-in-arm, giggling, having some fun. The door closed behind them while another girl, with a rose in her hair, remained on the stoop.

Graham whistled to the lady, waving her over. She gestured back, saying that she had to work. When a Jackson was held high, she abandoned her station and swaggered across the two lanes, stopping traffic, her stilettos clicking across the asphalt.

"Hey, blue eyes," she said as a greeting to Jonah. "Always did like that scar over your eyebrow. Sexy," and she smiled at the teenager before turning to Graham. "What's up?"

"Rosebud, I've got a proposition for you," Graham said.

"I'm the one suppose to make the proposition, sweetheart," Rosebud said.

"Take this," and Graham handed her the camera, "and go back inside and take a couple of pictures of those last two customers."

"What?" Rosebud said. "You mean the cop and his friend?"

A nod.

"You been smokin' that wacky tobacky again?"

"You'll have to use the flash," Graham said as a reminder.

"So you want me to march into their room, say 'cheese' and light up the place with this here camera."

"Yeah."

"All Jews as crazy as you?"

He took out another twenty. She tapped the sidewalk with the toe of her high heels, holding out her hand in demand. He reached deeper and unloaded two more Jacksons into her palm before she consented.

The woman sauntered back across the street, counting her money along the way. Upon reaching her usual spot on the brothel's stoop, she settled into her routine, hustling passersby.

Graham raised his arms, wondering what was the delay. Rosebud ignored him as she continued flirting with potential customers. Frustrated, Graham stepped back to take a seat on the bench next to Jonah.

"What's going on?" Jonah asked.

"I think I've just been fleeced."

"I guess even a Jew can make a bad investment. You should be more careful where you..."

"Wait," Graham interrupted as his eyes locked onto the scene across the way. "Rosebud, you are one clever whore."

The prostitute handed a kid the camera, gave him a bill and escorted him inside.

"What's Jimmy doing over there?" Jonah asked when he spotted the local runt.

Jimmy was about twelve going on twenty as far as street smarts. He had been known to do various dirty jobs in the hood from time to time.

Five minutes later, the kid sprinted down the stairs and slipped the camera to Rosebud. She placed it inside her skirt as Sergeant Maloney, in nothing but a pair of boxer shorts, came racing out the door.

"Where'd the punk go?" Maloney asked Rosebud, panting.

She nodded down the street, adding, "That kid sure can run."

The half-naked patrolman sprinted off while Rosebud stepped from the stoop and sashayed back across the thoroughfare to Graham. "Here's your precious Brownie," Rosebud said.

Jonah intercepted the camera and inspected it while the prostitute renegotiated the price. "How's about an extra Jackson?" and she held out her palm to Graham. Again.

"For what?"

"Shipping and handling."

He waved her off, arguing that she was no better than those crooks downtown.

"Honey," Rosebud said, "do those politicians look like this?" and she patted her rear.

"Depends on the angle." Graham, however, had to admit she had a point and forked over another bill before retrieving the Brownie from Jonah.

From the porch of the brothel a Negro put on his coat while another approached in his boxers. "Where's the kid?" Papa Al asked Maloney.

"He...he disappeared," the cop said, struggling to get his wind.

"Well, this is indeed a conundrum," Papa Al said.

"Can't...let...those...photos...get...out," Maloney said between clumps of air. "I...got...a...wife...and...kids."

Papa Al scoured the area. He spied Rosebud across the way with Graham. The duo appeared deep in conversation. The mobster's curiosity grew.

"Let's take a stroll, shall we?" Papa Al said to Maloney.

"But my clothes?"

"This is no time for formalities."

Graham looked up to see the pair coming his way. "Take Rosebud up to my office," he said to Jonah.

A sedan slammed on its brakes, honking at the man in his briefs. Maloney yelled at the driver before reaching the other side of the street.

"Get that skank back here," Maloney said as he approached Graham.

"You got a warrant?" Graham said, stalling. "Actually, it appears that you don't have much of anything, do you, sergeant?"

He presented his jacket to the policeman as a substitute for a pair of pants, but Maloney slapped the offer away, his manhood standing limp. At the sight of five security guards blocking the front entrance, the sergeant thought better of storming the dance hall. He chose option two and slammed Graham against the bench.

"I know you're involved," the cop said as he frisked the Jew.

The wrangling drew a crowd. Voices crisscrossed over each other until an African American in a cashmere coat made his way to the scene.

"It would seem that a spectacle of sorts is on display," Papa Al said.

"Is it common for your puppet to wander the streets with his testicles swaying in the breeze?" Graham said.

"She lay naked in her bed / And I myself lay nearby / No veil but curtains about her spread / No covering but I."

"Very poetic," Graham said, "but your prose is perhaps better suited for a different scenario."

"I most heartedly agree," Papa Al said. "I might add that nakedness should be reserved for the fairer sex. This is, indeed, a pitiful sight," he said as he motioned to the sergeant.

"Found this on the Jew," Sergeant Maloney said to Papa Al.

Papa Al took the camera and escorted Graham to a quiet corner. The horde began to thin out. With order restored, the mobster opened the Brownie and examined it before showing his findings to Graham.

The music promoter leaned forward in disbelief. Empty. He remembered Jonah's possession of the camera for a brief moment. I'll be damned, Graham thought as a knowing grin worked its way across his face.

"I would be remiss if I didn't say that I am more than a little disappointed," Papa Al said.

"It was all in fun," Graham said, adlibbing along the way. "Never was any film. I thought I might turn the tables on you gentlemen." He stonewalled for a moment before adding, "The show your henchman put on, however, far exceeded my expectations."

"I'm sure it did," Papa Al said with doubt in his voice. "While we are on the subject of *expectations*, there are rumors that the permit for your dance hall may not be renewed."

"Your threats aren't worth piss to me."

"As your community liaison, I would be within my power to file a number of complaints against your establishment, all of which would find their way to Mr. James McGinnis of the Redevelopment Agency. Hasn't there been enough carnage in the neighborhood?"

The toe of his boot crushed the stone expression of Abraham Berkowitz. Jonah stared at the jagged creases of the photo, cursing his fate, a fate that would forever hang by the dead limb of his family tree.

⅄

Big Momma Wright sat on her porch thinking how the times had changed. Papa Al's greasy prints were everywhere, all done with the blessing of downtown. She pondered her fate when a voice sounded from the bottom of the stoop.

"Mrs. Wright?" Jonah said as a hello.

"What you want?"

"Have you seen Otis?"

No response.

"I need to talk with him."

"Haven't seen that shifty son of mine goin' on two days."

Jonah climbed a step to let her know that he needed more.

"Could be over at the whorehouse, spendin' his paycheck," she said. "When you catch up with the lowlife, you tell him to come home. Got work to do."

"Yes, ma'am." Jonah started to retreat to the sidewalk when Big Momma reminded him that Otis's military notice had arrived in the mail.

"What the army want with another black man anyways? Ain't they got enough?"

"Yes, ma'am."

"You don't have nothin' else to say?"

Jonah pondered who was worse off, Otis or him. He figured it was probably a draw though he was tempted to give himself the edge, knowing what a dirtbag his father could be.

Halfway down Fillmore, thoughts of parenthood besieged him. It was hard to fathom that he was alone in this miserable world. He felt cheated. If he had grown up in the Richmond— or the Sunset District, he might have gone to one of those ritzy private schools where the worst violation of human conduct was grabbing a smoke in the john. He might even have had normal friends, the kind who didn't treat juvie like a revolving door.

Jonah reached inside his shirt pocket to retrieve a cylindrical object. The word *Kodak* showed as if it was the gateway to the apocalypse. He grew anxious, knowing the significance of what he was holding.

He hurried back toward the Fillmore Auditorium. A block away he spotted Sergeant Maloney standing guard outside. Rumors had spread that Rosebud had skipped town to visit a sister in Sacramento until things cooled down.

Papa Al probably had men searching the City for him as well, Jonah guessed. He slipped down Ellis Street, thinking.

On the one hand, he didn't want anything to do with it. It was Graham's idea to have some fun with the local thug, not his. Voices inside Jonah's head, however, kept badgering him: *You think the man is taking on city hall just to please himself? The Fillmore Auditorium is for each and every critter left in the neighborhood, including you. If you were to ask me, I'd say you owed the gentleman.*

"Shut up!"

⅄

A Washington slid across the glass counter. "There's another one just like it if I get the prints within the next thirty minutes," Jonah said.

The guy behind the register wasn't much younger than Jonah, perhaps sixteen. A smile began to take shape around a wad of gum as the employee scooped up the cash.

⅄

Jonah surveyed the area before entering the pawnshop. He flew up the stairs to his bedroom where a record album, chards of glass and a mangled photo still littered the floor. He studied the disorder, remembering the theft of his military file by his father. The warning hanging on his doorknob (KEEP OUT) seemed hollow. His privacy had been stripped from him. He picked up *Summer in the City*, wiped it clean with the sleeve of his Pendleton and returned it to its proper place on the shelf.

After straightening the other albums, he turned his attention to the envelope from Andy's Photo Shop. He pinched the prints from the casing to study them for the first time. The black and white snapshots caused him to blink. Bare-breasted women sat atop the laps of a S.F.P.D. sergeant and the Redevelopment Agency's community liaison.

He scanned the room to hide the photos but nowhere seemed safe anymore. With a sense of panic, he fled downstairs, locked the front door and went to the storeroom. Appliances, cases of booze, unwanted memorabilia and other items came under his examination. He rolled away the dirty clothes bin and peered upward into the cavity of the laundry chute.

This might do, he thought. He began to search for masking tape when voices from the lobby stopped him. Jonah thought about slinking to the light switch to turn it off but froze. Footsteps trailed off to the card room where the chatter came to him from the overhead duct. Jonah squeezed past the laundry bin, pushed an empty crate into position and stepped atop it. Though he was just a few feet off the ground, it felt much higher. While battling his fear of heights, he cocked an ear toward the vent.

"What are we gonna do now?" said a husky voice from the other side of the wall.

"Now is not the time to panic," said another. "One must never respond immediately to stimuli. What is required is control of the obstructing instincts."

"Don't need your bullshit," said the first voice.

"Let us analyze the facts," the second voice said. "First, we now know that there was indeed film in the camera. Second, the prints are in the possession of Jonah Berkowitz."

Impatient, the first voice said, "Maybe we should reacquaint him with Charles Sullivan."

"Another unexplained death at this juncture might give cause for downtown to come snooping around. We do not need that case reopened," the second voice said.

"I got some contacts up north," the first voice suggested. "Sheriff along the Russian River...name is McGee...owes me a favor."

"While an accident outside the city limits would dissuade a local investigation," the second voice said, "perhaps a less volatile act might be a more appropriate choice at this juncture."

"Sheriff McGee is in my debt big time," the first voice persisted.

The pair continued to debate the topic when the sound of crashing glass alerted them. They went to the lobby, but it was empty. Each looked at the other with puzzled looks until a band of light from the storeroom sent an invitation.

"What're you doing back here?" Sergeant Maloney said upon reaching Jonah.

"Nothing," Jonah said in a jumpy tone. "Just wanted to get a head start on tonight's card game."

Maloney studied him harder. "That so?"

No response.

"Diligence is one of the more sacrosanct virtues of mankind," Papa Al said from the entrance. "I applaud your dedication."

No response.

"This is quite a mess you have constructed here," Papa Al said as he stepped over broken whiskey bottles.

"Fell over a crate," Jonah said as he hiked up his shoulders. "Shit happens, right?"

"Indeed it does."

"Guess I better get busy." Jonah tried to exit but Maloney blocked his path.

Papa Al studied the crate, its positioning under the air vent. He stared into the eyes of Jonah and said, "Spying is not a noble trait."

"I…I didn't hear a thing."

"I wish I could believe you," Papa Al said. "However, your people have had a long history of bending the truth in the name of survival."

"I won't say a word…to anyone. Promise."

"I came across Jimmy this morning," Papa Al said. "I can hardly admonish the youngster for wanting to better himself. In fact, I admire his tenacity and told him that directly. That bit at the brothel with the camera took spunk."

Jonah spotted a box cutter resting atop a TV and took a step sideways.

"I purchased some rather interesting information from the lad," Papa Al said as he squared up to Jonah, trying to catch any sign of treason in his expression.

Jonah stood rigid.

"Jimmy reminded me that when film inhabits a Brownie, a number is displayed. No number, no film. The kid distinctly remembers a '1' appearing in the little window of the camera."

"Maybe you should hire Jimmy for your next photo shoot," Jonah said.

"*Maybe* I should slap you around," Maloney said as he hoisted his baton to strike. Jonah dove for the box cutter but the policeman was too quick. He swept the weapon aside before slamming the boy against the TV.

"Tsk, tsk," Papa Al said to Jonah.

Maloney retrieved the weapon and held it against Jonah's throat.

"Oh," Papa Al said in a nonplus tone, "I was remiss regarding one detail."

Jonah tried to refocus under the pressure of the blade.

"My sources revealed to me that a young man with sandy hair, blue eyes and a scar over his left eyebrow walked into Andy's Photo Shop at 1550 Ellis Street and bribed the employee to rush an order."

"Interesting," Jonah said in a weak tone.

"Very," Papa Al said when the voice of another came from the doorway.

"What's going on here?" Abraham Berkowitz asked.

"Ah, the father has arrived," Papa Al said. "We were just discussing the latest crimes of your wayward son."

Maloney withdrew the weapon. Jonah coughed as he rested on the TV.

"What's the bastard done now?" old man Berkowitz asked.

While Papa Al was updating the father with a lengthy rendition of the day's events, Jonah opened an unhinged panel of the TV and dropped an envelope inside.

"You must assume responsibility for your son's actions," Papa Al said to the old man. "His folly is yours as well."

The old man went to Jonah and grabbed him by his shirt. "Where are the prints, you little shit?"

No response.

The old man shoved Jonah backward into a crate. The buckle-end of a belt came slashing down. Jonah pushed with his heels against the concrete floor, trying to escape the onslaught.

"Where are the prints?" the father repeated as he continued to hit his son.

No response.

The father hoisted the TV and tossed it. Jonah took the blow with defiance. Papa Al saw that the effort was futile and gestured to Maloney who lifted the old man off his quarry. Still breathing hard from the beating, Jonah glanced to the TV. It remained in one piece. Good.

Papa Al ordered Maloney to search the ground level while old man Berkowitz was sent to the living quarters. Thirty minutes later both returned empty handed.

"Nothing down here," Sergeant Maloney said while Abraham Berkowitz confirmed the same for the upstairs.

Papa Al pivoted to the father, saying, "Your son has sand. I'll give him that."

The father spat at the feet of Jonah who remained seated on the cold slab.

"'If one has a rebellious son," Papa Al said in a preacher's tone, "the father shall take hold of him and bring him out to the gate of the place where he lives to purge the evil from his midst'...Deuteronomy, chapter 21."

The cop was accustomed to the routine. Without further instructions, Maloney clutched onto Jonah, stood him up and pulled him toward the exit.

⅄

From the middle of the street, Papa Al turned to his partner. "Sergeant, if you would, please," and the mobster motioned toward the store.

Maloney marched to the entrance of the pawnshop, opened it wide and told the first passersby to help themselves. A couple of lowlifes motioned to their buddies in the lot across the street. A rush of people soon began to storm the premises. Telephones, paintings and appliances sped from the store.

"What are you doing?" old man Berkowitz cried out to Papa Al.

"Purging."

The old man watched as an elderly woman hauled a case of booze away. "My things! I'll be ruined," Abraham Berkowitz said.

"*Things* aren't much to hang your hat on," Papa Al sermonized. "A far more onerous penalty would be the destruction of our arrangement. I would hate to take my business elsewhere."

Abraham Berkowitz received a tidy sum for helping to launder Papa Al's drug money through the pawnshop. "Punish him," the old man said as he pointed to his son. "He's the one with the photos."

"'Fear has a far reaching arm as Socrates once said." The mobster paused before adding, "You and your son are one and the same."

With this admonishment, Jonah realized that there was truth in what this thug was saying. Items of personal value did indeed reside within the building. *Crap!*

A person in a black suit with matching colored tie and hat stepped from a sedan with government plates. He walked to a quartet of men standing in the middle of Fillmore Street to inquire about the commotion.

"Who might you be, my worthy friend?" Papa Al asked.

"Agent Harris, Federal Bureau of Investigation," he said as he displayed a badge. "And you?"

"I am Allan Theodore McCollum the Third, the Redevelopment Agency's community liaison," and he offered his hand.

Agent Harris accepted the offer before asking if a Mr. Abraham Berkowitz resided nearby.

"Maybe," the old man said.

The agent approached the person, saying, "Did you call our local office?"

Jonah saw an opportunity and rushed forward before his old man could answer. "Yes, he most certainly did," Jonah said as he placed his arm around his old man. "My father called you to teach me a lesson in civics, having only my best interest at heart."

Papa Al caught the boy's intent and said to the agent, "I don't believe there is anyone of interest to you here."

"Oh, but I believe there is. I'm Jonah Berkowitz and I plead guilty to *borrowing* my file from the Oakland Induction Center."

"He didn't mean anything by it," Papa Al said, "just a teenager's forgetfulness. Didn't we all make such errors in judgment during our youth?"

"I wouldn't know," the agent said.

"Sergeant Maloney here will take full responsibility," Papa Al suggested as he pivoted to his confederate for confirmation.

"You have my word, Agent Harris," Maloney said. "I'll personally deliver the boy to your office by 5:00 p.m. today."

"Well, there you have it," Papa Al said, holding up his palms like a minister behind a pulpit.

The agent pondered the situation, thinking that perhaps he could save himself a load of paperwork. "If the boy is willing to sign the proper forms stating that he promises to report to Oakland next Tuesday for military assignment, we can be done with the matter straightaway."

"That won't be a problem," old man Berkowitz interjected. "Will it, son?" and he shot Jonah a glare.

"Oh, I'm afraid it most certainly will, father," Jonah said before turning back around to the agent. "Sorry, Mr. Harris, but my conscience won't permit me to sign such documents."

Annoyed, the agent nudged Jonah toward the government car when the boy asked permission to pack a few things before they departed.

"I haven't got all day," the agent said as he escorted Jonah back to the pawnshop.

Riffraff scoured the ground floor, snatching up whatever valuables lay nearby. A young kid ran blindly from the storeroom and crashed into someone at the exit. A television tumbled to the ground.

The young kid started to complain but stopped in mid-sentence when he identified the human obstruction. Jimmy gaped at Jonah, panicked and fled down the sidewalk. Jonah yelled at the kid, calling him a snitch, a weasel, a fink. The tirade occupied Jonah's attention until he caught sight of photos spilling from the broken TV.

"Let's get a move on," Agent Harris ordered while Jonah rushed to scoop up the prints.

Papa Al grew suspicious. With Sergeant Maloney at his side, the mobster made his way back to follow the agent and Jonah upstairs to the living quarters.

Papa Al saw Jonah holding the envelope with the photo shop's logo on the front. "Mind if we have a private word with the young man?" he asked the agent.

"He's in my custody now," Agent Harris said. "You'll have to wait outside."

Within the doorframe, Papa Al turned and said to Jonah, "It matters not how strait the gate / how charged with punishments the scroll / you are not the master of your fate / for I am the captain of your soul."

Jonah flashed him a smug look before raising his middle digit in a farewell salute. The agent closed the door to better control the situation while Jonah walked to a rack of empty shelves. A scream wailed through his head. Not an album remained—Big Brother, Percy, the Dead—all gone.

"We need to be on our way," Agent Harris said.

But Jonah didn't hear him, gazing at where his prized collection once rested. A rage rose within. With renewed determination, he brought the envelope to his inspection.

"Mr. Berkowitz," the agent repeated, "gather some things and let's go."

Jonah packed his tape recorder plus some garments into his backpack and carried it to the restroom. Agent Harris stayed close by.

"Do you mind?" Jonah said to the agent before closing the door.

The agent heard the click of the lock and took a step back.

Jonah turned on both faucets to create white noise. He opened the window and gazed down thirty feet to the backyard. His phobia roiled inside. Too far to jump. On the clock, he hurried to the linen cabinet to remove a number of bed sheets, which he tied together. He secured one end of the line to the radiator and tossed the other out the window.

The agent knocked on the door. "Time's up."

"Can't a guy take a dump in peace?" Jonah answered.

Another minute or two passed before a vile wretchedness came to the agent from the other side. The din of hurling and puking filled the air.

"You okay in there?" Agent Harris asked as he tapped on the door.

The spewing of bowels continued uncontained. "Need help?"

The suffering subsided. The agent pressed an ear against the door and overheard the speech of two distinct persons.

"You got somebody in there with you?" the agent asked as he banged on the entry.

No response except for the ongoing dialogue.

The agent lowered his shoulder and busted down the door. He rushed passed a laundry chute and a linen cabinet to the window. A homemade line dangled outside against the rear of the building. With a curse he spun around and took in the scene. Voices spilled from a tape recorder, which rested on the toilet seat. He pushed the "Off" button and started to leave when he noticed the shower curtain quiver. He loosened the strap on his gun holster. In one motion, he swept the plastic drape aside—nothing but the breeze from the opened window.

⅄

Dead quiet returned. Jonah listened for any sign of activity. He waited another ten minutes before crawling out of the laundry bin. With a deliberate step, he walked to the exit of the storeroom, eased open the door and peeked into the lobby. It appeared dark with the exception of a band of sunlight that entered through the front door where a "Closed" sign hung.

He went to the register to empty it before opening the floor safe. His father had not yet made the weekly bank deposit. Jonah collected a medal and over three thousand dollars in cash. Good but not good enough to start a new life, he thought.

Chapter 6

Jonah strapped on his backpack and made a beeline along the Panhandle, a narrow strip of grass and trees that ran parallel with the Haight District. He pushed up the collar of his Pendleton and slumped inward as might a turtle in hiding. Vehicles whizzed past. He peeped sideways, wondering if the next car would be the one. Paranoia leaked into his psyche as he zigzagged over to Central Avenue. The quiet of the residential area soothed him until he realized that he was the lone pedestrian—an easy target.

There was no returning to the Fillmore, he thought. While he wanted to say a final goodbye to his childhood friend, it would have been too risky. Otis's place would be the first stop for Papa Al. Jonah needed to get out of the City, but first there was the matter of a debt owed him.

He came to Buena Vista Park, the eastern border of Psychedelphia. A ring of flower children sat on the knoll, passing around a joint, taking a breather from the crowds down at Hippie Hill.

The scene looked inviting, but he resisted the temptation and pushed down Haight Street passing the Drogstore Café. Moonlights wrapped around the structure showcasing a kaleidoscope of colors—purples, reds and yellows fused together in a borderless mass. Like so many of the buildings, the once pristine lady had been subdivided into tiny boxes to squeeze out as much rent as possible.

Greed, Jonah thought. Is there ever enough?

A patrol car eased down the lane. Jonah ducked inside behind a rack of magazines, holding an issue of *Time* to his face. A police officer poked his head out the window of the cruiser and scanned each storefront with a thorough examination.

Jonah eyed the black-and-white until it disappeared. He started to return the periodical to the rack when he noticed the cover's title—SUMMER OF LOVE.

Jonah let loose a private laugh as he stepped outside. A long ago banner boasted those same three words, hanging over Stanyan Street at the gateway to Golden Gate Park. It was the annual reminder to sign up for the Catholic Youth Organization's (CYO) summer camp. Now the corporate types had stolen the catchy phrase, wanting to cash in.

Everything's for sale, Jonah thought, as he headed toward Shrader Street on the western edge of the district. The money-grubbers better hurry if they want their piece of the pie. Not much time left. Jonah knew the district couldn't handle the hundred thousand kids who had besieged the area. The whole thing could collapse on itself at any moment.

He arrived at The Psychedelic Shop. A mixed bag of posters decorated the display window. The Dalai Lama, Jefferson Airplane, a nuclear missile, and a burning monk fought each other for space. Stacks of *Electric Kool-Aid Acid Test* rested nearby.

Jonah saw two familiar guys wearing leather outfits and entered. "Hey, Spike, how are you?" Jonah said to the biker who was studying products in a glass case.

"Want some peyote?" Spike asked. He was a burly man, tatted up, wearing a Fu Manchu.

"No thanks."

"Mushrooms?"

"You seen Sonny?" Jonah asked.

"Should be at the headquarters," Spike said. "He's pissed at you. Wouldn't go over there right now."

"I need to see him right away," Jonah said.

Spike sensed the urgency in Jonah's voice. "You in a fix?"

"I have to leave town for a while."

Spike thought that Jonah was in more trouble than he was letting on and as a warning the biker said, "The cops are always keeping tabs on Sonny. They're probably watching the place as we speak."

"Are you still enjoying that Grateful Dead album? It was my last copy," Jonah said.

Spike took his meaning and all three went to the storage room where Spike told his fellow Angel to strip off his clothes. With a grunt, the recruit obliged, knowing he didn't hold rank to complain.

⅄

Spike and Jonah strutted past the I/Thou Coffee Shop and the Xanadu leather store. They kept pace with a cluster of hippies, trying to blend in. Jonah, however, felt conspicuous in his three-sizes-too-big biker attire. The sleeves of the black leather jacket dangled past his fingertips as he held up the pants.

Jonah noticed another black-and-white. The squad car turned onto Shrader Street and parked in front of the Hells Angels residence. Spike and Jonah pushed their way into the middle of the pack as it headed toward Hippie Hill.

Young people, wearing daisy chains in their hair, lay stretched out across the grass at the entrance to Golden Gate Park. The sound of pennywhistles, harmonicas and guitars accompanied toddlers as they ran in circles chasing their shadows.

Jonah looked back over his shoulder. From this vantage point, he could keep track of the patrol car as it sat at the corner of Haight and Shrader.

A scrawny guy with scruffy facial hair and wild eyes stepped atop a wooden crate. "Can you catch those small-minded words, can you?" he said as he pointed to another holding up a transistor radio for all to hear. The lyrics to the Jefferson Airplane's "White Rabbit" floated across the meadow.

"You all think it's just *one happy Saturday afternoon*, don't you?" Wild Eyes said, parroting a phrase from the song. "Well, let me tell you something. There ain't no *yellow clouds rising in the noon.* Just gray skies, my brothers and sisters."

No one paid much attention to him. There were many who held similar appearances, most of them burned-out vets coming home from 'Nam, descending upon the Haight in search of a dumping ground for their nightmares.

While Spike flirted with a pretty thing in her buckskins, Jonah drifted toward the mysterious man with pupils as big as cue balls.

"I was born of a teenage prostitute," Wild Eyes preached. "Spent most of my years at McNeil Island Penitentiary. I've learned a thing or two about life. You understand me?"

Jonah couldn't withdraw as if stuck in some strange gravitational pull. While the message's content offended him, the delivery was spellbinding.

"The Summer of Love is dead, my friends." Wild Eyes raised his head to include the others at his feet.

A gaggle of women gazed back with a wandering look, tripping. Their heads swayed in awe, as if this figure before them was the muse they never had.

"Look around you," Wild-Eyes added. "Is this the nirvana that the Human Be-In promised? Is it? The black man is threatening to rise up and destroy us all. Wipe your brain clean. See the light before the candle burns down to its very nub."

Wild-Eyes blew on a conch shell to pull others in. "Every last one of you, turn to the west and witness the final sparks of civilization before the Negro has his way with you…and your women…and your offspring. The day of reckoning is upon us!"

Spike pricked up an ear. "I love this guy," he said with a smile as the sermon of hate continued.

Jonah backstepped. While Spike and the other Angels were the unofficial guardians of the district, Jonah never grew comfortable with their stance against minorities.

The patrol car moved on from the Angel's headquarters. Jonah gave Spike the all-clear signal and they drifted east one block.

A behemoth answered the doorbell and approached a locked gate. He acknowledged Spike's presence before asking who the runt was.

"You remember Jonah, right?" Spike said. "He does spot work for Sonny."

Jonah tried to stick out his hand in a greeting but it lay buried within the jacket's sleeve. The guard squinted, not sure what he was looking at.

"Spread 'em," the guard said.

Jonah held out his arms and widened his stance as if in a lineup. The guard frisked the teenager before sifting through the backpack. T-shirts, jeans and underwear landed on the walkway. The sight of banded wads of cash caused the guard to balk. He leafed through the cash before inspecting an envelope.

Satisfied no weapons were present, the guard motioned for them to go ahead. Jonah gathered his things and followed Spike up a granite staircase where another musclehead waited. After a second body search, Jonah was allowed inside.

A skinny type, wearing a black T-shirt, leather vest and biker boots, approached. A cigarette dangled from the corner of his mouth while bags beneath his eyes told of someone who had been on an all-nighter.

"Where've you been?" Sonny Barger said to Jonah. The founder of the Oakland chapter rarely showed a smile, all business. He wore chin whiskers and a receding hairline, as if raked back by years of riding into the wind. A dagger, a death-skull and a cross decorated his frame. At 5-foot-9 and 140 pounds, he was not an imposing figure but his demeanor said otherwise.

"I've been busy over at the pawnshop," Jonah said.

"Be busy here."

"I came to give my notice."

"Is that so?" Sonny said.

Spike came forward on behalf of the kid, saying, "He's hot. Cops are looking for him. That's why we switched out his clothes."

"Cops are looking for everyone," Sonny corrected.

"I'm here to collect the back pay you owe me," Jonah said.

Jonah had been a faithful worker, putting in his time, not asking too many questions.

"Okay," Sonny said.

Jonah eyed Spike with a grin.

"Soon as you do one last job," Sonny added.

Short on time, Jonah started to walk away.

"Where do you think you're going?" Sonny said.

"I quit."

"You quit when I say you quit."

⅄

Jonah began to gather clumps of Mexican weed—stems, leaves, seeds and all. A sprinkling of Coca-Cola acted as a binding agent before the batch was placed in a presser. From there, Jonah wrapped the "bricks" with purple cellophane.

His mind drifted, thinking how bad things were. The death of Sara shook him up. She believed in him and would have expected more than what he had become. These thoughts and others kept harassing him until a curious sight brought him out of his melancholy. A coworker was stuffing an empty soda bottle into the middle of a brick of weed.

"What're you doing?" Jonah whispered.

"Trying to save on inventory," the employee said.

"That ain't cool," Jonah said.

"You work your side of the table and I'll work mine."

"Boss wants to see you," an Angel said to Jonah.

Jonah wiped his hands on his Pendleton and followed the Angel to a backroom. Sonny looked up from his paperwork, put down his pen and pointed to an emblem on his vest.

"See this. This is a 1% patch. Know what it means?"

"Probably not," Jonah answered.

"The American Motorcycle Association is like the Elks Club of biking—prim and proper, full of themselves. They bragged that 99% of bikers are clean-living folk but condemned the rest of us as scumbag barbarians. And that's just the way we like it. We're the 1% you don't want to hassle with. Got it?"

"Not much room for interpretation," Jonah said.

Sonny ran the whole show up and down California. That went for colors and patches, bike runs, meetings, and especially when it came to drugs. The Haight was a new venture for the Angels. The club walked a thin line as it sought to expand its operation into the LSD market.

So far the San Francisco chapter had managed to keep a low profile, even capturing the hearts of the locals as *protector non gratis*. Sonny intended to keep it that way. Rules were rules and the number one rule was don't mess with Sonny.

The Angel ordered the kid to deliver product to a place along the Panhandle. "Don't muck it up, kid."

"Right."

"Spike will accompany you," Sonny said.

"No problem," Jonah said knowing he had little choice in the matter.

The duo started to gather up purple cellophane bricks from the workstations, Spike complaining the whole time. "Wanna hurry it up? I got a date with some primo crank across the Bay."

Jonah went back to work, filling a duffle bag when he felt an odd shaped item. He plucked it up and inspected the product. *What the hell?* Convinced that he would catch the blame for the sloppy workmanship, he unwrapped the marijuana, extracted the soda bottle from the center and redid the job.

At the exit, the behemoth caught the signal from Sonny and put out an arm to stop the kid. Jonah shrugged his shoulders, wondering what was up, but the guard didn't respond.

Sonny stepped in front of the teenager. "The backpack stays here," he said pointing to the carryall.

"But it's all I own," Jonah complained.

"Your money will be waiting for you when you return," Sonny said.

Jonah thought about retrieving the envelope with the photos but decided it might be in safer hands here.

Chapter 7

"Ring it again," Spike said to Jonah as they stood in front of 1090 Page Street. The kid did but there was no answer.

Spike cussed as he glanced at his wristwatch. He paced along the sidewalk, preening his Fu Manchu before taking another peek at the time.

"Gonna get stuck on the Bay Bridge," Spike said. He gave the buzzer another try but with the same result as before.

Spike shook his head. "Gotta make sure that old lady of mine don't snort up all the crank."

"I can hang around," Jonah offered.

"Sonny would have my balls if something happened to the shipment," Spike said.

"I know the people. It'll be okay." Jonah owned a relationship with Big Brother and the Holding Company, using his connections with the *S.F. Chronicle* as an excuse to get close to several bands.

Spike checked his watch again, thinking. "All right, thanks, kid."

"You bet."

"Make sure you report back to Sonny with the return package."

"*Return package*?"

Spike explained the deal, ordered the kid to do right and then left on his Harley, racing down Oak Street toward the freeway.

Jonah returned to the door and knocked. Nothing. He swung around to leave when a curious sight materialized from a window. Fishnet stockings and red stilettos adorned an eight-foot long limb.

A female straddled the fiberglass leg. She wore stringy hair and a pock-marked face while bits of antique glass and crystal beads hung from her neck. She leaned out, saying hello.

"Hi there, Jonah. What do you think of my new sex toy?" Janis Joplin said, fondling the fake limb as if making love to it.

"Congrats on the trip to Monterey," Jonah said. "No stopping you and the band now."

Big Brother was in demand after their bit at the Monterey Pop Festival the previous year. Among the five hundred groups playing in the City, they were near the top of the heap, becoming the house band at the Straight Theater on Haight Street.

"Everything comes with a price tag," Janis said, holding a bottle of Jack. "Just yesterday some crazed fan jumped out of his car, pulling on me, trying to claw the clothes right off my back. It's nuts," and she took a swig.

"That's the cost of fame, I guess."

"What are you doing in that getup?" Janis said as she studied the sagging leather outfit.

Jonah bypassed the lengthy account that would come with answering such a query and said, "Actually I'm here with a delivery," and he held up a duffle bag.

"In that case, let's get those pretty blues of yours up here," she said, waving him on.

Jonah climbed three steps to an unlatched entrance. "Hello," he called out as he stepped inside. "Anyone home?"

His echo bounced off the walls of the living room, which had been converted to a dance hall. Laughter came to him from the rear of the house. He made his way down the hallway to a chamber. Janis Joplin and the members of Big Brother lay naked atop a poster bed, clumped together in a grand pose.

"Get in here and shut the door," Janis said. "The draft's nipping at my tush."

Another, who wore glasses and a scholarly look, approached. "My name is Robert Crumb."

Jonah introduced himself before saying, "You did that comic strip, *Fritz the Cat*, right?"

"Nice of you to remember," Crumb said.

"Robert will be doing the cover for our next album," Janis interjected.

The artist brought Jonah to an easel where a painting rested. "What do you think?"

"Actually," Jonah said, "I'm in kind of a hurry. Just wanted to drop off a shipment."

"Nonsense," Crumb said. "Now have a look."

The more Jonah hesitated the louder the demands came from around the room. Outvoted, he consented and surveyed a rendition of the proposed album jacket—fleshy bodies were surrounded by cartoon images of the band members. One-eyed guitarist James Gurley stood next to an organ on a dinner plate with the caption "Piece of My Heart". Janis stood in prison stripes, dragging a black orb under the title "Ball and Chain".

Jonah peered beyond the artwork, opting to study the live scene before him. "I think it's just fine."

After exchanging opinions, everyone retired to the dance hall in different stages of nudity. Jonah tossed the duffle bag to the wooden floor. Some of the band members inspected the bricks.

After a taste test, Janis nodded her approval and handed over a batch of Dexedrine as payment for the weed. "This should satisfy those sons-a-bitches," she said before reclaiming one of the caps and downing it with swig of Jack.

"I was under the impression," Jonah said, "that Sonny wanted LSD in exchange for the bricks."

"Speed's always been the drug of choice for the Angels," Janis said. "Besides, I'll be damned if I know where Ken Kesey's delivery boy is. He was supposed to be here yesterday."

"I'm not sure this is going to fly with Sonny," Jonah persisted.

"Have you always been this loyal to duty?"

"Had it whipped into me from the get-go."

"You're kinda cute," Janis said before bouncing to a girl who was fawning over guitarist James Gurley.

The two women locked onto each other, their lips pressed together. Then Janis pushed away the girl, attached herself to the guitarist and began to howl.

"Come on / come on / come on / come on /
Didn't I make you feel like you were the only man ."

The lyrics poured out soulful and bluesy, the music jumping through everyone. Jonah was familiar with the rendition, a cover song of Erma Franklin's release last spring. This, however, was something else, and Jonah shook his head in awe.

The music grew until the bleeps of sirens and the demands from a bullhorn sounded from the street. Jonah gathered up the bricks of weed, stuffed them back into the duffle bag and disappeared down the hallway toward the rear chamber.

Men in blue streamed up the steps and rushed inside. One ordered the revelers to put clothes on. Another asked if any drugs were being used.

"What brought you here?" Janis asked.

"Got a complaint about a lot of screaming going on," a sergeant said.

"That wasn't screaming," guitarist James Gurley corrected, "that was Janis Joplin."

"Doesn't seem to be much difference between one and the other," the sergeant said.

"What would your Irish ass know about music?" Janis said.

A hard expression took hold of the sergeant. He waved on his men. They began to search the flat, upturning furniture, rugs and mattresses. Cupboards, closets and crevices held nothing of interest. In the middle of the shakedown, a familiar voice could be heard from the entranceway.

"What's going on here?" a man in a suit said alongside his bosomy companion.

"The cavalry has arrived," Janis said before stepping to the new arrival, putting her arm around him.

"Who are you?" the sergeant said to the stranger.

"I am Terence Hallinan, attorney at law," he said as he picked a business card from his wallet.

The sergeant scanned the ID before tossing it to the ground. "Your clients are under the influence."

"I would certainly hope so," Hallinan said. "I'd hate to think that this was their normal behavior."

An officer returned from a bedroom with a young man in a leather outfit. The sergeant examined the winged skull stitched on the back of the suspect's jacket.

"You're kind of puny to be a Hells Angel," the sergeant said.

Jonah lowered his head from the attention.

The sergeant noticed the duffle bag. "Whaddya got in there?"

"Ah, well ah…," and Jonah stalled out.

Hallinan stepped between the two and said to the policeman, "Not this young man nor anyone else will be answering your questions today."

The sergeant threw a stare at the attorney.

"You have no probable cause to search these premises," the attorney added.

"What did you say your name was again?" the sergeant asked.

"Hallinan, Terence Hallinan."

"Didn't I see you down at the city jail last weekend with those two no-counts from The Grateful Dead?" the sergeant said.

"Mr. Robert Weir and Mr. Ronald McKernan would be their preferred titles," the attorney said.

"Are you any relation to Vincent Hallinan?" the sergeant asked on a hunch.

"He's my father, or at least that's what my mother keeps insisting."

Vincent Hallinan was a lawyer as well. But unlike his son, the father was hardened as to the way of local politics. A former rugby bruiser, the senior never backed away from the SFPD or other heavyweights downtown.

With the verification of who this suit guy was, the sergeant bristled. Not wanting to take the chance of an official reprimand on his record, he ordered his men to clear out.

Claps and whistles escorted the lawmen to the exit where the sergeant turned around to the throng. "We'll be back."

Taunts continued to chase after the men in blue as they retreated to the sidewalk. Janis went to the open window, caressed the fiberglass leg and started singing.

"Come on / come on / come on / come on /
and take another piece of my heart…"

The patrol cars eased down Page Street while everyone inside crowded around Hallinan to express their gratitude. He took a grand bow, showing off for his girlfriend. Janis flipped the woman a smile, scanning her bountiful body.

Jonah picked up his duffle bag of weed. "I'm out of here," and he started for the door.

"What about the dope?"

"I told you. Sonny wants acid, not your Dexedrine."

She hounded him all the way down the front steps. "Hey, blue eyes, can't you give a lady a break?"

"Wish I could."

At the sight of a vehicle coming up the street, Janis said, "Here comes our boy now."

A guy wearing a tie-dye T-shirt disembarked from a VW bus. "Sorry about the delay," he said. "Bear's been experimenting with a new batch. It's the bomb," he said as he surrendered a paper bag to Janis.

Owsley Stanley, a.k.a. Bear, had moved up the ranks from soundman for The Grateful Dead to Ken Kesey's leading chemist, producing over ten million doses of LSD within just the last two years.

"It ain't me you need to apologize to," Janis said to the delivery boy before gesturing to Jonah. "This gentleman has had to wait on you, forced to listen to my *screaming*."

Jonah counted out the tabs. Satisfied, he gave the weed to Janis in exchange for the acid.

"You sure you don't want to come back upstairs?" Janis said, wetting her lips in play.

"Can't," Jonah said without an explanation.

Janis jiggled her pelvis at him, but he refrained and said goodbye. "You take care of yourself," he said.

"What are the chances of that?" she said before retiring to Big Brother's pad.

Jonah stood there and gazed at the place where she once stood. He didn't want to let go of the moment, not knowing if he would ever be this close to greatness again. While in this catatonic state, a familiar voice came to him in bits and pieces from behind.

"What, you daydreamin' or somethin'?" Otis said.

"Where'd you come from?"

"Been standin' behind you for maybe a lifetime," Otis said before adding, "You got the jimmies?"

"I thought we weren't speaking to each other," Jonah said.

"That's yesterday's news."

"I've been asking around," Jonah said. "Nobody's seen you. I thought you might be…might be…"

"Might be needin' my best friend?" Otis said finishing Jonah's sentence.

"I wouldn't go that far," Jonah said when another reminder came to him. "Your momma's been looking for you."

"I negotiated a sweet deal with a couple of whores up the street. Had to take them up on their offer. Been backed up for weeks. What was I suppose to do?"

"Your momma seemed pretty upset," Jonah added.

"What's in the paper bag, dude?" Otis said trying to change the topic.

"Nothing." Jonah slid the sack to his side.

Suspicion filled Otis. "Why don't we let the brother have a look-see?" he said in the third person as he gestured to the paper bag.

Jonah turned to leave when Otis reached out. His fingers split open the casing. Tabs of acid poured out. Jonah hurried to the ground, scooping up tiny squares of foil.

"Didn't know you was on the job," Otis said as he bent over to help. "Why didn't you tell the brother?"

Jonah hustled to corral the product, eyeing the area for any danger. Not until the tabs were reclaimed and stashed inside his pockets did Jonah answer his friend's question.

"You're right, I should trust you," Jonah said, trying to rekindle what they had lost.

"Damn straight," Otis said as he handed over some tabs.

The boys talked out their differences. A bond that stretched back to their births began to revisit them when Otis asked about the future. Both realized, however, that too many uncertainties blocked the path to such clairvoyance.

"You got time for a meal?" Otis asked knowing what the answer would be.

"I have to collect my things down at Sonny's."

"Guess this is it then," Otis said. There was no way he would accompany Jonah to the Hells Angel's headquarters. Those boys would just as soon put a .38 into a black man as look at him.

They shook hands and Otis walked away. Jonah was starting to realize the ramifications of his decision to dodge the draft. He was abandoning his past and everyone in it. Some of those folks he couldn't give a rat's ass about, but many had been friends from the beginning.

Jonah turned to catch a last glimpse of his childhood friend. Instead of continuing east toward Fillmore Street, however, Otis swerved up Clayton toward the heart of the Haight. Jonah thought this was odd knowing Otis was in enough trouble with Big Momma already.

Jonah began to search for an answer to Otis's actions when an alarm jolted him. A woman's screech sounded from the open window of Big Brother's place. And another.

Jonah sped back up the staircase and through the entrance to see Terence Hallinan sprawled across the floor. Jonah spied the fear in the lawyer's bosomy girlfriend.

"He...he's unconscious," she said. "Somebody do something."

Jonah shifted his look to Janis.

"Not to worry," the singer said. "Was his first go with smack." She paused as everyone stared at her in disbelief. "I might've given him a stiff shot is all...He'll survive."

Without a care, Janis started to undress Hallinan's lady in front of Jonah. Embarrassed, he excused himself, leaving the fate of the young attorney in the hands of others.

⅄

He lugged along Oak Street, thinking that what he had just witnessed was messed up. Perhaps the doomsayers were right, perhaps the music of the City would collapse on itself, that there would be no need for the underhanded tactics of mobsters and politicians. He arrived at the Angel's place and walked past the security guards to find Sonny Barger in the assembly room.

"You're late, kid," Sonny said.

"I had to wait an extra thirty minutes for Kesey's delivery boy," Jonah said before shoveling the tabs of acid from his pockets.

Sonny made a full accounting. "Fifty short."

"Can't be." Jonah took a look for himself, but the tally was correct. His mind raced back over the exchange—the lengthy conversation with Janis, the struggle with Otis. *Crap!*

In a hurry, Jonah thought of a compromise. "How about you give me my things and I won't ask for that back pay you owe me."

Sonny picked a white T-shirt and a pair of jeans from Jonah's carryall and flipped them to the kid. "Put them on. The new recruit wants his leathers back."

"What about the money I brought with me?" Jonah said as he began to slip off the borrowed outfit.

"I told you not to muck up the job, kid."

"Can I at least have the envelope with the photos?"

⅄

He roamed Haight Street looking for Otis and the missing LSD tabs. He had to set things right with Sonny. Without a get-away stash, a run from the authorities would most likely end before it started. But a part of him was angry. For the time that he was employed by the Angels, he had done his best, always putting quality first. The incident with the jerkwad and the coke bottle set him off. Why the hell should I give a crap about Sonny's weed, Jonah thought, if this is the reward I get? But reality was reality, and he resumed his search.

Jonah remembered Otis veering away from his momma's place and heading toward the Haight. But why? Jonah worked his way along the main thoroughfare. A six-foot-three black guy wearing a feathered fedora and burgundy cloak should be easy to spot, Jonah thought. He scampered through the district, peering into storefronts and alleys, but Otis was nowhere to be found.

With one last effort, Jonah mounted a flatbed to gaze over the sea of hippies. One or two Negroes came into view but they were too beefy to be Otis. Frustrated, Jonah gave up the search and started to climb down from the truck when he spotted a familiar car cruising toward him.

He darted into the nearest shop. Between the blinds of a window shade, a black Caddy appeared. Sergeant Maloney sat behind the wheel while Papa Al occupied the backseat.

Jonah retreated deeper into the store to gather his thoughts. In a far corner, he played the role of a customer and fingered a collection of paisley shirts, keeping an eye on the entrance.

While contemplating his options, Jonah noticed a young girl acting suspicious near a stand of ankle boots. She tilted her head one way and then another in frenetic twitches. With a stealthy touch, she slipped the footwear into her handbag.

"No reason to behave that way," Jonah said in a paternal voice. "Everything here is free for the taking."

"Mind your own business, mister," the adolescent said, her eyes popping with dysphoria.

"The Free Store was set up by the Diggers," Jonah continued. "No profit-hungry jerkwads here—just a little insurrection is all."

The Diggers were a radical left-wing group of activists. They were anarchists who blended free services and goods with a community consciousness, of which The Free Store was the most notable example.

Jonah lifted a beaded cardigan from a nearby hanger and presented it to the adolescent. "This would go nicely with the ankle boots."

"Asshole." The girl snatched the sweater and waltzed toward the exit.

"A thank you would have been nice," Jonah called out.

An employee approached and said, "She's high is all."

"Sorry?" Jonah said.

"The little shit-kicker, the one with the ankle boots," the employee repeated. "She's on crack or something. I see her type all day. Probably headed over to the Crystal Palace."

The Crystal Palace, Jonah repeated in his head. Of course.

Chapter 8

Letters on a neon sign hummed. H-O-T buzzed with electricity while the E and the L flickered. Didn't matter. Everyone knew the reputation of the place, long ago tagged as the "Crystal Palace Hotel". Mystery engulfed the four-story structure. Many believed it had connections far beyond the crooks downtown.

Jonah bounced through the door and approached the manager. A three-day old stubble and sunspots hung on his face. While he often handed out free samples of LSD, peyote, mushrooms and other psychedelics, the narcs never seemed to bother him. It was as if the place was off limits to the authorities. To add to the riddle, he had no known connection to Owsley Stanley or any other drug supplier. If such was the case, where did he get his product and how did he keep his business afloat?

"Hey, Jolly," Jonah said to the manager, "have you seen Otis?"

"Try 4C," Jolly said.

"Thanks."

"Careful," Jolly warned.

Jonah mounted the staircase, skipping steps. On the second floor landing, shrills and wails began. Up another flight, a gaunt face with stark eyes appeared from a half-opened door. Jonah stepped over the zombie and gazed into the smoke-filled apartment.

"Otis, you in here?" Jonah called out.

In the living room, which was bare of furniture, he spotted a feathered fedora sitting atop a half-conscious black man. Jonah reached out to roll him over. The man was wearing the soiled uniform of a Marine.

The empty eyes of a schizophrenic greeted Jonah, but it wasn't his schizophrenic. In the veteran's hand was a rusty-tipped needle. His jaundiced face glistened with perspiration while fresh tracks festooned his arm. Without a warning, the veteran jerked up and grabbed onto Jonah.

"Are you with them?" the junkie whispered.

"*Them*?" Jonah asked.

And the junkie gestured downstairs to indicate his meaning.

"Where's Otis?"

"Leave me alone. No more. Please," the junkie said before releasing his grip and flopping back down.

Jonah placed a blanket over him and removed the feathered fedora from his head. Perhaps the rumors were true, Jonah thought. It had been speculated that the hotel was a government laboratory, that the CIA and others were studying the effects of super hallucinogens upon humans. To make matters worse, many of these guinea pigs ended up at the Free Clinic, treated for strychnine and insecticide poisoning.

The thought sent Jonah's heart racing as he picked his way. Syringes and soft-drink cartons laced with white powder littered his path as he gagged from the stench of urine.

A bark, sharp and evil, lured Jonah to a bedroom. With a tentative touch, he nudged open the door. It moaned, mixing with the other sounds in ominous rhythm.

A stripped-down Otis cowered in the corner on all fours, baring his teeth, growling. He clawed at a wooden plank with his bloodied fingernails.

Jonah approached with his outstretched hands, saying, "It's me. You're going to be okay. Just give me the extra tabs and..."

Otis lunged at the intruder, snapping, grinding his teeth. More blood.

Jonah played along, taking a chance. "That's a good boy," talking in a cadence as if conversing with a mangy mongrel. He reached out once more, landing his palm on Otis's matted Afro. "What a pretty boy you are. You're the prettiest," and more pets.

Otis responded and rolled over exposing his belly.

"Look what I've got for you," Jonah said as he presented a familiar looking hat.

⅄

The duo lumbered down the windy staircase. Howls and cries trailed after them to the lobby where Jolly said his goodbyes.

"You take care. Good luck over in 'Nam."

Jonah, struggling under the weight of Otis, turned halfway around and threw out a sneer before exiting. They shuffled three blocks west while Otis flared out his nostrils at pedestrians. A hippie leaned forward to examine the feathered fedora when Otis bit the invading nose. The man yelped.

At the corner of Clayton and Haight, creeping Jenny drooped from planter boxes, which rested below bay windows. Chipped pillars supported a portico that was guarded by an iron-gate topped with razor wire.

Jonah pressed a buzzer while glancing up and down the street. After several more tries, a mechanical hum sounded. They climbed the stoop, jumping a line of thirty to the lobby. The Free Clinic was open just one day per week, treating over two hundred patients during the twenty-four hour period. Jonah felt fortunate he didn't have to haul his friend across town to the ER at S. F. General. *Fortunate?* Jonah thought, *give me a break*.

The air was oozing with a stew of body odor and patchouli oil. Jonah fanned the foul odor before writing "Otis Wright" into the log. Greeting cards lay near the register inviting all to "The Funeral Of The Hippie". Jonah flipped to the backside: "PLACE: Buena Vista Park / DATE: Saturday, August 26th, 1967."

That's today, Jonah thought. *Funeral of the hippie*?

A fever-flushed woman, wearing nothing more than a blouse and panties, sat on a couch spewing her bronchitis into a fern pot. Next to her, an infant bawled, frustrated by her mother's dried-up breasts. A couple of junkies twitched and scratched. Above rested a sign that read: "No dealing, no holding, no using."

Jonah shepherded Otis to a bench. A couple nearby was wrapped in a blanket. Bare arms, shoulders and ankles peeked from the covering. They sat as one, she facing him, sitting on his lap. They appeared to be in quite a bit of pain. With each movement, the teenagers groaned in unison as if the parts of one were attached to the parts of the other.

Dr. Smith came in from a backroom to study the pair before calling for assistance. The young lovers were lifted as a single creature onto a wheelchair and rolled past the registry.

Jonah, with Otis's head resting on his shoulder, shrugged in disbelief. A wrinkled lady in her eighties adjusted her arm-sling, saying, "*Mentula captivus*."

"Excuse me," Jonah said.

"*Mentula captivus*," the woman repeated. "It's Latin for 'captive penis'."

"Uh, I don't think I need to know…"

"The muscles of the woman's genitalia," the senior persisted, "contract in blissful rhythm at the moment of orgasm. On the rare occasion, the penis can become stuck by the clamping vagina." A grin appeared on the old lady as if remembering a passing fantasy. "Sometimes, you can even have…"

Jonah pretended to hear his name being called and excused himself before lifting Otis to his feet.

"Sir, you can't go in there," a voice sounded from behind the registry as the boys headed down the hallway.

DETOX ROOM showed on a door's brass plate. Jonah entered and studied the patients. He conjectured that he might have gone from the proverbial rabbit hole into the Mad Hatter's Ball. An adolescent bounced off the four walls, her naked bosom flinging to and fro. Another hurled her body against the window bars. Otis let out a cry.

Enough. Jonah exited with his friend, went back to the front desk and demanded to see the doctor. As expected, he was told to wait his turn.

With time wasting away, Jonah threw out an influential name. "Otis here is a personal friend of Bill Graham's."

The admittance person cocked her head sideways at the mention of the music promoter. She closed a ledger and parted to the examination room.

A person, donning a white mock, soon appeared and with a hooked finger motioned for the two young men to follow him.

"I am Doctor Smith," he said after closing the door behind him. The introduction sounded muffled until he lowered his surgical mask to repeat his name.

"We've met before," Jonah said, "at the fundraiser last weekend."

"Ah, yes. That was very kind of Mr. Graham to offer his Fillmore Auditorium for the benefit. The proceeds will keep this place open for a few more months. After that, I don't know."

"I thought I read where Mayor Shelley promised to fund the clinic."

Dr. Smith glanced over to Otis, guessing that there wasn't an emergency and added, "The money never arrived. In fact, due to the false publicity, donations have dried up. If Mr. Graham would care to host another event, the clinic would be most grateful."

"I'll pass on the word," Jonah said knowing the likelihood of seeing Graham anytime soon was small.

The doc pinched on a fresh pair of rubber gloves. "Let's have a look at your friend, shall we?" He cleaned the abrasions and applied bandages after which he took the patient's vitals. Next, the doc went through the usual drill for suspected psychotic disorder.

"Has he consumed any food within the last two hours?"

"Not sure," Jonah said.

"Alcohol or antacids or barbiturates?"

A shrug.

"It doesn't appear too serious," and the doc hung his stethoscope around his neck. "Just to be safe, I would like to give him thirty milligrams of Thorazine."

He went to the medicine cabinet while a growl sounded from behind. "Perhaps I should put a muzzle on him."

"That would be fantastic," Jonah replied.

"Just kidding," the doc said with a grin.

Jonah grumbled as if disappointed. The doc dabbed Otis's vein with a pad and poked him. A bark and a snap.

"He might persist in this state for a while," Dr. Smith said. "Best thing to do is to talk him thru it." He started to fill out a form, saying, "Try to provide a peaceful environment—someplace quiet, out of the way."

"*Out of the way*," Jonah repeated. "My thoughts exactly."

"Here is a prescription for an antidepressant," the doc said as he handed the paperwork to Jonah plus a few tablets for the meantime. "Your friend should take the pills orally every twenty-four hours, increasing the dosage until his normal functions return. This could take up to three days at which time you may start to decrease the quantity. He may encounter..."

A call from the lobby interrupted the doctor's recital. He paused before continuing: "He may encounter some issues with body movements, dry mouth or dizziness."

Another harangue came to him and he left to investigate. A Negro wearing aviator sunglasses was crowding the receptionist.

"What is it?" Dr. Smith said to his employee upon drawing closer.

She squawked, sounding excited, saying that the man threatened her.

"I find that a loud voice often makes for poor harmony and ruins the song," the Negro said.

From the examination room, Jonah heard the familiar voice and tiptoed forward. He peeped through the crease of the opened door and spied the thug and the crooked cop. *Crap.*

"Time to split," Jonah said to his groggy friend.

Some of the bark had escaped from Otis and he submitted to Jonah's guidance. They went out the rear and started down the stairwell.

Back in the lobby, Dr. Smith asked the visitor what he wanted.

"Permit me to introduce myself. I am Allan Theodore McCollum the Third, but the locals simply refer to me as Papa Al."

"I know who you are," the doc said.

"I was merely inquiring from your receptionist the whereabouts of a young man when she spotted my weapon. I beg your forgiveness for any discomfort your employee may have experienced."

"If you'll excuse us," Dr. Smith said, "I have patients to tend to."

"Of course you do," Papa Al said, "but I am here on official business as community liaison. Sergeant Maloney and I are searching for Jonah Berkowitz. He apparently disappeared earlier today. More than a few people are concerned." Papa Al produced a photograph of the young man and asked Dr. Smith if he had seen him.

"You and your henchman should leave," Dr. Smith said as he included the policeman with his look.

Papa Al ignored the request and meandered to the far end of the room to open a window. He began to put a match to a cigar when he spotted a couple of characters lumbering along the alley below. The mobster retraced his steps to the doctor, excused himself and sped down the flight of stairs with Sergeant Maloney.

⅄

A casket filled with trinkets led a parade down the middle of Haight Street. A priest swung a crucible of incense anointing the mourners in a blessing. An altar boy walked beside him hoisting a cross. A black Lincoln Town Car hearse came next with youngsters in flowered denims and bright colored bell-bottoms close behind.

Jonah urged his friend forward, but Otis cringed and clawed at the limbs of mourners. The duo lost itself within the procession as Jonah peered backward, sideways, to the open space ahead.

A band of three hundred arrived at Buena Vista Park. The hearse sat by the curb while the priest and altar boy stood near the top of a grassy knoll where a makeshift stage stood.

A Digger stepped forward. "My fellow flower children, we are gathered here today before the eyes of God to proclaim the death of the hippie."

A roar swooped up alongside streams of bright lights. Newsmen jockeyed for position. A tour bus stopped, blocking traffic.

"The hippie no longer lives within the confines of the Haight-Ashbury," the Digger continued.

Another roar.

"He lives within the soul of every being who has experienced the miasma of his existence." The Digger locked his stare onto a reporter's camera. "He is within you," and he extended his index finger as if to include all those in TV land. "There is no longer any need for you to visit us. Spread the word within your community. Bring the revolution to your church, to your school, to your neighborhood, but do not come here. The hippie is forever dead," the Digger said as he raised both arms in homage.

The priest slid in front of the Digger. "My dear brothers and sisters, we do not scorn those who have trespassed upon our sanctum. We do not mock those who have spun our message of love into tales of decrepitude and decay. We ask only that you allow us to care for our own." With that proclamation, he motioned for the altar boy to circulate the masses with the offering basket.

"Let your hearts dictate the level of your generosity." The priest swept the crowd with his hallowed expression. "Release the burden from your wallets so that we may tend to the needy."

The Digger shook his head before reminding everyone that the purpose of today's procession was not to pay tribute in the form of money.

"But if the mood strikes you," the priest interrupted, "do not be deterred."

The congregation looked at each other with puzzled gazes. Confusion began to morph into anarchy as other speakers mounted the podium, trying to clarify the day's message, but it was too late.

Jonah spotted Papa Al moving around a hedgerow, scouring the brush along the north end of the park. Sergeant Maloney approached from the south, searching the coves of entranceways and garages.

Otis remained unsteady. Frantic, Jonah lugged his friend toward the rear of the hearse.

On the knoll the altar boy and the Digger fought for control of the offering basket. The priest descended to try to reclaim the situation, swaying his smoking crucible over the heads of the nonbelievers.

The disturbance brought Papa Al and Sergeant Maloney to the scene. Jonah lifted Otis into the back of the funeral coach and locked the door.

The priest suggested to his assistant that they should depart. The altar boy agreed and, with donations in hand, the pair made tracks for the hearse.

⅄

A pair of parrots squawked as Bill Graham entered. He passed the glassy stare of other fowls and sidled up next to Marion Sullivan at the counter.

"I heard John Handy is no longer playing at your club," Graham said.

"He's taken his sax and fled to Oakland."

"Who would've thought that the East Bay would be a more inviting place than the City of Love," Graham said.

"What about your Fillmore Auditorium?" Marion Sullivan asked. "What's happening there?"

"Downtown is still threatening to deny my permit renewal," Graham said.

"Without your dance hall," Sullivan said, "there won't be a lick of music left in the district."

"So much for Harlem of the West," Graham said. "I'm glad your brother didn't have to see this day."

"Me too," Marion Sullivan agreed.

"What'll it be, boys?" Leola King asked.

"Coffee for me...black," Graham said.

"Make that two," Sullivan said.

"I suppose you want water with that," Leola said.

"That'd be nice," Sullivan said.

"Big friggin' spenders," Leola said. She exhaled a huff and left, mumbling a Jesus-this and a Jesus-that to herself.

Squawks from above the entrance announced the presence of new patrons. Sergeant Maloney sneered at the parrots before marching alongside his colleague to the bar.

"Has either of you gentlemen," Papa Al said to the patrons at the counter, "seen young Jonah Berkowitz? He was to arrive at the Federal Building this morning with an F.B.I. agent, but such was not the case. The father is filled with worry over his son's unexplained disappearance."

"Haven't seen him," Marion Sullivan said.

"And what about you, Mr. Graham?" Papa Al said.

Bill Graham ignored the question, staring into the mirror behind the bar, sipping his coffee.

"As you are probably aware," Papa Al continued, "Jonah has serendipitously come into possession of some very photogenic mementos, photos that came from the very same camera, which you, Mr. Graham, claimed was void of film at the time."

Graham took another sip.

"Their value is of a personal nature, as I am sure you are aware," Papa Al persisted.

The music producer lowered his mug, peered at the image standing behind him in the mirror and said, "Don't you have something better to do than to shadow an old Jew like me around town?"

"Believe me, when I say that you are indeed deserving of such attention," Papa Al said.

"*Yah pin noteph ziva,*" Graham said.

"I am an avid proponent of culture," Papa Al said. "Do enlighten us."

"It's Yiddish for 'gonorrhea dripping penis'."

Chapter 9

The funeral coach sped around the curves of the Marin Headlands, crossing the double yellow as it passed a string of vehicles. Curses sounded with each jolt of the vehicle.

"For Christ's sake, slow down," the altar boy said to the priest.

The conversation made its way to two stowaways hiding in the rear. "Not the kind of talk you expect from churchgoers," one stowaway whispered to the other while bracing himself through the turns.

"If...you...say...so," the second stowaway responded as he bounced off the wheel well.

"The drugs should be kicking in anytime," the first stowaway said. "Try not to throw up all over..."

But a wrenching seized his friend. Vile blue matter exploded. Two days worth of debauchery coated the steel ribcage.

"Did you hear that?" the priest said to the altar boy. Without waiting for a response, the cleric turned into a pullout near Muir Beach.

A creek found its way through the grasslands to the Pacific. An ivy-clad lodge stood under a sign that read Pelican Inn.

The priest exited and stomped through a pothole of rainwater to open the rear panel doors.

"What in the name of Jesus, Joseph and Mary?" the priest said at the sight of two teenagers sprawled across the bed of the hearse.

"Good evening, Father," the white boy said.

"Good evening, my ass. What're you two scalawags doing in there?" the priest said.

"Well, I'm resting," the white boy said, "and my partner here is regurgitating what's left of his bowels."

"Get out."

The white kid guided his friend to the bumper, flopped his legs over the side and gave him a shove. The black mass thumped to the feet of the priest.

"What's wrong with him?" the priest asked.

"Just needs another day's rest is all," the white kid said.

The Father scanned the inside of the hearse. "Jesus, All-Mighty. You've got the place smelling like gutted fish."

"Sorry?" the white kid guessed.

The altar boy exited the passenger side and stepped to the rear where he studied the collection of misfits. "Who are they?"

"Reprobates," the priest said. "Evidently they've hitched a ride with us."

"Well, get rid of them," the altar boy countered.

"Could you at least give us a lift to the next town?" the white kid asked.

"We don't need this," the altar boy said.

"My friend is in bad shape," the white kid persisted. "I don't know if he's up for a hike."

The priest leaned forward to better examine the Negro before saying that he did indeed look sickly.

"But...," the altar boy started to say.

"We'll have none of that," the priest interrupted. "Where is your Christian spirit?"

The white kid was thankful for the offer of a ride and gathered up his friend and helped him into the backseat. The altar boy inspected the rear of the coach, closed the doors and returned to the front.

"Is this yours?" the altar boy asked as he held up an envelope to the white kid.

The stranger reached out and snatched the paper casing away.

"You're welcome," the altar boy said in a sarcastic tone. "Some people," he said as he shook his head.

Jonah ignored the comment, checking the contents of the envelope, counting the photos. "All here," and he sighed his relief.

"Did you honestly think I'd steal some silly photos?" the altar boy asked.

"Not sure," the white kid said before adding, "Maybe."

The altar boy pivoted back to the priest. "I've got a bad feeling about this."

⅄

The vehicle cruised along a serpentine route to the coastal town of Stinson Beach. A hush swallowed all until the altar boy said to the priest, "At least you could have made them ride in the rear."

"And have them sit in their own filth?" the priest said.

"It's what they deserve," answered the altar boy.

"I'm Jonah Berkowitz," the white kid said, but the altar boy refused to acknowledge the greeting. Jonah motioned to his friend, saying, "And this reject is Otis, Otis Wright."

No response.

"And what about you, do you have a name?" Jonah asked the altar boy.

Nothing.

"Rene," the priest interjected. "His name is Rene."

"Renaé?" Jonah guessed, trying to get the pronunciation right.

"R-e-n-e," the altar boy corrected, dragging out the word. "The last e is pronounced as a long vowel like the e in ego," and he repeated his name. "Rene, got it?"

"He's French," the priest said as a way of a shorter explanation.

"Ahhh," Jonah said. "Makes sense." Something wasn't quite right about the kid, but Jonah didn't think the matter deserved much thought and swung his attention back to the priest who introduced himself as Father Paul Giguere.

"I am French as well. We hail from Quebec," and he pulled into a parking space.

They left the sleeping Otis in the hearse and walked along a raised sidewalk. The salty breeze engulfed them. In the distance, waves lapped onto the shore in a soothing cadence while a soft hum sounded from above as lampposts came alive.

The trio passed a market and a saloon before arriving at the Sand Dollar Café. Jonah opened the screen door for Rene who held his chin up in a haughty pose.

The Western façade, uneven hardwood floors and weathered windows told of another era, perhaps from the twenties. The group sat at a table with a red-checkered oilcloth. Father Paul yanked his coattails out from under him and sat in a chair.

"Welcome to Stinson Beach," the waitress said as she popped her gum. "Always nice to see the good Lord in our midst."

"Thank you, my dear," Father Paul said, "but I am a mere messenger of His word."

"Good enough for me," the waitress said. "Can I start you off with something to drink?"

"By any chance would you have any of the devil's nectar in stock?" the priest asked.

"Got no hard liquor. Just beer and wine."

"That is indeed a misfortune. The day has challenged us with a long list of trials and tribulations," the Father said with a fallen look.

"Not to worry," and she disappeared out the door.

"Aren't we here to eat?" Rene asked.

"Patience," Father Paul said with a grin. He began to count out loud as if playing some sort of game. Before he reached to twenty, a sweaty glass sat before him.

"Compliments of Smiley's next door," the waitress said with a pop of her gum. "Been here since 1851. Not Smiley, the store," the waitress clarified. "Will bourbon be okay?"

"*Merci, mon cher*," and the priest raised his drink to her.

"Oh, my, you speak French too," the waitress said with a smile.

"*Je veux être avec toi*," Father Paul added. "The birds of heaven pale in comparison to your beauty."

"Aren't you the one," and the waitress slapped him on the shoulder in play.

Rene threw out a theatrical cough to catch the waitress's attention. "I'll have a ham and cheese on wheat."

"Same here," Jonah said.

"Make that *trios*, my dear," Father Paul said in French, pouring it on.

The waitress repeated the order, winked at the priest and wiggled away.

"Lovely girl," Father Paul said as he studied her backside.

"I didn't think priests were allowed to flirt," Jonah said.

"That was not flirtation, my son," the Father said. "That was merely admiration for God's handy work. The Lord is truly a fine sculptor. Wouldn't you agree?"

"She did have curve appeal," Jonah said.

"Are you two nitwits through?" Rene said.

"Unfortunately, we're probably just getting started," Jonah said.

Father Paul agreed with a *par excellence*. "You have a sharp wit about you, my son," the priest said before turning to the altar boy, insisting he could learn a thing or two from their new friend.

"*Une conasse*," Rene said with his shaking head.

"What?" Jonah asked.

"He said that you are an asshole," Father Paul illuminated in a flat tone.

"Well, even assholes have feelings," Jonah said with a smirk.

"You are such an ingrate," Rene said.

"*Ingrate*?" Jonah repeated before adding, "An interesting word choice for a puny altar boy...How old are you, anyway?"

"That doesn't concern you," Rene said.

"You've got the complexion of a twelve-year-old but the disposition of a cranky old dirtbag."

"I've had just about enough of your insults," the altar boy said as he started to rise.

Without warning, another cleric entered the restaurant. The altar boy suspended his intent and reseated himself. Father Paul turned around, eyed the fellow priest and allowed a moment for thought before inviting the stranger to join them. An additional chair was brought over by the waitress who inquired whether or not the new arrival spoke French as well.

"*Juste un peu*," the new arrival said, pressing his index finger and thumb within an inch of each other to indicate his meaning.

"This handsome hulk," the waitress said, pointing with her eyes to Father Paul, "speaks the lover's tongue too. How about that?"

"Let me introduce myself," the new arrival said. "I am Father James Duggan from St. Brendan's Parish in San Francisco."

Additional salutations made their way around the table while sandwiches arrived. Another bourbon was ordered as well as a couple of shakes and a glass of water. Over the course of the meal, the conversation drifted toward the purpose of everyone's journey.

Father Duggan volunteered that he had church business further north. "I am speaking at a dear friend's memorial. He met with a tragic accident at sea."

"Was he a fisherman?" Father Paul guessed.

Father Duggan nodded before relaying the specifics of how a sleeper wave caused his friend's boat to capsize, of how the body was never recovered.

"Please," Father Paul started, "let us make a donation on behalf of the dearly departed," and he pulled out his wallet.

Father Duggan refused the gesture but did state that such an offering could be sent to "The James O'Farrell Memorial Fund", Saint Theresa Avila Church, Bodega. Father Paul wrote down the address before repeating the information aloud to make sure he got it right.

At the end of the meal all departed together, making small talk, until Father Duggan bade farewell and headed toward a two-tone Mercury. Father Paul studied the departing cleric, noticing that he had placed his jacket inside the front seat before walking toward the beach.

"Do you still have that gallon of water in the hearse?" Father Paul said to Rene.

With a grin, Rene acknowledged the implication and left.

Oddities filled Jonah's head regarding his traveling companions. It was then that he spotted Rene near the rear of the two-tone Merc. The altar boy unscrewed the gas cap and tipped a plastic container to the lip of the tank.

Upon Rene's return Jonah threw him a scowl before saying, "What do you got going here?"

Rene turned to Father Paul. "We should have left him and his friend back on the road."

"But you have to admit," Father Paul said, "he does have a certain *avoir du.*"

"Nothing stylish about him at all," Rene said. "Just another fast-talking lowlife." Rene didn't let up and continued to fester and complain.

Not wanting to upset the altar boy further, Father Paul relented, saying that perhaps it might be best if everyone parted ways. "I hope there are no ill feelings," Father Paul said to Jonah.

Jonah turned to the altar boy and said, "Happy now?"

"Very much so," Rene said.

A few minutes later, Jonah accompanied the priest and the altar boy to the funeral coach where Jonah helped Otis exit from the backseat.

"Good luck, my son," Father Paul said. "May God be with you."

Jonah guided Otis to a nearby bench while the priest and the altar boy boarded the hearse. The vehicle started to roll down Main Street when a white envelope appeared from the passenger window.

"Hey," Jonah called out, "that's mine," and he sprinted after the hearse.

⅄

"Here," Jonah said as he offered leftovers to his friend. "You should eat."

"Thanks," Otis said, struggling to get the word out.

"That's the first complete sentence I've heard you speak in almost twelve hours."

"Nice to be back," Otis said.

"Since you're feeling better, I've got something for you," and Jonah punched his friend in the nose.

"What you wanna do that for?" Otis said as he put his hand to his bloodied face.

"The Hells Angels withheld my get-away stash as ransom for those tabs of acid you stole," Jonah said.

"Maybe this would be a good time to reconsider your options," Otis said.

This last statement started Jonah thinking. "Did you rip me off to get high, or to keep me from leaving the City?"

"Which answer will keep the brother's nose on his face?" Otis said.

"Unbelievable," Jonah said. He looked away in disgust when he saw Father Duggan return to his vehicle. The two-tone Mercury backed up and motored north out of Stinson Beach.

⅄

The boys hitchhiked along Highway One, walking past tidelands. The full moon put a spotlight on egrets pecking from the mud, their movements resembling that of a thingamajig made of hinges and spindles and whatnots.

A mile further down they came to the Audubon Canyon Ranch. Nests the size of laundry baskets decorated the surrounding trees while a weedy path led to a farmhouse. Shutters, in varying degrees of disrepair, outlined the windows where bands of light streamed out onto the porch.

"Whaddya say?" Otis asked, winded, short of breath.

Jonah surveyed the place. "What? You think some nice country folk are going to open their doors to the likes of us, is that it?"

"Not for me, that's for sure. For you, maybe."

With no traffic on the road for the last hour, the likelihood of catching a ride was slim. Tired, Jonah climbed the stoop to knock on the door. A little girl, maybe five or six, answered while licking on an all-day sucker.

"Hi, is your mommy or daddy home?" Jonah asked.

The tyke hiked up her shoulders. Lick, lick.

"An older brother or sister?"

Another shrug. Lick, lick.

"Can you go get someone, anyone? Please?"

The girl shook her head as if to say no.

"Why not?" Jonah said in a loud tone before lowering his voice and trying again. "Look, here's a buck," he said as he handed her the dollar.

The girl disappeared behind the closed door with her newfound riches. Jonah waited...and waited. The shrill of an off-key piano could be heard. Jonah knocked before ringing the doorbell again. There was no response except a growing melody. He signaled to Otis who was encouraging him on from behind a shed.

Jonah crept to the side of the house. He began to raise his head up the clapboards toward a window. Young eyes met his at the edge of the sill. A scream.

Jonah started to sprint toward the shed when he heard the blast from a shotgun. With his hands raised high, he pleaded for leniency.

"Don't shoot. I didn't mean any harm. Just wanted..."

"Turn around so I can get a look at you," a female's voice said.

Jonah obliged, saying, "Sorry if I scared you. I noticed your light was on and thought you might help me with some directions."

"You did, did you?"

"Well, I mean..." Jonah started to fumble over his phrasing before saying, "At the time it didn't seem like such a bad idea."

"So, you're not in need of food or shelter or drink? Just some silly old directions?"

"Well, I wouldn't be disrespectful and turn down such an offer if it was to come my way," Jonah said.

"In that case, I guess you'd better get in here."

Jonah lowered his hands and took a step forward when the woman behind the weapon added, "You might as well bring your friend too," she said pointing the barrel toward the shed.

"He's black," Jonah said.

"Thanks for the warning," the woman said before returning inside, leaving the entrance open.

⅄

The little girl clutched onto a Washington.

"You don't have any right to that," Jonah said, motioning to the dollar bill.

"I see you've met my baby sister," the young woman said as she returned from stowing away the shotgun.

"Darling thing," Jonah said.

"Some people might disagree with you," the young woman said as she let her hand rest upon the crown of her sibling. "This is Kaarina. It's Greek for chaste."

"You sure?" Jonah said.

"And I'm Adelpha. Our parents run the place on behalf of the Audubon Society." She was seventeen with raven-black hair, a Mediterranean complexion and a welcoming smile.

Jonah introduced himself before gesturing to his companion. "This is Otis."

The little girl stuck out her tongue at the black man who returned a snarl.

"Excuse my friend," Jonah said. "He sometimes gets weird for no reason at all."

Otis showed a glassy look, blinking. With a shaky step, he walked toward the far wall.

"Is he okay?" Adelpha asked.

"Probably not," Jonah confessed.

Adelpha stepped closer to Jonah and whispered, "Would your companion like something to..." But before she could finish her sentence, Otis collapsed.

Jonah rushed over and felt his buddy's head. "He's burning up."

"Let's get him to the bedroom," Adelpha said as she led the way.

Jonah placed Otis atop a twin bed. Adelpha covered him with a blanket before sending Kaarina to the bathroom for a cold compress.

"I didn't mean to bother you like this," Jonah said.

"Yeah, right," Adelpha said.

A flustered Jonah searched for another apology. "Ah, well, he should be fine in another hour."

"Don't be ridiculous," Adelpha said before Kaarina returned with a damp washcloth.

While applying the cold pad to his forehead, Adelpha asked if Otis was taking any medications. Jonah produced the few tablets he had remaining from Dr. Smith's office.

"I've got a prescription but haven't had time to get it filled," Jonah said.

Adelpha told him not to worry, that she knew the local pharmacist. "He stays open late tonight. I'll take care of it."

Jonah said thank you before stepping to the window where he lingered for several minutes.

Adelpha spied his stiff demeanor. "Is something the matter?"

Chapter 10

"Feeling better?" Adelpha asked as the morning sun pushed its way through the window.

"Nothin' the brother can't handle," Otis said in the third person as he leaned against the bedpost.

"Hungry?"

"My stomach's gurglin' up a storm."

"Then I suppose you'd be interested in breakfast."

"Got ice cream?"

"Of course, apple pie as well," Adelpha added with a chuckle. "But first you'll have to shower."

"Tryin' to say the brother ain't fixed right?" Otis said before taking a whiff under his armpit.

"Has to have been a while, right?" Adelpha suggested before pivoting to Jonah to include him with her look.

Everyone climbed the staircase to the washroom where Adelpha turned on the hot water for the stall before asking her baby sister to fetch some extra towels.

"Don't waste the water," Adelpha said to her guests before seeing the blank expressions on their faces. "We've got some issues with the well…All I'm saying is—don't be afraid to shower together, understand?"

The guys mumbled their objections as they withdrew a step from each other. Sideway glances told of their discomfort.

"What a couple of sissies," Adelpha said with that broad smile of hers.

"Us city types don't…" Otis started.

"Get in there or no ice cream," Adelpha interrupted, folding her arms across her chest, waiting for them to strip.

⅄

Each occupied a far end of the stall. Eyes stared off into the deep crevices of nearby tiles.

"Amazin' what a man will do for a sweet," Otis said.

"Think I liked you better when you were barking on all fours."

"Appreciate you rescuin' me from my demons," Otis said as he passed the bar of soap.

"Any wild critters still roaming around upstairs?" Jonah asked.

"Heads not cleared up all the way, but I don't have the urge to growl or bite anyone."

"I guess that's a start," Jonah said as he rinsed himself.

"That 'bout enough time?" Otis asked.

"I think we got most of the stink off," Jonah said as he stepped out of the shower.

The absence of their clothes caught his attention. He pinched a towel around his waist and went to the exit to investigate. He eased open the door when an all-day sucker landed on his chin. Startled, Jonah fell backwards into Otis. The pair tumbled to the ground. Towels went flying. Flesh met flesh.

"Get that thing off the brother," Otis yelled as he kicked his friend in the leg.

"What the hell?" complained Jonah.

The two pulled themselves off the floor, crisscrossed their hands over their privates and turned in unison to a huddle standing within the frame of the door. Kaarina stood on a chair next to a much older man.

"I'm Christo Constantinides," the man said.

No response.

"Perhaps you boys would like to get dressed and join my family and me downstairs for a meal," Mr. Constantinides said. "Adelpha's washing your clothes. These will do in the meantime," he said as he passed different ensembles to them.

More silence.

Without wanting to build on the existing embarrassments, Mr. Constantinides retreated down the hall with his daughter.

Otis began to put on a pair of overalls while Jonah slipped into jeans and a white T-shirt.

Otis gazed at his outfit. The waistline was four sizes too big while the pant legs came to mid-calf. "I be lookin' like farmer Jones," and he shook his head. "Good thing my peeps ain't here to witness this."

⅄

China and silverware sat atop white linen. Jonah picked up a fork to inspect it. The utensil possessed a rounded handle. *Nice.* He ran his tongue over the tines—polished with no rough edges. *Excellent.* On the back was stamped 18/10 (18% chromium, 10% nickel). That much nickel was used only in the finest flatware. He started to inch the fork to his lap when a voice sounded from behind.

"The silverware has been in our family for five generations," Adelpha said. "My grandparents brought it here when they emigrated from Athens in 1919."

Jonah nodded with an awkward smile and returned the fork to its proper place. In need of a distraction, he turned to the patriarch of the family who was in the middle of a history lesson.

"In the early sixties," Mr. Constantinides said, "Marin County was pro-growth," and he passed around servings of lamb. "This ranch was to be subdivided for development."

Without asking, Adelpha sprinkled tzatziki sauce onto Jonah's roasted lamb, adding garnishes of diced tomatoes and onions. He gazed down upon the mound of food while Otis started in with a whirl.

"...The lagoon where the egrets feed was to be asphalted over in favor of a four-lane freeway. Then a group, including myself, came in to save the area."

"Seems like a shit-load of trouble for a couple of birds." Otis forked another piece of meat. "My momma used to say that we need more zeros instead of heroes, know what I mean?"

"Your mother," Mr. Constantinides said in a patient tone, "sounds like an enterprising woman."

"Every bit, and I aims to grow from the experience of workin' alongside her," Otis said as he buttered a potato.

"What does your mother do?"

"She's in the pharmaceutical business. So's me. Got my own territory. Fixin' to branch out soon as I get back from kickin' the shit outta some slant-eyes."

"Slant-eyes?" Mr. Constantinides asked. "I'm afraid I don't…"

"Gooks, Tunnel Diggers, Charlie," Otis said. "We're goin' to 'Nam."

"Maybe it's time for your medication," Jonah interjected as he placed a glass of water and a tab of Thorazine in front of his friend.

Mr. Constantinides asked if the boys wanted an extra helping of lamb. Otis, after popping his pill, inquired about the apple pie and ice cream, wondering if it was still part of the offering.

Adelpha excused herself but not before requesting Jonah's help. In the kitchen he opened the back door a crack and scanned the area.

"There's something out there that scares you, isn't there?" she said.

"We're just on vacation, taking some time off before…before…," and he stalled out.

"*Before* Uncle Sam delivers you to Vietnam?"

"Right."

"You come here on foot in the middle of the night with just the clothes on your back and you expect me to believe that you're on holiday?"

"It's the only part of the story I thought you might believe."

"I loaded an overnight bag with your clean garments as well as a few additional items," Adelpha said. "Perhaps they'll come in handy on your journey." Another reminder came to her and she said, "Oh, I was able to get your prescription filled out," and she showed a small plastic bottle before placing it inside the carryall.

"Thanks," Jonah said. "I'm not used to people doing stuff for me. Usually have to fend for myself, if you know what I mean."

"I think I do," she said.

Another thought came to Jonah and he said that he and Otis better skip dessert. "We should be on our way."

They looked at each other with a knowing look. Perhaps if there was more time, they might have gotten to know each other, even grown to like one another.

⅄

It took two hours for the boys to catch a ride north along Highway One. They sat in the back of a pickup, which rumbled through a grove of Eucalyptus trees before entering a straightaway flanked on either side by fields of golden grasses. Jonah turned to take in the countryside when the overnight bag caught his eye. He opened it and peeked inside. A complete set of silverware sparkled before him.

"I'll be damned."

"Most likely," Otis said in agreement. He spotted the bag, which reminded him of the young woman who had cared for him. "That Adelpha's got some nice cheekbones. Not all puffed up with Big-Macs and such."

"How do you do that?" Jonah asked.

"What?"

"Make a compliment sound ugly."

"Same ways you turn a positive into a negative," Otis said.

Jonah fell silent with his thoughts, gazing at the passing pastures. Waves of wild wheat rolled across the land. Hills overlapped each other, spotted with meadows and redwood forests. The surrounding tranquility set him to thinking of the few good people who had brought peace into his life. Sara, Bill Graham and now Adelpha. It was a short list, but one that he would not soon forget.

The Olema Druids Hall whizzed past and, after another ten minutes, the truck cruised into a Chevron at the west end of Point Reyes Station. An attendant talked with the old timer behind the wheel before filling up the gas tank while another started to clean the windows.

The boys hopped out of the back, went to the office and got a key, which was attached to a hubcap.

"They 'fraid somebody gonna snatch their precious key?" Otis said as the pair walked around to the rear and entered the restroom.

"That's probably reserved for you," Jonah said as he gestured to a trash-can with the words "Monkeys piss here" spray-painted on its exterior.

"You're a funny dude, know that?" Otis said as he unzipped. "Outta be a comedian or somethin'."

"You think Sonny lookin' for us?" Otis said, eyes fixed straight ahead at the white tile.

"You *did* steal his LSD," Jonah said.

"That was the devil stole his drugs."

"We're probably not worth the trouble," Jonah said. "Besides, he's got my get-away stash as compensation."

"How much compensation we be talkin' 'bout?" Otis asked.

"About three-thousand dollars worth."

"Dude, you be havin' trouble holdin' onto money."

"Funny how that happens, isn't it?" Jonah said.

"What 'bout Papa Al and that crooked cop?" Otis said as he veered away from the latrine to urinate on the nearby graffiti.

"What about them?" Jonah asked.

"Why was they chasin' us through the Haight?"

"Uh, I, uh," and Jonah stumbled over his phrasing before saying that the thugs were always mad about something. Why should that day be any different?

"Then why we on the run?" Otis gave a good shaking before packing it in.

"We're not on the run," Jonah said before adding, "We're on vacation, remember?"

"The brother's kidneys are doin' flip-flops in the back of hearses and trucks, wearin' some farmer's clothes, and you say we're on *vacation*?"

"Shut your pie-hole."

The pickup continued north past Hog Island Oyster Company. An inlet stretched for five miles alongside Highway One.

"People say that the San Andreas Fault runs under Tomales Bay," Jonah said.

"What people?" Otis said. "Not my people."

"That the Pacific Plate has been slipping north for millions of years."

"Ain't that a bitch."

"See that shoreline over there," Jonah said gesturing to the far side of the bay. "It was part of southern California at one time."

"Someday Rodeo Drive hotties gonna be sittin' next to my peeps in the Fillmo', that what you tryin' to tell me?"

"Where'd you learn to talk like that, at some Panama City, one-hump school for pimps?"

⅄

The boys slid across the steel bed as the truck sped past Nicks Cove. Within another mile or so, Tomales Bay faded behind them when a familiar vehicle came into Jonah's line of sight.

"That's Father Duggan's car," Jonah said as he pointed to a two-tone Mercury parked alongside a row of Cypress trees.

Otis shrugged as they slipped past the sedan, its hood up. "Who's Father Duggan?"

"Had dinner with him back at Stinson Beach," Jonah said.

"Well, whoever you be talkin' 'bout, doesn't look like he stuck around."

"No it doesn't." The puzzle begged for answers. Jonah massaged his temples, trying to kick-start his brain. He retraced conversations and scenes—the dialogue at the Sand Dollar Café, the sharing of everyone's journey, the James O'Farrell memorial.

"Why those sons-a-bitches," Jonah said out loud.

"Ya talkin' 'bout my people again?"

"How do you feel about doing a little sightseeing?" Jonah asked.

"Say what?"

"It'll give you a chance to play tourist," Jonah added.

"You tryin' to whiten me up?"

Chapter 11

"Mr. Berkowitz," Papa Al said as he paced the lobby of the pawnshop, "have you had any contact from your wayward son?"

"Wait till I get my hands on that little shit," old man Berkowitz said.

"I will take that as a no," Papa Al said. "What about your son's friend? Otis Wright is his name, I believe."

"His mother hasn't heard from him in three days," old man Berkowitz said. "She thought maybe he was shacked up with one of those whores up the street, but she didn't think he had that kind of stamina in him."

"The ways of the female will indeed wear one's soul," Papa Al said in agreement. "Let us pause to revisit the facts, shall we? First of all, we know that the boys were together near the Free Clinic recently. I saw them with my own eyes. Secondly, they have not been seen since. This would lead one to conjecture that...," but Papa Al stopped in mid-sentence at the sound of the bell clanging over the front door.

"Got a tip from a local mortuary," Sergeant Maloney said as he entered. "Turns out that one of their hearses went missing."

"And this would be pertinent because?" Papa Al asked.

"It's been ID'd as the same vehicle that took part in the parade down Haight Street the other day," Maloney said.

"Where our boys were last spotted," Papa Al added as he resumed his pacing. "Interesting."

"Any connection?" old man Berkowitz asked.

"Not sure," Papa Al said. "Could be a mere coincidence. Hard to tell. Perhaps we should put out an APB on the vehicle."

"I'm on it," Sergeant Maloney said before exiting.

⅄

Jonah knocked on the roof of the cab. The old timer steered the pickup to the side of the road and stopped. The boys jumped out and waved goodbye before starting down Bodega Highway, a two-lane deserted road. No vehicles appeared from either direction. The land stood vacant. It was hard to imagine that a town would be close at hand. Jonah began to doubt himself, wondering if he had correctly remembered the priest's conversation back at the Sand Dollar Café

Boredom filled Otis's head as he snatched the overnight bag from Jonah. "You got any of my things in here?"

Resting next to his fedora was a set of polished utensils. "Did you steal her silverware?" Otis said. "Dude, ain't you got no respect for family?"

"It was a gift," Jonah said.

"Why you lyin', dude?" Otis showed a disgusted look before taking his hat and stepping toward the brush to take a dump.

Jonah peered down the lane. Nothing. Could be stuck here for hours, he thought. Anxious to get going, he called out to Otis. "You done yet?"

"Not talkin' to you," a voice sounded from behind a tree.

All of a sudden, a ten-wheeler appeared. Jonah stuck out his thumb. With a rush of air from the brakes, the rig came to a halt. Jonah turned and let out a teamster's whistle. Otis hopscotched from the brush, pulling up his bell-bottoms along the way. The man behind the wheel looked in the rear-view. Burgundy pants hung around the knees of a black guy while a pimp-like hat sat atop a mass of wiry hair. The driver shoved the semi into first.

Balls of exhaust settled upon the teenagers. Jonah wheezed and coughed, fanning away the stench with his hand, while Otis brought up a wad of phlegm and spat at the vehicle in the distance.

The boys trudged along the country lane. They passed a series of chicken coops leaning against each other. Clucks and chirps sounded an alarm as turkey vultures circled above. Jonah observed Otis tracing the flight of the large birds.

"They're not interested in you," Jonah said.

"That so?" Otis said.

"Not enough meat on those bones to satisfy a cockroach let alone those boys," Jonah said as he gestured to the flock of scavengers.

Skeptical, Otis put up a hand to shade his eyes, keeping track of the activity in the sky. A ragged hedgerow bordered the sloping hillside as they neared a wooden bridge. Without warning, a rustle sounded from the creek bed below. Startled, Otis skipped backwards as a covey of quail dashed across the road in single formation, their head notches dancing in rhythm to their speedy retreat.

"Think the brother's had enough vacation," Otis said in a jumpy tone.

"The wildlife's getting to you, is it?" Jonah said with a grin.

"Go ahead and laugh," Otis said. "We'll see who gets back home alive."

"You're going to make the Marines proud," Jonah said, soaking it up.

The comment sparked a reminder. "I got my orders," Otis said. "Gotta report next week…How 'bout you?"

"Not sure," Jonah said.

"As far as I can see, you got no choice," Otis said. "Best you surrender yourself before the FBI catches up to you. Maybe that way they'll go easy on your ass."

⅄

They hiked another half mile to a crest in the road. A one-block village announced the beginning of Freestone Valley. The sun's light splashed over the meandering landscape, which gave way to a redwood forest in the distance.

Heads of locals pivoted at the plumage parading through the center of town. Otis showed off his street shuffle, strutting with swagger. With his chest puffed up, he tapped the brim of his peacock-feathered fedora, saying hello to the onlookers. Jonah fell in line, thinking that they weren't much different than other critters of this earth.

Otis sashayed past Potter Elementary, oblivious to Jonah's docent-like speech. "…and when the children came screaming out of the school, Hitchcock had stringed paper-crows to the kids to make it look like birds were chasing them…Not much in the way of special effects back in '63."

"Saw the movie," Otis said. "Don't need to hear no more 'bout murdering birds and such."

For a distraction, he kept marching, trying to ignore the rambling from his partner. He would have walked right through that backwater town to the far reaches of the valley if he hadn't felt a tug on his burgundy cloak.

"That must be St. Teresa's," Jonah said gesturing to a steepled building resting atop a knoll. "Let's go."

"What you want with some church anyways?" Otis asked. "Ain't even Sunday."

"It's all part of the tour," Jonah said with a smirk.

In protest, Otis entered and made his way to the rear pew with Jonah. Words came to them from a robed person at the pulpit.

"*Bonjour*, my fellow worshippers. My name is Father Paul Giguere. I have the honor of filling in for Father Duggan who unfortunately has been stricken with the flu. He sends his deepest regards to the family and friends of his late departed friend, James O'Farrell."

The priest cleared his throat. "Jesus said: 'I am the resurrection and the life. He who believes in me will live, even though he dies; and whoever lives by believing in me will never die.' John, Chapter 11, Verses 25-26."

Father Paul spewed out a string of clichés about how the good die young before finishing with the Lord's Prayer. "And now, Mary Sullivan, President of the Ladies Guild, has a few words she would like to share with you."

A geriatric woman used her cane and limped to the pulpit where she thanked Father Paul Giguere before leaning into the mic. "Jasper O'Farrell, James's great-great grandfather, donated this site for Saint Teresa's in 1862. The church was later deeded to the Archbishop of San Francisco who named a street on behalf of the O'Farrells."

Mary Sullivan caught her breath and restarted: "Over the years the church has fallen into disrepair. Just this last summer, the choir loft was judged unsafe and dismantled. The bell tower has deteriorated.

"I am most pleased to say that the money raised on behalf of the James O'Farrell Memorial Fund will address these issues. As requested, the Ladies Guild of Bodega and the Saint Teresa's Restoration Committee will administer the effort."

In a final burst of energy, she said, "From the heart of this structure shall rise the soul and spirit of our dearly departed parishioner. God bless James and his entire family," she said as she pointed to the O'Farrells sitting in the first row.

A young person in his black garb traveled up the center aisle to each and every pew, reaching out with an offering basket. Sealed envelopes and cash poured into the receptacle. Those in attendance gave generously for all knew the legacy of the O'Farrell clan.

The altar boy continued until he came to the back row where he caught the simper of a familiar face. Eyes locked onto each other. Jonah waved. Startled, the acolyte fumbled with the handle of the basket. He recovered and scuttled back to Father Paul where the two engaged in quiet conversation before departing to a rear chamber.

⅄

"What do we do now?" Rene asked Father Paul.

"Jonah and Otis have no business with us. There is little need for these emotions."

"Well, I sort of…" and the altar boy fizzled out.

"Yes?"

"I might have taken something from the white kid."

The priest was about to ask for clarification when Mrs. Sullivan entered, saying that the congregation was waiting. The priest held his hand up to ask for a moment. Mrs. Sullivan pleaded for him to hurry and left.

Father Paul turned back around and spotted Rene with a frantic expression on his face as he stared out the window. "What is it?"

"*La police est ici*," Rene said.

The priest rushed to take a look for himself. A policeman was talking with a man of the cloth in the parking lot.

Father Paul pulled on Rene's sleeve. "*Allons-y*!"

They hurried from the sacristy and traveled across the apse. The priest surrendered the sign of the cross to the mourners before rushing out a side door. A couple of teenagers, one white and the other black, rushed down the center aisle in hasty pursuit. Parishioners gazed at one another. Questions floated on the air.

The white kid stopped near the pulpit where a woman leaned on her cane. He dug into his backpack while his partner motioned for him to hurry. Before long a polished set of silverware rested inside the offering basket.

"This gift is donated on behalf of Adelpha Constantinides from down the road near Stinson Beach," the white kid said. "She would want you to have it," and he fled before the geriatric woman could reply.

⅄

"Where are my photos?" Jonah said as he caught up with the altar boy in the parking lot.

"Get in," Rene ordered.

"Not before you…"

"The cops are here," Rene interrupted, pointing to a man in blue on the far side of the church.

All jumped into the funeral coach. A black-and-white scurried to block the exit when the hearse veered thru a fence into a pasture, bouncing over craters before flying up a berm and onto Bodega Highway. Barbwire, posts, grasses and cow pies garnished the hood and front grill.

In the backseat, Jonah and Otis peered through the rear window, spotting the police car with its lights flashing, siren blaring. Then, without explanation, the hearse slowed down.

"What the hell?" Jonah called out.

Father Paul remained silent, his concentration fixed on the development ahead. An oncoming tractor, towing a harvester, slogged its way toward them, motoring down the center of the double yellow with a caravan of cars lugging behind.

Panic invaded the hearse as the black-and-white gained ground. The altar boy screamed. Otis cursed. The priest froze. Within the chaos, Jonah saw a moneybag on the floor. A hasty plan rushed forward. He unlaced the strings and released the cash out the window. Sharp words crisscrossed each other inside the vehicle as bills floated on the breeze behind them.

The tractor screeched to a halt. Sedans and coups swerved across the country lane. Motorists exited their cars and scurried over the blacktop, wrestling Washingtons from one another. Demands from a police car's bull-horn went unheeded.

Jonah tossed the empty moneybag to the front seat as the funeral coach made its way past the congestion to the open road. The distance between them and the sheriff's car grew as they sped through the valley.

"Damn you," the altar boy said to Jonah.

"This is some kind of jam you've placed us in, son," Father Paul said in agreement.

"That was not your money," Rene said to Jonah.

"Don't see how it was yours either," Jonah said.

The altar boy clenched his teeth, sat stiff, too mad to know what to say while Jonah reminded everyone that the good Lord probably wouldn't take kindly to false witnesses stealing from His worshippers.

"I'm confused," Otis said.

"These yahoos are nothing but a couple of con artists," Jonah said, "posing as priest and altar boy, looting from the religious weak."

"Still," Otis said, "it wouldn't done any harm to have kept the money for a while."

"And that phony sermon back in the City," Jonah said to Father Paul, ignoring Otis, "preaching about how people should open their wallets to tend to the needy—what a crock."

"That was a lot of bones you threw away back there," Otis persisted. "Not to mention Adelpha's silverware. Why don't you send some of that generosity the brother's way, huh?"

"I'd be willing to bet," Jonah continued with the priest, "that you and your altar boy stole this hearse as well."

"Don't pretend you're the high and mighty one here," Rene interjected. "You sit there accusing us of this and that when you show up uninvited. You're nothing but a two-bit crook on the run. And an amateur at that. At least we've got *panache*," and he threw an envelope to the backseat.

Jonah extracted the prints from the casing and made a quick accounting.

Otis peered over his buddy's shoulder. "Whaddya got there?"

"Yes, Jonah," Rene interjected, "do tell. I'm a bit curious myself."

"It's nothing," Jonah said as he stuffed the prints back into the envelope.

"You be goin' to whole lot of trouble over *nothin'*," Otis said. "The brother's "thinkin' that those photos got somethin' to do with why we be stuck in hicksville."

Otis lurched at the envelope, but Jonah was too quick for him, holding the casing over his head in a game of cat and mouse.

"Ah, keep your lousy pictures," Otis said, giving up. "Prob'ly just snapshots of some old Jews anyways."

Jonah relaxed and brought the object back to his lap when Otis pointed out the window. "Look, a fox."

Jonah peered sideways. Otis stole the envelope.

"Should be ashamed of yourself. Oldest trick in the book," and he placed his back to Jonah, examining the photos of Papa Al and Sergeant Maloney at the brothel.

Surprise filled Otis's face. He turned and slapped the pics into the chest of Jonah, saying, "Are you serious, dude?"

No response.

"Those boys ain't gonna let this go, no way."

Rene threw out a smirk while Jonah slumped into his seat. Silence shrouded the hearse until Otis started up again with his buddy, saying, "You lied to me. You said we was goin' on vacation. Said we deserved some fun before 'Nam." Clumps of air surged from his nostrils. "Just wanted some dumb-ass Negro to cleanup after you, that it?"

"Not it at all," Jonah said in a whisper as he caught another snicker from up front. "I didn't want to get you involved, but I had no choice." He paused, letting the sentiment take hold before adding, "What was I suppose to do, leave my best friend at the Crystal Palace Hotel to wither away?"

Otis took in Jonah's sentiment. "Best friend?"

"Hard to believe, right?" Jonah said.

"What 'bout all your music pals?"

"Nope."

"Bill Graham?"

"Nope."

"Or that Sara?"

Jonah rubbed his chin in thought. "Hmmm, you might have a point there."

Otis punched him in the shoulder. Jonah yelped.

"How it feel?" Otis said before thinking about their present reality. "Guess we're in this thing together."

"Guess so," Jonah answered.

"Where we gonna go now?" Otis asked.

"Can't go too far. Not on an empty wallet," Rene interjected.

Jonah fell quiet at the truth of the matter while Rene poured it on, saying to Father Paul, "It's about time we parted ways with Frick and Frack once and for all. They're nothing but a couple of..."

"Wait," Jonah interrupted as he reached into the front pocket of his Pendleton. It was still there, a mustard-colored leaflet he had kept for just such a day. "Some whacked-out hippie at the Oakland Induction Center gave this to me a couple of weeks ago," Jonah said as he passed it forward.

"Morningstar Ranch?" the altar boy said as he perused the flyer.

Chapter 12

A man in blue opened the passenger door to a Caddy and leaned in. "Got a call from a buddy down at the station," Sergeant Maloney said to the person in the driver's seat.

"Do tell," Papa Al said.

"A Lincoln Town Car hearse has been involved in some sort of disturbance up north in the town of Bodega," Maloney said.

"What sort of disturbance?" Papa Al asked.

"Had something to do with a memorial mass that went sideways. Local police gave pursuit."

"Any arrests made?" Papa Al asked.

"Not to my knowledge," Sergeant Maloney said.

"Was that *our* stolen hearse?"

"Witnesses saw a white teenager and a Negro flee in the vehicle along with a priest and an altar boy."

⅄

Daisies, rainbows and peace symbols decorated the outside of a VW bus as it motored out of Freestone Valley along Bodega Highway. The four-cylinder engine sputtered up a steep grade. The passengers, however, were in no hurry, busy arguing about which one of them was the biggest asshole. The driver, a longhair named Nevada, waved other vehicles past, flipping them off each in turn.

A hawk's feather hung from the rearview mirror while LOVE decals adorned the windows. In the rear a guitar case sat atop bedrolls, dirty laundry, empty whiskey bottles and a scattering of potato chips.

They referred to themselves as the Crazy Three, and for good reason. Besides the unpredictable Nevada, there was Gypsy whose eyes appeared scary large while Running Bear was a sixteen-year-old girl who fantasized about being an Apache.

Boasts circulated the van regarding how the group had been booted out of a commune up in Oregon, proud of themselves for bringing chaos to the Tolstoy Farm, saying that the inhabitants were nothing but a bunch of losers. However, their brief sojourn in California had not treated them much better. Picked up by a local sheriff for possession of illegal contraband, they had bedded down with Bruno in the butt-hut at the Sonoma County jail. Nevada brokered a deal with the law. In return for the trio's cooperation, all charges would be dismissed.

"There's no way I'm gonna play the part of a fink for some low-life sheriff," Running Bear said.

"Yeah," agreed Gypsy as he cleaned his fingernails with the tip of his knife. "All bullshit."

A former rodeo champ, Nevada was equipped with an attitude to backup his threats. "Either of you say one more word and it'll most likely be your last."

The stench of patchouli oil, weed and body odor filled the pause that followed. The smell sat heavy within the close confines. Running Bear went to roll down the backseat window but the handle was missing. She screamed until Nevada threw her a glare.

The bus eased into fourth gear as it crested the hill. On the descent, the Crazy Three, including the driver, raised their hands in unison, letting out their best roller-coaster wails.

The hippie wagon bottomed out after another quarter mile where they headed north for a short distance to Graton Road. A dusty driveway and a patch of level land, which served as a parking lot, soon came into view. Nevada drove past a sign that read NO VEHICLES BEYOND THIS POINT. Gypsy stabbed the console with his knife while Running Bear let out a war cry in anticipation of battle.

The bus putt-putted up an incline and stopped at a closed gate. Over the entrance hung a piece of driftwood with a painted rendition of the northern star and a lotus flower. Between the symbols was inscribed "Morningstar Solar Legation and Economic Council". A young woman, wearing nothing but lightning bolts on her thighs, welcomed the band with a smile.

Nevada yelled at her to move aside. Gypsy leered at her from the window, wiping his blade with his tongue. Screams sounded from the backseat. Undaunted, the naked lady sidestepped to the passenger window, reached up on her tiptoes and hung a daisy-chain necklace around the stranger.

"Like the tats," Gypsy said, scanning the ink on her legs.

"I'm Ocean," the girl said with a glazed-over expression.

Nevada disembarked and walked to the gate to open it when a fleshy tower appeared from nowhere. "No motorized transports allowed on the property," the six-foot-five black man said in an even tone. He too was naked with the exception of a red ribbon tied to his dong.

"You gift-wrapped for Christmas?" Nevada said.

The Negro squared up to the visitor. Gypsy hopped out of the passenger seat with his blade.

"You ain't nothin' but some bar floozy's reject," Nevada continued.

The black man, however, discounted the insult as an emergency filled his vision, pointing to the loudmouth's vehicle. Nevada turned around to see his van slipping backwards down the driveway. Nevada cursed on the run as he tried to get to the driver's side, but he was too late. With a thump, the bus came to a crashing halt, wedged between a six-wheeler and a Rambler.

⅄

With strings of flowers around their necks, the Crazy Three followed Ocean. Gypsy commented on the young woman's tan buttocks, saying that perhaps the deal that Nevada made with the sheriff wasn't such a bad idea after all.

Nevada punched him in the chest.

"What was that for?" Gypsy asked with a growl.

"No one mentions anything about the deal, got it?" Nevada said with a stare.

They passed tents, sleeping platforms, lean-tos, and huts made of various discarded materials such as tarps, cardboard, plywood, and sheets of Plexiglas. Animal carvings adorned a tree house while a Chevy's packaging crate housed more folks.

Cabbages, turnips, lettuce and onions sat in tidy rows within a vegetable bed. Girls lounged in the buffalo grass, sewing colorful dresses. A shaggy sheepdog played with a knot of children while passersby swayed with a breezy pace.

The new arrivals came to an open-air dining hall, which Ocean simply referred to as the Lower House. She gestured to a tin can, suggesting that a donation would be nice. Nevada scoffed before elbowing Running Bear to put away her money.

The Crazy Three made their way down a buffet line with their trays. A server dumped a load of beans and rice onto their plates while another offered fresh greens.

"Ain't you got any real food?" Nevada complained.

"Mother Earth provides all that is necessary for our needs," the server said.

Everyone sat at weathered 4' x 8' sheets of plywood, which rested atop sawhorses. The dining hall and the wraparound porch could accommodate almost fifty people at a sitting.

A person, wearing a pair of drawstring cotton pants, addressed the crowd. "For those of you who have just arrived, my name is Piano Player and this is Aurora," he said while gesturing to a pregnant woman beside him. "We welcome you to Morningstar Ranch where no one is turned away. In return we ask only that you respect this property and all who inhabit it...Welcome and enjoy your meal."

Gypsy spooned white corn to his inspection before flipping the food across the room. The vegetables splattered the feathered fedora of a black guy who raised his arms with a challenge.

Gypsy rose halfway and threw the Negro a look. The black man stepped forward when another in a Pendleton hooked onto his arm.

"Cool it," Jonah said to Otis.

"You see that fool?" Otis said.

"We can't draw anymore attention to ourselves, savvy?"

Otis relaxed and fell back into the chow line while Jonah's vision followed Gypsy. The stranger reminded Jonah of that character on the soapbox in Golden Gate Park espousing the virtues of racism. Same chilling eyes, same madness.

Ocean stood by the tin cup with her lightning bolts, playing hostess, requesting that the next batch of arrivals make a contribution.

Otis gestured to his friend. "He'll pay."

"What?" Jonah said.

"Saw you lift a couple of bills from the bag before you tossed the cash out the car window," Otis added.

With a curse, Jonah pulled out a five-spot from his jeans and placed it into the collection can. Father Paul reminded him that there were two more in the party and gestured to himself and the altar boy. Jonah huffed before surrendering more money.

"You're not a very good thief, are you?" the altar boy said with a laugh.

"Nobody asked you," Jonah said.

"First of all," the altar boy persisted, "you need a partner to provide a distraction."

"I work alone," Jonah said shuffling his way toward the server's table.

"I agrees with the altar boy," Otis said to his friend. "The FBI nabbed you for lifting your induction file and then you go and steal from that sweet Adelpha. No class, dude."

"I told you," Jonah said, "I didn't take her silverware. It was a gift."

"And now look at the mess we're in," Otis said. "All 'cause you got caught developing a roll of film. You should pick another line of work, dude."

"Those photos are the only safety net we have," Jonah interjected as he picked up a plate.

"How's that?" Otis asked.

"Haven't figured that part out yet."

"That be 'bout the only part there is, Einstein."

⅄

Workers picked the last of the Gravenstein apples from the orchard. The Diggers of Haight-Ashbury had entered an arrangement with Morningstar Ranch. In exchange for tending the trees, the anarchists would be allowed to harvest the fruit, which was needed to feed the masses that had descended upon San Francisco.

In this spirit of collaboration, Jonah and Otis pitched in after lunch with the painting of the Lower House's exterior. The Crazy Three, however, had a different notion on how to treat the afternoon and retired to drink a bottle of Ripple.

"What's your take on them?" Otis said, eyeing the trio.

"Hard to say for sure," Jonah said as he slid his brush along the grain of the redwood.

⅄

A bong sounded in the distance. Dozens ceased working and gathered in a circle within the orchard. Chanting began. The residents clapped in unison, facing the entrance to the combine in anticipation. Jonah and Otis put down their tools and stepped off the porch to see what all the fuss was about.

A gray bearded person in an orange Kurta sat atop a makeshift throne, which was carried by the red-ribboned black man and three others who were dressed in different stages of nothingness. The Swami greeted columns of people from his ceremonial chair as he traveled across the meadow to the orchard. All responded with a fifteenth century mantra as the commune came alive.

"Hare Krishna Hare Krishna.
Krishna Krishna Hare Hare.
Hare Râma Hare Râma.
Râma Râma Hare Hare."

The bearers delivered the flowery throne to a temporary platform. The swami remained seated while acknowledging the welcome.

Piano Player, with the pregnant Aurora at his side, introduced his guest to the throng. "Swami Bhaktivedenta has graciously consented to honor us with his presence today," he said before motioning for the religious teacher to come forward.

The swami bowed in the direction of Piano Player and Aurora before turning to the crowd. "Your greeting is most pleasant. For this I am in your debt." He pressed down the air with his palms, asking everyone to sit.

"Growing up in the slums of Calcutta," the swami started, "I could not foresee what Buddha had in store for me."

"A red dot between the eyeballs," answered a heckler from the rear.

Piano Player scanned the area while the swami continued: "I was a typical yes-man, eager for the material things of life. I started a pharmaceutical business, had a wife and three children. Perhaps I was much like those whom you have fled from."

"You're black, wear funny clothes and smell like curry," yelled the heckler. "You ain't nothin' like us."

Piano Player retook the podium to remind everyone that a religious man was present.

The swami bade a thank you to his host before revisiting his message: "In 1950 I adopted a life of pious renunciation, pledging my dedication to Buddha with love and devotion. Last year I founded the International Society for Krishna Consciousness, or the Hare Krishna Movement as you Americans are found of saying."

"No place for pagans in this part of the world," the heckler said in a slurred voice.

The swami embraced the heckler, saying, "Today I may be Hindu, tomorrow Christian or Muslim. In this way faiths are interchangeable, but Dharma is a natural sequence or connection that cannot be changed."

He stepped down from the throne and held out his hand in an invitation for the nonbeliever to come closer. "Join us to taste the nectar of divine love in the holy name of Bhakti. Come and dance with cymbals and drums in glorious celebration."

The heckler waved off the offer and went back to his Ripple. A duo joined him, joking and laughing.

With the conclusion of Swami Bhaktivedenta's deliverance, chants of Hare Krishna filled the orchard as hippies swished their arms to and fro, their feet floating on the bliss of Buddha's love. Piano Player excused himself and climbed the knoll to the hecklers.

"LATWIDNO," he said to the trio as he approached.

The blank expressions on the strangers begged for an explanation.

"LATWIDNO," repeated Piano Player. "It's an acronym for 'Land Access To Which Is Denied No One."

"Catchy," one of the hecklers said.

"This is my property. All are welcome."

"But?"

"There are no *but's*."

"In that case," the heckler said, "I guess we're good here," and he motioned for Piano Player to leave.

"Who are you, my friend?" Piano Player asked.

The heckler thought about his arrangement with the sheriff's office and decided to change his tone. "I'm Nevada, and we are the Crazy Three."

"Yes, well, I'm sure you are," Piano Player said before adding, "*Crazy* is one thing we're not in short supply of here."

"Don't have to convince me," Nevada chuckled as he gathered in the confirmations from his companions.

"I request that you allow space for the insanity of others as we have you," Piano Player said.

"You're a trip," Nevada said. "You know that?"

"You are free to indulge on your own journey while you are at Morningstar but be mindful of others. Good day," Piano Player said before traveling the few steps to a permanent structure named the Upper House.

Within minutes, Bach's "Ave Maria" drifted from a keyboard. Jonah gazed up from the orchard toward the top of the knoll. The classical arrangement was enticing, washing over him with an angelic melody. While Jerry Garcia and Janis Joplin had rocked his existence, this haunting piece healed his troubled soul.

He followed the music to the Upper House and started to take a step up the stoop when a bottle crashed against the side of the bungalow. Screeches and taunts followed, demanding that the noise stop. Jonah walked to the disturbance and told the Crazy Three to shut their pie-holes.

Nevada showed a sneer, asking Jonah if he was up to the task of enforcing such a demand.

"Maybe not," Jonah said, "but I don't mind giving it a try."

A voice called out from the nearby porch. "You," and Piano Player pointed to the teenager, "won't you join me for a toke?" he said, holding up a joint.

Jonah withdrew from the Crazy Three. Inside, Jonah and Piano Player sat in the Spartan-furnished living room, taking turns on the smoke.

"Are you always this patient with people?" Jonah asked as he gestured outside to the Crazy Three.

"I've seen a lot during my travels," Piano Player said. "Most folks mean well, but sometimes they are overwhelmed with the minutiae of everyday life."

"No amount of suffering justifies that kind of rudeness."

"The wound is often the place where the light enters the strongest."

"And was your wound large?" Jonah asked, guessing that Piano Player was speaking from personal experience.

"The music business was a cruel mentor for me. It was when the almighty dollar took control that I chose another path, leaving Lou Gottlieb behind and becoming Piano Player."

Jonah took a drag on the joint before saying, "I recognize the name," and then he repeated the man's moniker—"Lou Gottlieb"—as if making sure it sounded right. "Of the Limeliters?"

"Correct."

"What brought you to this place?" Jonah asked.

"The road got to us," Piano Player said. "Three hundred days away from home every year, and for what, a little extra coin and some fame?"

"When did the group breakup?" Jonah asked.

"We went our separate ways in sixty-three. Yarbrough went on to become a successful solo artist. I dropped out and came up here."

"When did you know what you wanted to do with your life?" Jonah asked in his best reporter's voice.

"Life isn't something you can pin down. It's constantly evolving, changing. If you don't move with it, it'll roll right over you."

"So we are at the mercy of our environment, is that what you're saying?" Jonah said.

"In order to get a good shot at what you want to take from this journey, one must not let the rulings of yesterday fix you to the ground."

Jonah thought of his yesterdays, of a past unfulfilled by the absence of a mother and a caring father. Melancholy started to settle in when Piano Player asked about the music scene back in San Francisco.

"I understand that The Grateful Dead are doing great things these days," Piano Player said.

Jonah welcomed the diversion, saying, "They've hooked up with music producer Bill Graham."

"Yes, I'm familiar with the man," Piano Player said. "He has held several fund raisers at his Fillmore Auditorium on our behalf and that of the Diggers." He saw the curiosity on Jonah's face and added, "Much of the food you see growing here is for the benefit of the Haight. Mr. Graham believes in the cause and in return he simply asks that we save him a healthy supply of apples. It appears that this particular fruit has a special place in his heart."

"I've heard the story," Jonah said.

"And are you a fan of The Grateful Dead?"

"I've seen everyone of their concerts," Jonah said, bragging.

"Well, I suppose you'll be going to their concert this weekend at the Fillmore."

"I'm afraid that won't be possible," Jonah said.

"They're opening up for Jefferson Airplane. Should be quite a show."

A clean-shaven man wearing a cleric's collar called from the other side of the screen door, asking if anybody was at home. At the sight of the priest, Piano Player rose from his chair to invite him and his companion inside.

"Welcome to Morningstar, Father," Piano Player said.

"That is most kind of you," and then the clergyman spied Jonah and said to his host, "I see you have met our friend."

"You know each other?" Piano Player asked.

"Unfortunately," Jonah said.

"Let us not let the past impinge on this beautiful day." The priest side-stepped any further acrimony with introductions. "I am Father Paul Giguere and this is my assistant, Rene. We are returning to Canada and thought we might impose upon your legendary hospitality to grant ourselves a respite from the road."

"We were just discussing such a life," Piano Player said. "It can indeed be a challenge."

"Especially when those whom you have tried to help along the way, end up being the scourge of your existence," Rene said as he threw Jonah a look.

"Well, there certainly seems to be a tale here to be told," Piano Player said before recommending a glass of lemonade.

"Would you happen to have anything a bit stronger?" Father Paul asked.

All retreated to the living room where the adults sipped from snifters of brandy alongside gossip and various accounts of adventure.

"And so we find ourselves at the mercy of the Lord once again," Father Paul said at the conclusion of his wild story of how a band of no-account drifters had stolen their money, which the Church had entrusted to them.

Jonah lowered his eyes in disbelief. *And I thought my so-called father had a monopoly on bullshit. Jews have nothing over Catholics.*

"Please stay until God has other plans for your services," Piano Player said.

"That is very generous of you," Father Paul said while Jonah excused himself, his head reeling from the drivel.

He stepped out onto the porch when he overheard a murmuring from the side of the house. At the end of the porch, he leaned over the railing to spot the Crazy Three slouched below an open window, eavesdropping on the conversation inside.

What the hell?

⅄

The residents of Morningstar gathered for a feast in honor of Swami Bhaktivedenta. Cornish hens, breasts of chicken, sirloin tip and smoked salmon infused the air with a galaxy of scents. After a nondenominational prayer by Father Paul, the festivities started. Flutes and cymbals provided background music for various discussions, which ran the gamut from religion to anarchism to baying at the moon. Sugar cubes, laced with acid, made the rounds. Flower power and brotherly love engulfed all.

In the middle of dinner, Jonah noticed the Crazy Three as they slipped out the back and into the night. Leave them be, Jonah told himself, but he couldn't let it go.

The laughter faded as Jonah followed a trio of shadows ducking in and out of the compound lights. At the Upper House the Crazy Three slinked inside and disappeared for several minutes.

Jonah knelt behind a redwood when the Crazy Three reemerged on the porch. They hurried down the stoop and rushed around the perimeter of the ranch to the various shelters. The trio whisked through lean-tos and makeshift shacks. At the open-air tree house, Jonah overheard them argue the merits of some deal they had brokered with the law. Gypsy and Running Bear seemed to be at odds with Nevada, arguing that it was time to make the phone call and be done with it.

Jonah added up pieces of the conversation, realized their intent and started to bolt in the opposite direction when he banged into an inky figure. The two fell to the ground as one, entangled in each other's hold. Alarmed, Jonah tore at the other person's clothing, trying to free himself, when he recognized the other's voice.

"Stop that, *espèci d'idiot*!" the person said in French.

"What're you doing here?" Jonah asked as he stared down Rene who stood there with his shirt ripped in half.

"I might ask you the same question, sneaking around in the dark like some common thief. I always knew you were a…"

"You should cover up," Jonah interrupted as he pointed to a nipple.

Rene looked down and gasped. "Turn away!"

Jonah did as requested, talking over his shoulder, "Well, this explains the raging hormones, the drama."

Rene hurried to refasten the ace bandage around her chest before buttoning her shirt.

"Why the disguise?" Jonah asked.

"I don't owe you an explanation."

"I believe you do."

Dead air crowded the space between them. The awkwardness grew.

The altar boy surrendered, saying, "All right, but you mustn't tell anyone, agree?"

"Sure," Jonah said in a cavalier manner.

The altar boy pushed him. "I'm not kidding."

"Okay, okay," Jonah said. "Just get on with it."

With the release of a clump of air, an explanation started forward of how posing as an altar boy would be good cover. "Besides it's safer to travel on the road as a male."

"What's your real name?" Jonah asked.

"Renée, Renée Giguere."

"Father Paul's daughter?" he said with surprise in his voice.

"*Stupide.* What else?" she said, shaking her head.

"Renée? Not Rene?" Jonah pondered this development, saying, "Who would've thought it possible to change one's sex by simply adding a single letter to a name."

⅄

There had been increased pressure from neighbors for the public authorities to shut down Morningstar Ranch. Complaints ranged from public nudity to septic stench to illegal drug use to noise pollution.

The information that Jonah provided the commune's council of elders confirmed that a visit from the sheriff's office was imminent. The council voted against banishing the Crazy Three, opting to use the trio's ploy to the combine's advantage.

⅄

The red-ribboned black man escorted Nevada and his two comrades to the parking lot, away from the compound. With the false knowledge that their earlier search of the ranch had gone undetected, the Crazy Three accepted bottles of Ripple from the black man as well as an offer to help with the repairs on their VW bus.

With the confidence that the Crazy Three would be out of earshot for the next couple of hours, the council of elders initiated a plan of action. Piano Player organized several work details. Otis volunteered to join forces with the beautiful Ocean while Jonah and Renée led a small contingent to the various abodes.

Vacuums hummed. Brooms, mops and rags swooshed away grime, urine, and traces of discarded weed. Buckets of bleach aided in the hiding of unwanted aromas. Hippies searched backpacks, suitcases, toiletry kits and wardrobes. Drugs that were not consumed on the spot were hidden in the nearby forest. The "cleansing" took on a merriment of its own with Christians working hand-in-hand next to Hindus, with whites and blacks banding together in common purpose.

Chapter 13

At the dining hall, Swami Bhaktivedenta bestowed a blessing upon the gathering: "May Buddha align your vibratory essence with life and transmute all hindrances into love."

Father Paul, with Renée standing next to him in her altar boy outfit, rendered an invocation, giving thanks to the Light above. Jonah hadn't shared his revelation as to Renée's true gender with Otis. Normally the boys shared everything, but Jonah had sworn a vow of secrecy.

Piano Player congratulated everyone on a job well done and as a way of a thank you he circulated the last of the "blue juice". Jonah stole the LSD from Otis's grasp and handed it to Ocean.

"I told you before," Otis said to Jonah, "I already got a mother."

"Yeah, but she doesn't love you like I do," Jonah said. "Besides, I'm not prepared to pick up the pieces again."

A possum had been offered up as a tribute to the cleanup efforts. To the chagrin of most, the chef, who was on acid, overcooked the nocturnal beast. Its meat was tougher than usual, driving many from the ceremony in search of edibles to satisfy their ravaging appetites. In the middle of this exodus, a cloud of dust rose from the entrance, accompanied by a string of mechanical rumblings.

Piano Player and his pregnant lady led all toward the front gate. Below in the parking lot Running Bear was trying to collect parking fees from a cluster of lawmen. A sheriff was questioning Nevada in some detail before the entire contingent, some twenty strong, advanced up the driveway to the entrance of the ranch.

"That's him," Nevada told the sheriff, pointing to Piano Player.

"Are you Louis Gottlieb?"

"Yes."

"Mr. Gottlieb, I'm Sheriff McGee. I have in my possession a search warrant for these premises."

"There is no need for that," Piano Player said, nodding to the document. "Welcome to Morningstar Solar Legation and Economic Council where access is denied to no one."

Sheriff McGee showed a curious look to his colleagues. The group included not just deputies, but representatives from the Health Department, Juvenile Corrections, Building and Permits, and Narcotics as well as photographers from the *Press Democrat.*

A bureaucratic buzz filled the compound the likes of which these rural parts hadn't seen in some time. The residents appeared fully clothed. They remained calm, cooperating with search parties while neighbors crowded the perimeter.

Officers spread out over the ranch, shaking everyone down. They searched the linings of jackets, wallets, purses and backpacks. Even personal items such as tampons, gels and the soles of footwear were subject to inspection.

The Morningstar inhabitants formed a circle, linking hands in prayer outside the Upper House as deputies stormed inside. They probed electrical sockets, checked floors and walls for cavities, and emptied flour tins and cereal boxes.

From the edge of the property line, an old rancher studied the collection of hippies, shouting, "Degenerates!" Other labels such as "aliens" and "animals" drifted across the meadow.

The hippies abandoned their circle to address the disparaging remarks. With their cones of hair and colorful rags, they approached the gawking neighbors. Bells, beads and trinkets were given as peace offerings. A yogi perched himself on a fencepost while shell-decorated goddesses jingled like wind chimes.

One of the flower children sympathized with a neighbor's horse and started to trim the mane from its eyes. A rancher scolded the girl, saying she had ruined the horse's chances for a blue ribbon at the county fair.

A yell from inside a lean-to sounded an alarm. Officials, reporters and cops dashed to the scene. A deputy stood amidst a mound of rubble, holding up an ancient paper of speed as if he had just unearthed the Holy Grail.

"That's it?" Sheriff McGee said.

The raid had not gone as intended and the sheriff ordered his men to clear the area. There was a grumble as the procession made its way through the front gate and down the driveway to the parking lot.

Feeling that he had perhaps been double-crossed, the sheriff gave orders for the Crazy Three to be escorted to the nearest squad car. Gypsy cursed an objection while Running Bear let out a war cry. Nevada wheeled around and clocked the girl. Blood squirted from her mouth as deputies wrestled Nevada to the ground and cuffed him.

"Mr. Gottlieb," Sheriff McGee said, "I can see that you were well prepared for our visit. It seems as if someone has tipped you off. My congratulations."

"I seek no advantage over you or anyone else," Piano Player said. "We are all derived from the same molecules, sir."

"Everything seems to be in order with the exception of some minor infractions," Sheriff McGee said. "Besides the finding of small quantities of contraband, there could be an issue with your septic, which is overflowing. In addition, urine samples taken from toilets appear brown. Better have your people checked for hepatitis."

"Will do," Piano Player said.

"Oh, one another thing. The Building inspector was ready to throw the book at you but was impressed with the commune's organized nature. He suggested that you tear down some of those lean-tos and build yourself a tent community. No county ordinances against that."

"I appreciate the tip," Piano Player said.

"Personally, I've got more serious things on my plate," Sheriff McGee said, "but these neighbors of yours feel threatened. They're not going to give up, and they have the backing of Governor Reagan to boot."

"Understandable," Piano Player said. "It's culture shock."

"My hands are tied," the sheriff said. "Unless you comply with the sanitary codes for an organized camp, I'm afraid you'll have to cease operations.

"I can hold off the wolf pack for another seventy-two hours," the sheriff added. "Beyond that you're on your own." He handed over an official looking document before leading a caravan of squad cars from the area.

Piano Player read aloud the "Cease and Desist" order. The grievances of the locals were listed over a three-page spread.

Jonah remembered a passage from the Torah where God is always involved, where He continues to be present, affecting everything that mankind does. "Why don't you will the land to God?" he suggested to Piano Player.

"You keep thinking, Jonah," Piano Player said with a chuckle. "That's what you're good at."

"It might have some side benefits," Jonah persisted. "Ever heard of the courts trying to collect taxes from God?"

"Can't say that I have."

This second bit of rational caused Piano Player to give the matter some serious consideration. Both men started to head back toward the Lower House when Jonah asked about the fate of the Crazy Three.

"My guess," Piano Player said, "is that the sheriff will teach them a lesson about what happens to informants who don't inform. They might get a few days tacked onto whatever charge was originally hanging over their heads. Beyond that, probably not much."

"I almost feel sorry for them," Jonah said. "Getting played like that from both ends."

Piano Player and Aurora noticed that many of the neighbors remained nearby and walked over to reassure them. A fellow commune member, however, ripped off his clothes and pecked at the ground like a chicken. He chewed on pebbles, swallowing dirt, writhing on the ground, clucking away. A few of his brothers and sisters came over to calm him, chanting Hare Krishna.

A nearby resident started to escort her husband from the scene when he pulled away and smiled at a hippie who was in the family way, dancing in the buff.

The naked Aurora spied the flirtation. "Care to join us for a little music?"

"Come, Elmer," the woman said to her husband. "We best leave."

But Elmer didn't budge, struck by the girl's natural beauty. Piano Player returned a knowing grin before writing L-O-V-E with his finger on the dust of Aurora's robust belly.

"Disgusting," the woman said before storming off without her husband.

⅄

The Allman Joys and the Steve Miller Band began setting up while the residents gathered at the Lower House to celebrate their victory over the county. Grass and beer were in abundance while appetizers of peyote buttons, mushrooms and LSD circulated the throng.

The music blasted over the countryside. Young and old boogied. Jonah dragged the altar boy out onto the earthen floor while Otis gawked at the sight before shrugging it off. No big deal. Gender seemed to be the last consideration in selecting a dance partner.

"Allman Joys is forming a new band this month," Jonah said to Renée, the pair swaying to the sound. "Gonna call themselves the Hour Glass."

Renée whirled around, saying to Jonah, "In case you haven't noticed, I'm not dancing with you," and she latched onto a ten-year-old girl to prove her point.

Jonah smiled before continuing: "I'll have to tell my friend Hal Butler at the *Chronicle*. He'd love to do a piece on these guys. Have you ever read his column?"

Renée turned her back to him, listening to the lyrics.

"It could be a spoonful of coffee /
It could be a spoonful of tea /

But one little spoon of your precious love /
Is good enough for me."

"The lyrics are about man's search to satisfy his cravings," Jonah said. "See what you women do to us? That, of course, can only occur if you admit to being a woman in the first place."

With that last pronouncement, Renée traipsed toward the front gate. Jonah followed.

Otis spotted his buddy chasing after the altar boy. "You see that?" Otis said to Father Paul, but the priest did not reply.

At the top of the driveway, Jonah caught up with Renée. "Hey, I didn't mean anything by it."

She gazed out onto the parking lot and the redwood ridge beyond, folding her arms, her back to him.

"So you're an altar boy by day and a woman by night," Jonah said. "So what? No one cares." He figured she wanted some alone time and started to retreat when her words stopped him.

"My dad needs this," she said as she swung around to him. "He was dying of boredom back in Quebec and thought that there might be enough *forcé* left in him for one more trip."

"To relive some past?" Jonah guessed.

"It's all he's ever had," Renée said when another thought came to her. "Can I ask you for a favor?"

"What's that?"

"Continue to address him as Father Paul. He'd like that."

New arrivals caught his attention instead and without a response he dashed off.

⅄

"We're outta here," Jonah shouted over the music to Otis.

"Can't hear," Otis said as he passed a joint to the fleshy Ocean.

"Gotta go. Now!" Jonah repeated.

"Tell Ocean here 'bout Steve Miller's new contract with Capitol," Otis said ignoring the request. "Didn't you say it was worth almost a million?" He pivoted to the bare breasted woman, saying, "What would you do, darlin', with a million clams?"

Otis never heard her reply as Jonah hauled him away, saying, "Papa Al and Maloney are here."

"What? Why didn't you say so? We best be gettin' the hell outta here."

"Good idea," Jonah said in a sarcastic tone.

The pair said goodbye to Piano Player who sensed their vulnerability. "Use the back entrance," he said before embracing each in turn, telling them to take care.

They rushed past the apple orchard and across the meadow to a grove of redwoods. A worn path greeted them and they fled into the shadows.

Back at the front gate, Piano Player approached a burly white guy in a policeman's uniform and a Negro in a three-quarter-length coat. "Seems rather warm for such a wardrobe," Piano Player said to the black man. "May I take that from you?" he said, stalling.

"No, thank you. I'm afraid I've become attached to the darn thing." He scoured the compound with his inspection before saying to Piano Player, "My associate and I are looking for the driver of the hearse in your parking lot," the Negro said. "Would you happen to know where I could find him?"

"What is your interest in the vehicle?" Piano Player asked.

"It was stolen in San Francisco, perhaps harboring a couple of wanted fugitives." The Negro spotted the doubt in the man's expression and added, "It is a delicate matter. There is no need to go into the details other than to say that the citizens of the City would be in your debt."

"I may have to see some credentials before I can let you onto the property," Piano Player said.

The burly cop pushed past, saying, "Enough with the small talk," and he stomped toward a throng of merrymakers gathered at a weathered house with a wraparound porch.

"You'll have to excuse my partner," the Negro said. "He means no harm, just a bit over ambitious at times. I would hate to see his Irish fury unleashed upon your guests. 'A stone is heavy and the sand weighty, but the provocation of a fool is heavier than both.' Proverbs 27:3."

Piano Player let his vision linger on the black man as he walked away, thinking that if anyone held the rights to creepy, it was this guy.

⅄

"You're gettin' to be a regular pain in the ass," Otis said to Jonah as they trotted through the forest.

Jonah looked back over his shoulder. Nothing. Good.

"First you take the brother's drugs, then you pull him away from the most beautiful creature the brother's ever laid eyes on," Otis said in the third person.

Jonah peered behind him again as they came to a confluence of trails. He steered Otis to the left not knowing if this was the way to salvation, just wanting to keep on the move.

"That Ocean was into the brother," Otis said as he slowed his pace. "She had some decent proportions to her too. Could've salvaged somethin' from this trip. Know what I mean?" He paused as if pondering the answer to his own question before saying, "Woulda been better off stayin' back home."

"By home do you mean back in the City where the Angels would have been rifling through your dead body for their missing acid tabs? Is that the home you're referring to, huh?"

"Might be better than on the run from a thug and his cop friend," Otis said.

They stepped from the forest to peek down Dupont Road. The quiet felt reassuring and they started walking along the asphalt. After another mile, Dupont dead-ended at Harrison Grade. Otis did what he did best—jabbering about nothing and everything—when a putt-putt sounded from behind. A van came to a halt. Love-decals, rainbows and peace symbols garnished its side.

"Would you boys be interested in a lift to the next *ville*?" the driver said in French.

Jonah studied the VW bus. "Doesn't this belong to the Crazy Three?"

"With all these lawmen running willy-nilly over the countryside," Father Paul said, "I am surprised that you would elect to waste your precious time discussing the particulars of an automobile's ownership."

With that pronouncement, reality set in and the boys scurried into the backseat. Renée was still dressed as an altar boy, continuing to play the con.

"With Nevada and his compatriots headed to the garrison," Father Paul said, "I thought it best to give the bus a little run…to insure that the batteries did not go dead."

"How thoughtful of you," Jonah said.

"It seemed like the Christian thing to do," Father Paul said. "Besides, Papa Al was keeping a close eye on the hearse."

The van rolled down Harrison Grade, which ran parallel to a meadow where cattle grazed. After another mile, the vehicle dipped back into the woods, maneuvering through several S turns before returning to the daylight. At Bohemian Highway, they came to a village tucked between redwood-studded hills. Father Paul thought a bite to eat would be in order while Jonah insisted that they drive on.

"Nonsense," Father Paul said, "food is good for the soul."

"I've heard the same thing about breathing," Jonah said.

Chapter 14

The VW bus turned south on Bohemian Highway and entered the hamlet of Occidental. Negri's Restaurant and the Union Hotel came and went as the van hung a left, motoring a short block to Church Street. Father Paul steered the vehicle toward the backside of the one-block town and parked.

Jonah exited and perused a wooden placard, which read METHODIST EPISCOPAL CHURCH. "Otis and I will go visit God while you two round up some food."

"Nonsense," Father Paul said. "Half the enjoyment of a meal is the exchange of pithy dialogue. Sitting by one's self, conversing with a bowl of Bolognese, is not my idea of social intercourse."

Jonah's vision veered to Renée as if seeking her help. She shrugged, flipping him a wicked grin. Outvoted, Jonah joined the group as they retraced their steps back to the center of town where they drifted to Fiori's at the Altamont Hotel. Father Paul looked over the menu before spotting a handwritten note on the entrance: CLOSED FOR FUNERAL SERVICES OF JOSEPH DONATI.

"Well, on to the next Italian faire," Father Paul said.

They meandered a few doors down and entered a saloon. Blue-collar types in their overalls and soiled T-shirts sat on stools sipping whiskies. The edges of the bar-back mirror held business cards and political cartoons. One depicted LBJ setting Ho Chi Minh on fire with napalm. A miniature flag of Dixie stood limp nearby.

Father Paul garnered friendly nods while Otis received the old stink-eye from several patrons. Renée nudged Jonah to alert him. He kept Otis busy with idle chatter as they made their way to the reservation desk.

"Good evening," the receptionist said. She owned a kind face, which was mounted atop a plump frame some forty years old. "May I help you?"

"I am Father Paul. How do you do?" the priest said as he extended his hand.

"And I am Lucille Gonnella." She accepted his greeting, saying, "Nice to meet you, Father."

He held onto her while asking what was the house special. Lucille explained that the faire was southern Italian—family style.

"If you can manage to make your way past the minestrone, the anti pasta and the entrée," Lucille said, "an apple fritter will be waiting for you at the end."

Jonah scanned the main dining room and studied the faces at the tables. Father Paul continued to impose himself on Lucille, embracing her hand when a broad-shouldered man sauntered over, asking the woman if everything was all right.

Lucille drew her hand away from the priest's and slapped her husband across his chest. "Oh, Mr. Mahoney Gonnella, are you jealous?" She took in his protective glare before saying, "He's a priest for heaven's sake."

"It is indeed for His sake that we walk this earth, madam." Father Paul said goodbye to the couple as he and his party followed a waiter to a banquet room in the rear.

Jonah's head swayed to and fro, on the lookout. Renée caught his frantic search, telling him to quit it, that he was causing her to tense up as well.

"You don't know Papa Al," Jonah said.

"Whoever he is, he's got a hold on you." She trailed behind Jonah before leaning into his ear. "*Dans le pétrin!*"

Agitated, Jonah swung around. "Speak American."

"You're in big doo-doo, aren't you? You do know what *doo-doo* means, *oui*?"

He gave her a hard look as they passed under an entranceway, which read "Bocce Ballroom". The waiter noticed the priest's curiosity and added that the space had been built out of a single redwood from the Pannizzera Ranch. The employee went on—without anyone's request—and explained that the town had been settled by a criminal named Christopher Folkmann who had changed his name to Dutch Bill Howard after stealing a military boat and fleeing San Francisco in 1849. The waiter walked tall as if proud of his storytelling.

Jonah pondered how many more lawbreakers the area harbored. Hell, all he had to do was take a look at his fellow travelers—a pair of con artists, a drug dealer and himself, a pickpocket and errand boy for the Hell's Angels. But there were criminals and then there were criminals. The thief who stole the occasional boat was ranked well below the mobster who extorted, battered and murdered his way to the top of the heap. Or at least that's what Jonah told himself as he scoured the cavernous hall once again.

Candle wax dripped down the side of an old Chianti bottle, which sat atop a piano where a teenager played a Big Band tune. Jonah and the others shared a table with a family of eight. Must be Catholic, Jonah thought. Nobody else would breed such a horde, except for maybe those Mormons he read about in *National Geographic*, or was it *Popular Mechanics*. He couldn't remember and it didn't matter as he tried to keep his mind occupied.

"What'll you have?" a waitress with a mustache-shadow asked Jonah.

No response.

"Sir?" the waitress repeated.

Renée gave him a kick. Jonah hissed at her, asking what the hell was that for. She pointed to the lady with the notepad.

"Oh, ah, sorry." He smiled an awkward smile before saying, "Can you repeat the question?"

"Whaddya...want...to...eat?" the waitress said, dragging out the words.

Jonah asked the waitress to pick something for him. She recommended the house special, which he said would be fine, wanting to get on with things. The quicker they ate, the quicker they could leave.

Father Paul commented on the background tune coming from the piano, recognizing the melody as belonging to the old Ozzie Nelson Orchestra. "The band hit number one on the single's chart in 1935 with 'And Then Some'. Ozzie's calm vocals mixed well with Harriet's perky voice."

"Didn't they get married?" Otis asked. "Had two kids, right?" and he stared at the wall, trying to recall their names.

"David and Ricky," Renée volunteered. "I used to love the TV show."

"Heard the ol' man was a son-of-a-bitch," Otis said, "denying his boys a chance at college, tellin' them they owed it to the family to stay in television."

Jonah massaged his temples, not believing that the topic of conversation centered around *The Adventures of Ozzie and Harriet* while just three miles away, a pair of the meanest bastards this side of hell were on the hunt for them.

Without a word, he rose and left.

"What, pray tell, is wrong with your friend?" Father Paul asked Otis.

"Prob'ly just hormones."

⅄

The eighteen-year-old found a stool at the end of the bar under a Confederate flag. He ordered a Coke when an old timer, wearing bib overalls, objected.

"How old are you, boy?" the local asked as he put his meaty arm on the young stranger. "Must be at least eighteen, right?"

"Yes, sir."

"Old enough to get your nuts blown off in Dink Town, right?"

"Excuse me?" the teenager asked.

"Dink Town, you know, where the dinks live."

"Just took my physical," Jonah added before introducing himself.

"I'm Eddy." With a claw grip, the local squeezed Jonah's hand before turning to the bartender. "Get this man a proper drink. On me."

The employee nodded and went to pour a whiskey as Eddy announced to the crowd, "Jonah here is goin' to Vietnam to kick some butt. Ain't you, boy?"

Jonah flashed a smile, remaining silent, just wanting to be alone with his thoughts. A couple of rednecks, however, wouldn't hear of it and sidled up next to him.

"Those slope heads need to be taught some manners," Eddy said as he looked to his buddies for confirmation.

Jonah took a sip before deciding to play along, saying, "Yeah, I figured I'd go over there and get the scalps of some Gooks."

"*Gooks*?" Eddy said. "No...no...no. We don't much care for that term."

"Is that right?" Jonah said.

"Several of us fought in Korea, includin' yours truly," Eddy said. "*Mi guk* means 'American' over there. Later on it was shortened to gook. That's what they called us—gooks. Now the enemy in 'Nam is called that. Don't sit well with me, understand?"

"No gooks it is," Jonah said as he clanged his glass with several of the rednecks.

"Dinks. Charlie. Slope heads. Tunnel rats," Eddy offered, "all good. But no gooks."

"How about *MacGooks*?" Jonah said, "in honor of the new fast-food chain."

"You tryin' to be funny, boy?" Eddy said.

Jonah caught the change in the man's expression and apologized.

"We got enough jesters roamin' the countryside, tellin' jokes 'bout LBJ and such," Eddy said. "Won't have it."

"Heard that Defense Secretary McNamara resigned," a second redneck said, "along with four or five other top aides of the President. Nothin' but a bunch of quitters if you ask me."

Jonah nodded.

"Now you got these protestors marchin' all over the place," another added. "Some 200,000 paraded down Geary Boulevard in Frisco like they was doin' the world a favor."

Eddy signaled to the barkeep to order another round before saying, "Those dinks in Hanoi are gettin' the notion that they can win this thing, stormin' across the DMZ into the south."

Eddy brought Jonah in closer. "LBJ's gonna send 40,000 of you boys over there this year, bring the troop total to 'bout 700,000. That oughta do it."

⅄

Father Paul served up bowls of minestrone from a tureen while samples of antipasto made the rounds. Renée and Otis picked salami, cheese, and pickled veggies from a serving plate. Next came dinner salads and sides of ravioli.

By the time the entrées came around, most everyone was full. Otis had difficulty stuffing the last bit of a T-bone steak down his thin frame while Renée hid a portion of her uneaten spaghetti and meatballs under a napkin. Father Paul licked the remains of his cacciatore from his fingers before gazing at the untouched meal next to him.

"The good Lord would be disappointed if such a bounty lay idle," Father Paul said as he studied Jonah's roasted chicken dinner.

"We could box it for him," Renée suggested.

"What you care for anyways?" Otis said.

He's right, Renée thought, why should I care? She fell quiet, allowing the food to take center stage.

⅄

"You heard 'bout Tricky Dick, right?" Eddy said, the whiskey speaking for him, "He's over in Saigon tryin' to steal LBJ's thunder. Nixon don't belong there. Just a citizen like you and me."

Jonah wondered if he might find more peace and quiet back at the table with the Ozzie and Harriet show.

"Tricky Dick sweated bullets against Kennedy," another redneck volunteered, "and then he was defeated again…to Brown for governor. Just another loser," and he drained his drink.

Eddy switched up the conversation, asking, "Didn't you walk in with that colored fella awhile ago?"

Jonah gauged the yokel's tone and said, "My friend is signing up for the Marines. Wants to do his country proud. Go red, white and blue," and he raised his drink.

"*Semper Fi*," Eddy added as he clanged the kid's glass.

Jonah started to take another sip when he glanced outside. Papa Al and Sergeant Mahoney were exiting Negri's Restaurant across the street. Startled, Jonah began to rise when Eddy pushed him back down.

"Have another," the local said, waving over the bartender.

"I should get back to my dinner," Jonah said as he tried to get to his feet once again, but the result was the same as before.

"Might be the last civilized drink you have," Eddy said as he slid another whiskey in front of Jonah.

Papa Al and Maloney searched several cars in the parking lot before entering the Union Hotel saloon. Jonah lowered his head behind the cluster of rednecks as the two thugs headed toward the rear hallway.

Eddy noticed Jonah's twitchy behavior. "You hidin' from that Negro and his vanilla friend?" Eddy said as he nodded toward the out-of-towners.

Jonah didn't hear the question, busy studying the movements of Papa Al.

"Jonah?" Eddy said, shaking the boy's shoulder.

"Sorry," Jonah said as he blinked the haze from his brain. "What did you say?"

"Those two fellas, they botherin' you?"

Got to do something, Jonah thought, and then an idea came to him. "Ah, that was my daddy, the white one, but I guess you figured that out," Jonah said with a lie.

"And the Negro?" Eddy asked. "Is he your friend's pappy?"

"Y-e-a-p," Jonah said, dragging out the word, buying time to think. "Okay, yes, that would most definitely be Otis's dad. Yes, sir."

"They come to take you boys home?" another redneck asked.

Jonah expounded on the assumption, adding, "They don't want Otis and me to go to Vietnam. They think it's all a bunch of nonsense."

"*Nonsense*?" a third redneck repeated. "Nothin' nonsense 'bout protectin' home and country from those red commies."

"Well, sir," Jonah said, "that's exactly what we told them, but they are of the same mind as those protestors and peaceniks you were speaking of earlier."

"Oh, they are, are they?" Eddy said with a tightened expression.

"Otis and I just want the opportunity to give something back to the U.S. of A.," and Jonah put on a sad look.

The waitress approached with a serving tray. "Did you save room for an apple fritter?"

"That sounds just divine, my dear," Father Paul said.

Without warning, a Negro wearing a three-quarter-length coat and aviator glasses peered over the waitress's shoulder. "I believe they are finished with their repast, my dear."

"Papa Al!" Otis exclaimed as he started to rise.

Maloney put a hand on Otis and pushed him back down.

Father Paul spotted the fright on Otis's face and tried to intervene. "Allow me to introduce myself. I am Father…"

"My friend and I are in a bit of a hurry," Papa Al interrupted. "We require a word with the young lad here," and he gestured to Otis.

Renée guessed that these were the ones chasing Jonah, and she rose to her full height. "You are not welcome here."

Papa Al took in the diminutive figure and said, "For an altar boy… and a scrawny one at that…you certainly do possess a pair of rather large testicles."

Renée started to rush the mobster when a local in his bib overalls stretched out his meaty forearm like a crossing guard. "No need for that," Eddy said to the altar boy.

"Thank you, sir, for your intervention," Papa Al said, "but I think we have the situation under suitable management."

"You two ingrates can leave," Eddy said, staring down the strangers. "Your sons stay."

"*Sons*?" Papa Al said. "I am afraid I don't understand."

"You should be proud of your offspring," Eddy said as he brought Jonah forward to join Otis. "They just wanna serve their country."

"I am afraid there is a misunderstanding," Papa Al argued. "These are not our sons," Papa Al corrected as he gestured to the two teens. "Nor are they related to us in any manner. Rather, they are in possession of some very valuable evidence, which the SFPD is anxious to apprehend."

To back up the claim, Maloney pulled out his wallet and flashed his badge.

"Don't mean shit up here," Eddy said as he glanced at the ID. "'Sides, you oughtn't use your authority as an excuse to punish your own flesh and blood."

"We are here on official business," Papa Al reiterated.

"Again," Sergeant Maloney said to Papa Al, "you talk too much." He grabbed Jonah and Otis and pushed them toward the exit when a phalanx of rednecks blocked his path.

"Get outta the way," Maloney said to the group.

Eddy crossed his arms across his chest, silent, glaring at the city cop. And that's when all hell broke loose. Maloney reached into his back pocket for a leather-covered truncheon and skulled the redneck. Another came to the aid of Eddy and took a swing at the cop but instead hit a fellow patron. The local, thinking an old debt was being settled, sucker-punched the guy. The fight soon turned into a brawl—everyone man, woman and child for himself.

Lucille Gonnella and her husband came storming out of the kitchen with a couple of cooks, each brandishing a butcher knife or a frying pan or a ladle. Bodies went to the floor. Customers scattered. Chianti bottles and dinner plates flew toward various targets. Wives screamed while husbands wagered on the outcome. Dollar bills crisscrossed each other. Odds shifted with the exchange of blows.

Father Paul hauled in a roasted chicken and retreated to a far corner. Otis started to crawl to safety as well before an arm dragged him back into the fray. Jonah found himself entangled within a chokehold, coughing, gasping for air. Renée bit into the exposed flesh of a limb when Jonah's cry told her that she had ahold of the wrong leg.

"What the hell?" Jonah exclaimed.

"Everything's gotta be perfect for you, doesn't it?" she yelled over the caterwauling.

"I just don't wanna be bushwhacked by friendly fire," Jonah said before someone hooked onto his mouth and yanked him backward.

Adolescents stood by with stale fritters, eyeing their quarry. Each time a head popped up from the pile, the teens plummeted the fleshy cranium as if playing a carnival game.

Renée managed to get to Father Paul who objected to her interference, saying that he hadn't finished his meal. With urgency, she latched onto him. The pair weaved their way through the dining hall to a rear exit, but not before the priest grabbed an apple fritter. Once outside, they met up with Jonah and Otis and all sped to the VW bus, the priest noshing on the run.

Chapter 15

Thunder rumbled north along Highway One and over the Russian River at Bridgehaven. Harleys cruised alongside wetlands, scaring herons and egrets from their dinner. The band of fifty bikers rode in formation, two abreast, on a weekend joy ride. They crept into Jenner, a town of two hundred residents squeezed between an estuary and a coastal range. Summer cottages huddled on the bank while a handful of businesses lined the block.

The lead bike pulled in front of a half-century-old lodge. With the toe of his boot, Sonny pushed the kickstand down and finger-combed his wind-blown hair. Wearing their colors, he and a couple of bikers strolled past a tavern, a dining hall, a post office and entered the general store, which was bordered by abalone shells. The black-leathered group marched up and down the aisles, snatching up chips, cookies and other comfort food.

The sound of the crashing surf lured Sonny to a window. Waves reached the shore with a confluent thump of peace and force. Seals lazed on the beach where the river emptied into the Pacific. Probably advertise the area for honeymooners and other saps, Sonny thought.

A teenager in braces came to his side and studied the scene. "The soothing echo of the surf fills my heart with music." She smiled, showing off her grillwork.

Sonny turned to the oddity and growled, shooing her back to the safety of her father who wore a pair of khaki-colored shorts belted up to the high-water mark. The paternal figure wrapped his arms around his child as he shepherded her outside.

The biker retreated from the window and walked to an older guy who stood behind the register. Sonny gestured to a wired cabinet, asking for a quart of Jack Daniels. The employee pulled out a shotgun from under the counter and pointed the barrel to a sign that read: WE RESERVE THE RIGHT TO REFUSE SERVICE TO ANYONE.

"Well, hell's bells, partner," Sonny said. "Can't you see? We ain't just anyone."

"I called the sheriff when you pulled in," the old timer said. "Should be here momentarily."

The other Angels crowded in waiting for Sonny's signal. In an attempt to defuse the situation, he tried small talk as he pointed to an ancient photo. "That your grandpa?"

"Elijah Jenner was his name," the old timer said.

"Guess he thought enough of himself to spread the name around," Sonny said while motioning to shelves of knickknacks bearing the same monogram. JENNER BY THE SEA decorated T-shirts, coffee mugs, license plate frames, postcards and guidebooks.

"Granddad used to live on Penny Island part-time," the old timer said. "He loved fishing and boating. Before that there was a sawmill and a boathouse nearby."

Sonny examined the galleon windows, wheel beamed ceilings and twelve-inch oak plank floors, thinking the town's legacy was filled with craftsmen. The biker, however, stopped short of any further pleasantries, saying, "That was a damn fine history lesson. Now how about our whiskey?"

"Like I said, I gotta ask you to leave," the old timer said cradling the weapon in his arms.

"Is that because me and my boys aren't here on some honeymoon trip? That it, pops?"

"Good a reason as any."

Sonny leaned into the wrinkled face. "I'm afraid we need to clear the dust out of us. It was a long ride up the coast. Much appreciated if you'd handover a couple bottles of Jack."

"No can do," the old timer persisted.

Sonny motioned to a fellow Angel who slashed a chain across the counter before sauntering past the register toward the liquor rack. The old timer swung the shotgun around and pulled the trigger. A spray of rock salt pockmarked the right side of the biker's face.

"Shit! He shot off my ear!" The biker, holding his bloodied head, marched toward the old timer until the click of the second hammer sent a warning.

Sonny decided it wasn't worth the trouble. "I hope my man here"—and he motioned to the biker without an ear—"didn't mess up the place to your disliking."

"Cost of doing business, I suppose," the old timer said.

"I suppose," Sonny said before nodding farewell.

Outside, county deputies stood beside three cruisers.

"Good evening, sheriff," Sonny said as he approached. "What can I do you for?"

"What's wrong with him?" the sheriff asked as he pointed to the wounded biker.

"Had a minor disagreement with one of your local merchants," Sonny said.

"I'm Sheriff McGee. You boys need to move on."

"As soon as we stock up on some refreshments," Sonny said as a half dozen Angels drew weapons.

"I wouldn't advise that," the sheriff said.

"Go screw yourself," a biker said.

Deputies raised their service revolvers. Nearby, a couple of other Angels squared off against a second cluster of lawmen. An old-fashioned Mexican impasse ensued with each side measuring the resolve of the other.

"My men and I will escort you north," the sheriff said. "At the Mendocino County line another batch of officers will meet you."

"It doesn't seem that you've done the math," Sonny said as he included his comrades with his look.

"Oh, I've done the figuring all right," the sheriff said with a grin. "You better take a look behind us."

Sonny cupped his eyes to examine the neighboring hillside. Sparkles of radiance glistened off metal. At least twenty guns were trained on the patches of the Hells Angels.

Sonny hesitated before saying, "Well, guess we can wait a while for that drink."

"Sounds like a wise decision," Sheriff McGee said.

Without another word, Sonny mounted his Harley and kick-started it. The other Angels followed suit, waiting for the black-and-whites to take the lead. The patrol cars proceeded the short distance to a roadblock on the eastern edge of town. A line of vehicles a half-mile long waited for the entourage to pass. Angels flipped off the tourists before whistling at a group of schoolgirls aboard a bus, gesturing for them to come for a ride.

Sonny braked alongside a hippie van, recognizing a couple of faces inside. "Don't this beat all. The boys and I were partaking in a break from city life, enjoying the coastal scenery, and who do we run into? Ain't fate a bitch?"

Jonah leaned out the backseat window. "Just let it go, Sonny. You got my three thousand. That should make us square."

"What is the man referring to, my son?" Father Paul asked from behind the steering wheel.

"I see you and your nigger have hooked up with the church," Sonny said.

"Leave the priest and the altar boy out of this," Jonah said to Sonny. "They've got nothing to do with anything."

"I could use the van for a pickup in Cazadero," Sonny said.

"Don't do this," Jonah pleaded.

A black-and-white rolled up to the delay. "Let's get a move on," and the deputy motioned down the road to the rest of the pack, which was gradually disappearing around a bend.

"Sonny ain't gonna touch us with the cops here," Otis said to Jonah. "Let's just drive on."

"Shut up," Jonah answered. He knew where this could end up. If they ignored Sonny's request, the biker would hunt them down and reap his vengeance, priest and all.

But Renée had a different take on things and she vacated the vehicle and traipsed to the biker. "Who the hell do you think you are, mister?"

"I'm the one percent you don't want to mess with, kid," Sonny said.

The deputy approached and ordered the altar boy to return to the van, but Renée wouldn't listen and kept yelling at the biker.

Jonah jumped out, wrapped his arms around Renée, dragged her back to the bus and tossed her inside. "Stay there."

"*Stupide*!" she shouted.

Two additional patrol cars arrived. Deputies exited and unfastened their gun holsters.

Intrigued by the chaos, Father Paul inquired of the Angel what the law wanted with him.

Instead, Sonny said, "I could use your assistance up the road."

"Will there be any adventure involved?" Father Paul asked.

"Probably," Sonny said.

"Excellent," Father Paul said before another thought came to him. "Might there be whiskey forthcoming?"

"Absolutely," Sonny said.

"We are here to serve, my son," Father Paul said with a grin.

⅄

With lights flashing, patrol cars streamed through a stop sign and headed east on Highway 116, a two-lane country road, which ran parallel to the Russian River. Cattle grazed while rusty machines dotted the surrounding meadows. Clapboards, with their faded veneers, put on a sad face.

Workers and shoppers vacated the shops of Duncans Mills to gaze at the spectacle. Old and young lined the highway on both sides of the one-block town, speechless, awed by the presence of so much good and evil in one place.

The grassy hillsides began to give way to a forest. With the close proximity of bluffs and gargantuan trees, the entire fleet became lost in darkness. The sun dipped below the horizon as a guttural sound roared through the shadows.

A road sign came up fast—CAZADERO. An arrow pointed north. A lone Angel slipped away and gestured for Father Paul to stay close. Harley and hippie van cruised deeper into the hinterland as the rest of the caravan headed north. They motored alongside the twisting Austin Creek as redwood boughs arched over the road, forming a God-made tunnel. Dark shapes melded as the evening descended with a hurry.

"You think Sonny's still pissed 'bout his missing drugs?" Otis asked Jonah in the backseat of the van.

Jonah gave his friend that what-do-you-think look.

"I was gonna return it." Otis dipped his head in thought before adding, "Not my fault the devil got hold of me."

"That wasn't the devil," Jonah said. "He was an imposter. The real one is up ahead," and he nodded to the biker out in front.

Otis took in the rural isolation around him. Hillsides stood thick with trees, and he wondered if the sun had ever reached this piece of earth before.

"You could disappear in these parts and never be found again," Otis said.

"Thanks for the cheery thought," Jonah said.

"Was on your shift," Otis said, returning to the issue of the drugs. "You the one responsible for the shit."

Jonah's head pivoted sideways, disbelief in his eyes. "You stole fifty tabs of LSD, jerkwad." He threw up his shoulders as if to say no further explanation was necessary.

"Your delivery, your responsibility," Otis retorted.

"What you're saying is that I should have known better than to trust your black ass, is that it?"

"Just sayin', dude. You know how weak I can be."

Jonah tightened his lips before admitting to himself that perhaps there was some truth to the matter. It was indeed his delivery, his duty.

Renée overheard part of the conversation. "How many people are hunting for you two?"

"Well, there's Papa Al," Jonah started before Otis quickly added the crooked cop. "I suppose for good measure you could throw in Uncle Sam."

"While I do not appreciate becoming an unwilling partner in your little crime spree," Father Paul said, "I must confess that this is all rather exhilarating. I haven't felt this alive in years."

"And what about this biker fellow," Renée said to Jonah, ignoring her father, "should we include him as well in your list of pursuers?"

"Maybe," Jonah said.

"Maybe?" Renée said. "Is that all you have to say?"

"What else is there?" Jonah said.

"How about telling us what he wants with the van?" Renée said.

"I have no idea," Jonah said before spying Renée's doubt-filled expression. "I swear."

"First chance we get," Renée said, "Father Paul and I are out of here."

"I wouldn't do that," Jonah warned.

An uneasy quiet fell upon everyone. Jonah's deliberations shifted back to Sonny, to a man who was known for his unwavering demand for obedience. Jonah thought about the various scenarios that might lie ahead, but none looked promising as his vision lingered on the surrounding forest.

The van cruised past Elim Grove where a newfound excitement occupied Father Paul as he recited a biblical passage: "'They came to Elim, where there were twelve wells of water, and three-score and ten palm trees, and they camped by the waters.' Exodus, Chapter 15, Verse 27," Father Paul said before adding, "Elim refers to a place of spiritual refreshment where Moses and his followers stopped while fleeing Egypt."

Otis studied the stands of redwoods. "Don't see nothin' refreshin' 'bout it, just blackness."

"You stand corrected, my son," Father Paul said as he pointed to a nearby wooden placard—BERKELEY MUSIC CAMP. "Not even you can deny that a good melody can lighten up the darkest of places."

"What is wrong with you?" Renée said to her father. "You sit there philosophizing on the merits of music when we're stuck in some pithole with two losers and a psychopath."

"I know. Isn't it glorious?"

The mention of music spun Jonah's thoughts in yet another direction, and he felt his Pendleton for the envelope. Still there. Mail the damn photos to Graham and be rid of it, he thought, but then a reminder came to him. The prints were the only leverage he had with Papa Al. Once they were out of his possession, Jonah's worth would take a nosedive.

High beams put a spotlight on one structure and then another as they entered Cazadero. They motored beyond Berry's Saw Mill before circling back around, drifting past a post office, the Sky Room Saloon, and a café with EATS posted over its entrance. A one-pump gas station appeared and Sonny pulled in.

The attendant came out from under a bullet-riddled Coca-Cola sign. He was wearing grease-stained overalls while grime caked his fingernails.

"Evenin'." He spat out a wad of tobacco juice, which driveled down his beard. "Don't think I've seen you boys before."

"Where does Roy Cornett live?" Sonny asked.

"Roy ain't here no more, serving time down at Folsom on those counterfeit charges." Another spit, this one landing at the feet of the biker. "What you want with a fella like that anyways?"

Sonny stared down at his muddied boot before lifting his attention to the attendant. "How do I find his old place?"

"It's up on Fern Road overlooking the falls. You passed it comin' into town, quarter mile back."

Sonny started to ease his Harley from the station.

"Don't you want gas or something?" the attendant yelled.

Chapter 16

Mr. James McGinnis, head of the San Francisco Redevelopment Agency, gaveled the meeting back to order. "If there is another outburst, I shall instruct the sergeant-at-arms to clear the room. Now quiet, all of you."

A hum hovered over the crowd as they returned to their seats inside chamber No. 5 at One South Van Ness Avenue. The neighborhood was all there—Leola King, Marion Sullivan, the Black Panthers, The Grateful Dead, the whores and others.

They had traveled to the bowel of the beast. There was no love shared between downtown and the Fillmore District. Thousands of painted ladies had been torn asunder by the steel claws of government bulldozers. Rubble festooned the streets. Rodents roamed unchecked. Tourists, who not long ago flocked to the famed Harlem of the West, now whizzed past without a thought.

The grumbling continued as James McGinnis asked if there were any further speakers. Marion Sullivan nudged the man next to him who accepted the challenge and headed toward the microphone.

"Members of the Redevelopment Agency," the man started, "my legal name is Wolfgang Wolodia Grajonka, but you know me as Bill Graham. As a ten-year-old orphan in war-torn Europe, I walked from Berlin to Lisbon with nothing to survive on except rotten apples. I have endured Nazis, famine, and the demise of my entire family. We all have suffered in our own different ways to get to this point," he said with a gesture to include the people around him. "Our sacrifices will not go unfulfilled."

Up front, politicians leaned back into their cushy chairs. One thumbed through a calendar.

"Our Fillmore is here to stay," Graham continued, "to be inhabited by citizens who may not have the financial wherewithal that you possess, but who have invested far more than mere dollars and cents."

Mr. James McGinnis whispered into the ear of one of his cohorts before glancing at his wristwatch. Another yawned.

Graham noticed the detachment. "You may yearn for your afternoon nap or your three o'clock appointment at the local pub, but you cannot silence us with your crooked cops and thugs."

"How dare you…," James McGinnis started to say.

"Nor shall you," Graham interrupted, "stop the music. The beat shall roll on, no matter what."

"Are you threatening this agency, sir?" Chairman McGinnis said.

"I did not make my way across a withering ocean only to arrive at this place cradling idle promises," Graham said.

The throng stood and cheered. Black-power salutes stood stiff. Leola King and others broke out in song, singing "Amazing Grace" as the pounding of the gavel went unnoticed.

⅄

Bill Graham stood on the front steps of the three-story concrete building and put a match to a cigarette before picking a tobacco sliver from his lip. A puff of smoke drifted past a man with a slight build and a salt-and-pepper goatee.

"You think you can fight city hall, do you?" the man said.

Graham scanned the diminutive man. "What do you want, Berkowitz?"

"Just being friendly. Us Jews got to stick together, right?"

"Your kike ass hasn't seen the inside of the synagogue in a decade. So don't give me that Jew crap," Graham said.

"Jeez, no reason to get snippy."

Graham tilted his head and exhaled.

Abraham Berkowitz waited for the right phrasing to come to him before saying, "Those boys from Redevelopment got a heart on for your dance hall."

No response.

"You have to admit, it is prime real estate," Abraham said. "Easy to get on Geary and zip downtown." Another thought came to him and he said, "You haven't seen my boy around, have you?"

Here it comes.

"He left town in a hurry," Berkowitz said. "Probably with that Otis fellow, the one that sells crack for his momma."

Wait for it.

"I hope Jonah isn't in trouble," Berkowitz said. "He's not built for it. Did you know he's thinking about skipping out on his obligation to serve? Why, back in the day that wasn't an option. They'd string you out to dry. Yes, sir."

"Like I said, what do you want?"

"Well, I miss my son terribly. I just want to talk to him. Set him straight on a few things."

Bingo. There it is. Graham paused and studied Berkowitz's expression.

"Yeah, you know. Things like the war in Vietnam, things here at home. Stuff like that."

"By home, you mean your shop, making sure that it remains open? That kind of *stuff*?"

"Ah, sure. That's part of it. Gotta have a means of income. You can appreciate that, being a businessman yourself. You wouldn't want your precious Fillmore Auditorium to close, would you?"

Graham dropped his smoke to the asphalt. He started to leave when Berkowitz reached out and hooked onto his arm.

"You have to help me here," Abraham Berkowitz said. "You think these boys from downtown are tough, you haven't seen anything yet. If Papa Al…,"

"If Papa Al," Graham interrupted, "wants to deal with this, he knows where to find me."

"Jonah was in Andy's Photo Shop last week," Berkowitz said as he paused to let his meaning sink in. "Papa Al isn't stupid."

A full bearded guy wearing wire-rimmed glasses sauntered over to Graham. "What a circus in there, right?" he said while nodding to the government building.

"Clowns are the pegs from which a circus is hung," Bill Graham said with a wry smile.

"Your little speech won't endear you to downtown," Jerry Garcia said.

"It wasn't meant to," Graham said.

"Are we cool for this weekend?" Garcia asked.

"With all the heat from the Redevelopment Agency, we should probably cancel the show."

"The band had a request to play in Rio Nido along the Russian River. Maybe I can get the gig back."

"Go for it," Graham said.

"Isn't that Labor Day weekend?" Berkowitz interjected, making sure he had the date correct.

"Bill," Garcia said, ignoring the old man, "if the boys and me can help, please let us know, okay?"

Neither Graham nor Garcia noticed Berkowitz slip away.

⅄

A black Caddy pulled up in front of the Jenner Inn. A well-groomed Negro wearing aviator glasses exited with a man in blue. With fixed expressions, the pair marched past the post office, entered the grocery store and approached a man behind the register.

The Negro picked a couple of wallet-size photos from the inside pocket of his coat. "Excuse me, kind sir, but have you seen either of these two in your fine establishment recently."

"And who might you be?" the proprietor said.

"I am Allan Theodore McCollum the Third and this is Sergeant Maloney of the S.F.P.D."

"What was your question again?" the proprietor asked.

Impatient, the sergeant said, "He asked if you've seen these punks," and he pointed to the pics.

The proprietor took a hasty glance. "Can't say."

"The white lad in the photo," Papa Al said, "was seen this morning not too far away in Occidental. He has had a business relationship with the Hells Angels in the past and might have sought them out. We were informed that the biker club paid you a visit around the same time our suspects eluded the sergeant and myself."

"Listen," the proprietor said, "People in these parts keep to themselves. Now if you'll excuse me, I have to stock the shelves." He started to leave when Sergeant Maloney blocked his way.

"Perhaps I should rephrase the question," Papa Al said. "Would that help?"

"Don't matter to me," the proprietor said. "Answer's still gonna be the same."

"I can remember sitting on my grandmother's porch as a twelve-year-old when a bee started buzzing around my head," the Negro said.

"Well, what the dickens does some bee have to do with…," the proprietor started to say.

"My granny," the Negro interrupted, "saw the fright on my face and said, "Boy, that little ol' bee is a lot more scared of you than you are of him.' So I asked my grandmother, 'Does the bee know that?'"

"Listen, mister, I ain't got time for fairy tales. If you want something, then I suggest…"

"My grandmother told me how much she appreciated the power of that question. Ever since, a well-crafted query has become part of who I am."

Tired of the drivel, Sergeant Maloney cupped the back of the proprietor's head and slammed it down upon the photos. "For the last time, have you seen either of these punks? Yes or no."

With his face pressed against the snapshots, the proprietor struggled with his words. "They may have been…in the crowd…but I don't recall. Sorry, but there was…a lot of confusion…in here the other day."

"*Confusion*?" Papa Al repeated. "Please tell us more."

The proprietor, after the sergeant released his hold on him, told in great detail the altercation with the Hells Angels, describing the lead biker, saying that the local sheriff escorted the group back toward Santa Rosa and the county line.

"Now was that so difficult?" Papa Al said to the proprietor before turning back around to his comrade. "I believe our business here is completed."

Maloney started to retreat when he looked back over his shoulder and spied the proprietor stepping toward a weapon. Without a word, Maloney went behind the counter and busted the shotgun over his knee.

Chapter 17

Lights flooded the Depression-era shack, which sat on the edge of Fern Falls in Cazadero. Music flowed through open windows, blaring with attitude.

"Sounds like a party's goin' on," Otis said as a smile grew on his face.

Everyone unloaded from the van and followed Sonny past a parade of pickups, which were loaded with furniture, appliances, toilets and all manner of domestic wares. A handcrafted wooden ladder with carved rails demanded Father Paul's consideration. He thought it would be a nice souvenir of his journey, a perfect fit for his loft back home in Quebec.

Sonny slipped under the yellow crime-scene tape. His club patch and no-nonsense expression told all who was present.

A rube with stringy hair approached. "Welcome."

Sonny spied the outback leather coat on the yokel. "Nice wardrobe."

"You might say it's my calling card," the rube said as he opened his coat to reveal a couple of guns.

"Impressive," Sonny said in a deadpan tone.

"The ladies seem to…," the rube began before Sonny interrupted, asking what happened to Roy Cornett. The biker didn't trust the gas attendant's story and decided to double-check the facts.

"Ain't this where we're suppose to do the introductions?" the rube said. "Locals call me Mr. Sizzler, like the Steakhouse? Get you anything you want. Fresh t-bones, rib eye, filet, sirloin, tri-tip—you name it, I'll deliver it to your doorstep."

"Like I said," Sonny said, "where's Roy Cornett?"

"The law's put him away," Mr. Sizzler said. "Only matter of time. The local sheriff's got a lengthy memory. He was pissed that Roy got off for killing Helmuth Seefeldt back in forty-two. The Seefeldt family is still prominent in these hills, living up on Creighton Ridge near the Parmeters, running a sheep ranch. The Seefeldts did a lot for Cazadero back in those days."

"It's 1967, shit-for-brains," Sonny said.

"Oh, okay, sure," Mr. Sizzler said, trying to move forward with his thoughts, "Well, Roy Cornett continued to forge checks in Mr. Seefeldt's name long after the man was put under. Roy soon graduated to cranking out phony bills. Didn't take long before a local merchant turned him in. Never crap where you eat, right?"

"Anyone find the counterfeit money?" Sonny asked.

"The FBI most likely confiscated it when they searched the place last month."

"Why the celebration?" Sonny asked.

Mr. Sizzler went on to explain how Roy Cornett's last wish before the FBI hauled him off was for the few people whom he called "friends" to take his house and everything in it. It was his way of sticking it to the establishment's collective asshole one last time.

"As you can see, we took Roy's meaning literally," Mr. Sizzler said while pointing to a couple of associates who were dismantling the kitchen cabinets. Others started prying up the pine floorboards.

"By the time the FBI returns," Mr. Sizzler added, "ain't gonna be nothin' left 'cept the dirt under our feet." He grinned, glad to be a part of something.

With that Fillmo' swagger of his, Otis slid forward to partake in the celebration, sidling over to a couple of females. Father Paul joined him while Renée clamped onto Jonah's sleeve, pulling him aside.

"Well, Mr. Smarty Pants," she said to Jonah, "where are we suppose to sleep tonight?" She motioned for him to confront Sonny, to ask him about the accommodations.

"You're some kind of pushy broad, aren't you?" Jonah said.

The back hallway started to split apart from the rest of the house with a chorus of creaks and moans. Everyone rushed toward the scene, heads stacked on top of one another within the doorframe like a Chinese fire drill. The rear room tore away from its foundation bit by bit until collapsing in a pile of dust upon a trailer.

Jonah looked at Renée. "There goes your majesty's suite for the night."

Frustrated, she drifted outside to the deck. Moonlight shimmered in granite pools at the base of a waterfall. An owl hooted its presence. Jonah closed the French doors behind him and stepped to her side. He clasped onto the railing, leaned into the night and took a sniff.

"Smell that?" he said.

No response.

"That's the pure, unadulterated scent of peace."

"*Unadulterated*," she repeated. "Big word."

He smiled to the back of her head, admiring her tenacity. "You know, you're probably a good fit for the con game."

She turned quiet, unsure if a compliment or another scathing judgment was about to come her way.

"No, I mean it. You got grit. It's part of what makes you who you are, written into your DNA. Why deny it?" He paused before adding, "Of course, God knows who the hell you really are. Altar boy? Rebellious girl? Perhaps even…"

But before he could finish his thought, she reached up and brought his lips to hers. Jonah tasted the warmth of her mouth. He pulled her close. She wrapped her leg around his. Blinded by lust, they slid along the railing, doing a mating dance. They bumped into the French doors and pressed up against the glass. Without warning, the portals gave way.

Coupled together, they crashed onto the living room floor as one. Otis and Father Paul glanced at each other before returning their puzzlement to the spectacle.

Otis bent over his buddy. "Dude, what're you doin'?"

"It's not what you think," Jonah said before untangling himself from Renée.

"Seriously," Otis repeated, "no matter to me. Just wish you told me 'bout the switch."

"No switch. *You and me, the world on its knees*, remember?" Jonah saw the doubt in his friend's face and added in clumsy fashion, "Bros before hoes, right?"

"Whatever, dude," Otis said.

Renée threw Jonah a look. "*Bros before hoes*?" and she shook her head. "I'm out of here."

"Wait," Jonah said as he tried to catch up.

Otis eyed the exodus and decided to follow when a demanding voice stopped him.

"Where do you think you're going?" Sonny said.

"Ah, nowhere?" Otis guessed, searching for the right answer.

"You and me, we need to talk," Sonny said before leading Otis to a backroom.

⅄

With rage in her eyes, she stepped on the gas, grinding through the gears. Jonah slumped into his seat. The ensuing silence proved difficult and he caved in, blurting out that he didn't mean anything by it, that *bros before hoes* was just an expression.

"How's this for an *expression*?" and she gave him the finger.

He asked where they were going. It was a question he assumed was innocent enough, something to get them back on track.

"*We* are going nowhere," Renée said. "*I*, on the other hand, am going to get a bite to eat." She hoisted her chin in a haughty pose, staring into the darkness ahead.

"There's only one place open at this hour," Jonah said. He had explored this area two years previous, the only other time he had run away from home.

"And where would that be?"

"Oh, I could show you, but as you said there is no longer any *we* in this equation."

"*Stupide.*"

"Turn right here."

The VW bus jounced over potholes as it struggled up Kidd Creek Road. After another mile, they arrived at a two-story structure, parked and exited the vehicle. A needle-strewn path took them through a patchwork of gardens to an entrance where a sign read CAZANOMA LODGE.

A waiter seated the couple at a white linen table next to a window. He placed two menus in front of the customers, explaining that the special was beer-braised bratwurst with cabbage and roulade.

"The roulade," the waiter said, "is wrapped in thinly sliced veal around a filling of bacon, chopped onions, pickles and mustard, then browned and simmered in broth. Absolutely divine."

The waiter caught the male patron gazing out the window toward the pond below. "Or you could fish for your dinner, but I wouldn't suggest it. The mosquitoes are just horrific this time of year."

"Sounds perfect," Jonah said as he rose and latched onto Renée.

A stone mill anchored a wheel, which wound through the water with a lazy roll. Jonah handed Renée some fish food that looked like dog kibble. Trout began to float to the surface, sucking in the treats.

"Sorry," Jonah said out of the side of his mouth while tossing the granules into the pond. He couldn't remember why he should be sorry but knew enough from observing other couples that that particular word was sacred to the survival of the male species.

But Renée's countenance was fixed on the ripples, her look glazed over as if she was deep in thought.

"You can't stay mad at me forever," Jonah said. "It's against the laws of..."

"You men are such disgusting creatures," she interrupted.

Her stubbornness attracted him and he bent forward. She spied his boyish desires and slapped him across the kisser.

"How are you two lovebirds doing?" the waiter interrupted as he approached from behind.

Jonah backed away, blinking away the ache from his jaw while the waiter reached into the pond with a net and brought up a pair of trout.

"Good job," the waiter said in a patronizing manner as he sized up the prospective meal. He untangled one of the fish from the nylon mesh, brought it to a flat stone and hammered its head with a mallet. Splat. Matter squirted in all directions. The second trout was brought forth to the slab, but before the wooden truncheon found its target, the couple skipped down the path.

⅄

Stoners were sprawled across a water-stained mattress when a man dressed in a black T-shirt and a leather vest swung open the door and told the duo to beat it.

They gathered up a bag of weed and a bong and split. Sonny closed the door behind them before slinging Otis to the floor.

"You stole fifty tabs of LSD from me. Not cool," and Sonny lifted Otis up by the collar for a swat when, without warning, a longhair fell through the ceiling. Dust and plasterboard poured out.

The longhair coughed and hand-wiped the chalk from his body as he rose to his feet. "Hi," he said as he extended his hand in invitation, but Sonny shot him a cold stare.

The longhair held up a plaque, saying, "Look what I found in the attic. It's the old benchmark from Pole Mountain. Been missing for decades. It's on Cazadero's most wanted list. Might be worth something," he said as he skipped out with his treasure.

Sonny shook his head, thinking that these hills had acquired more than their fare share of crazies. He went to Otis and punched him in the face. "What I wanna know is, how are you gonna redeem me for the loss of those tabs?"

Then an idea came to Otis. "I got some product in the van."

"The van?"

"It's hidden inside one of the side panels."

Sonny marched to the hallway and called out for the priest.

"*Oui*?" came a reply from the living room.

"Get in here. Now."

The priest went to the backroom and inquired as to the nature of the emergency. "I have a brandy waiting for me, gentlemen."

"This nigger here says you got some product in your van," Sonny said. "That so?"

"Product?" the Father repeated.

"Drugs. LSD," and Sonny threw up his palms, frustrated.

Father Paul noticed the bruise on Otis's face and wheeled around, wagging a finger at the Hells Angel. "How dare you put a hand on this poor boy. Hasn't he and his kind suffered enough at the hands of you white baboons?"

Otis crunched up his face. "*White baboons*? Didn't know there was such a thing?"

"That is beside the point," the Father said before returning to his preaching, but Sonny cut him off and went outside.

He searched the parking area but couldn't locate the hippie van. Enraged, he returned to the cabin to ask the priest where the vehicle was.

"I have no idea," Father Paul answered.

"Your altar boy and his sweetheart probably took off with it," Sonny guessed. He started back in on Otis, giving him another swat or two, when a twenty-dollar bill floated down from the cavity above. The priest snatched onto the Jackson and brought it closer.

"Glory be!" Father Paul exclaimed before folding his hands together in prayer. "Thank you, Jesus."

Sonny stole the Jackson from the priest's grip and held it up to a nearby lamp. The hidden image of Andrew Jackson showed a peculiar smile, not the same starched look as on the outer skin of the bill.

"Yep," Sonny said, "this is Roy's work all right,"

In some bit of weird choreography, the trio peered upward as one. Another bill could be seen clinging to the jagged edge of the plasterboard.

Sonny ordered the priest to hoist Otis to the ceiling. The priest, however, refused the suggestion of manual labor, saying that such activity would be undignified for a man of the cloth. A sharp stare from Sonny, however, put the Father into motion.

The paunchy Frenchman quaked under the weight of Otis who stood on the priest's shoulders. "I didn't realize that a person of such light proportions could possess such girth," Father Paul complained.

With a struggle, Otis pulled himself partway up through the hole, balanced himself on a joist and lit a match. Within the flickering light, he saw a metal object protruding from a nearby wall.

"There's a ventilation fan up here," Otis called out before finishing his inspection and lowering himself to the floor.

"Most likely just an airway to the outside," the priest guessed.

"Nah," Otis said as he brushed dust off his cloak. "Don't think so."

"What do you mean?" Sonny asked.

"There was light coming from the other side of the fan," Otis said.

"Oh, how I love puzzles," Father Paul said.

On a hunch, the priest opened a closet door and pulled on a chain to a hanging bulb. Smudges, impeded into the hardwood floor, drew his attention. They were each two inches wide and two feet apart. A pair of brackets appeared above and in direct line with the markings underfoot.

The discovery sparked an idea, which in turn vaulted an earlier remembrance. "Please, come with me," Father Paul said to the others.

They made their way to the parking area. A pickup sat nearby, weighed down with furniture, appliances and domestic wares.

The priest patted a handcrafted ladder with carved rails. "I believe I have resolved our dilemma, gentlemen."

⅄

The priest placed the footholds of the ladder upon the markings on the closet floor. A perfect fit. With a knowing smile, he leaned its top end into the pair of brackets above.

"*Voila*," the priest said as he waved his hand like a magician.

Sonny growled an order to Otis and pointed to the ladder.

"The brother's tired," Otis said in the third person.

"The *brother*," Sonny said, "will do exactly as I say or else the *brother* will find his black ass lost in the woods…forever."

Otis perused the task before him. "The ladder leads to nowhere," and he gestured to the ceiling.

Sonny took a closer look. It appeared as if a section had been recently painted. He went to the living room, dismantled a chair leg and returned.

"Here, use this," Sonny said as he handed the instrument to Otis.

Otis mumbled out a few curse words and started to climb. When he reached the ceiling, he rammed the wooden peg upward into the ceiling. Bits of sheetrock fell like snowflakes. Otis clawed into a section and tore it loose.

A few Jacksons sprinkled downward. With the removal of the plasterboard, four duffle bags appeared under the soft glow of a nightlight. Otis handed a few of the carryalls before reaching for the fourth, which was wedged between beams. With a yank, the duffle bag sprung forward. Man, ladder and money crashed to the feet of Sonny Barger.

The racket summoned the revelers from the living room. Mr. Sizzler gasped at the sight of so much moolah in one place, guessing that it was from Roy Cornett's counterfeit operation.

"If this is what I think it is," Mr. Sizzler said as he picked up a bill, "you could probably fetch a good price for it around these parts. You know, as kind of a souvenir of Roy Cornett's newfound celebrity status."

"I got a buyer waiting for me," Sonny said. He had arranged a meeting with a fence in Rio Nido but wasn't about to release the details of the arrangement to this yahoo.

"Give you a sawbuck for one of 'em," Mr. Sizzler persisted. "The boys might want some of this action as well," he said while gesturing to the throng within the doorframe.

"Don't think so," Sonny said.

"How's about a trade?" Mr. Sizzler asked as he displayed a Colt .45 pistol and a sawed-off shotgun from under his outback coat.

"How's about we say there is no trade," Sonny said, "and I take those peashooters off your hands?"

Mr. Sizzler saw the threat in the biker's eyes and went for a weapon, but Sonny kneed him in the crotch before the pistol could be drawn. The rube buckled over in pain. With hands clasped together, the biker hammered the back of the rube's head, sending him to the floor.

Otis retrieved the .45 and raised it in the direction of Sonny. His hands quivered as he hesitated. With knowledge of the force behind this outlaw, he thought better of it and shifted the barrel to the collection of locals, saying, "Get the mofo outta here…now."

The crowd dispersed leaving their confederate behind. Father Paul went and locked the bedroom door. Sonny relieved Mr. Sizzler of his second weapon before nudging him with the toe of his boot. No response.

"Is he dead?" Father Paul asked.

"He'll live," Sonny said. "Just a bad headache is all."

"Now what?" Otis asked.

"Now we leave," Sonny said.

Otis scanned the room. There were no windows. The lone exit was via the hallway where the others would be waiting.

The trio got Mr. Sizzler in the upright position and used his dead weight as a battering ram. All sped toward the single wall construction as one and crashed through the knotty pine paneling and into the night.

Chapter 18

A batch of locals rushed through the screen door and into the parking area. Cusses followed Sonny who kick-started his Harley. Father Paul and Otis fled on foot down the road with duffle bags in tow. The mob yelled, promising damnation. Sonny brought out a shotgun and fired a warning shot. The locals came to a halt, studied the situation and raced on, waving knives and bats.

Otis and Father Paul, with the Angel protecting their backsides, came to Cazadero Highway. A hippie van approached, made a U-turn and pulled alongside.

"Get in the back, my son," Father Paul said as he pushed Jonah out of the driver's seat.

Otis jumped in as well and tossed four duffle bags into the face of Jonah. "What the hell?"

The angry pack flooded the main road. Beer cans, rocks and bottles hit the rear of the van as it pulled away. Agitated figures faded in the rearview before being swallowed whole by the darkness.

"What was that all about?" the altar boy asked the priest as they headed south.

"Nothing," Father Paul said. "Everything is just splendid." He looked into the eyes of the altar boy and added with a grin, "This is so intoxicating. I just adore a good road trip, don't you?"

"Something's not right." The altar boy pivoted to the backseat and asked what was in the bags.

"Merchandise," Otis said.

Jonah unzipped one of the carryalls and stole a peek. A Colt .45 pistol rested atop banded rolls of twenty-dollar bills.

"What's this?" Jonah said with a surprised expression.

"The gun is a gift from that Mr. Sizzler fella," Otis said. "The money is counterfeit, handcrafted by Roy Something-or-other. Guess he's a local hero. Rednecks wanted to offer real cash for some of the bills—you know, as keepsakes."

Jonah rifled through the cash, peered sideways at the other bags and asked, "Are they all loaded with…"

"Oh, yeah," Otis interrupted in anticipation of the question. "More cash than you've seen in your shitty life, I'm guessin'."

"But it's nothing but play money," Jonah argued as he fingered a Jackson.

"There you go again," Otis said. "Why the white brother always got to see the negative side of things?"

They motored down Cazadero Highway, cruising past the Berkeley Music Camp and Elim Grove. Anxious, Otis peered through the back window and spotted several vehicles in the distance.

"We got company," Otis said to all.

Jonah swung around. At least three different sets of headlights came and went as they sped through the bends.

With demands for an explanation from both the altar boy and Jonah, Otis told what happened to Mr. Sizzler. "His friends might be upset."

"*Stupides*," the altar boy said in French to everyone including Father Paul.

Father Paul pressed down on the gas pedal. "Relax and enjoy the ride, my dear." A smile grew on his face.

Otis had heard the priest refer to the altar boy before using those same words of endearment, but with the disquiet that pumped through his veins he wasn't able to give it any deliberation.

The altar boy looked into the side-view mirror. "They're gaining."

The night drew dark as clouds passed before the quarter moon. Fog wound its way through the valley floor. Objects became difficult to see. Father Paul leaned forward to better detect the movements of Sonny out in front when, without warning, the headlight of the Harley went black. The bike veered from the main road and crossed a two-lane bridge. Father Paul understood his intent and switched off the van's high beams as well. Once across Austin Creek, all rolled to the backside of a weathered barn.

Three pickups soon arrived, streaming along Cazadero Highway on the other side of the bridge. With their pursuers out of sight, Sonny and the others eased from the shadows and double-backed in a northerly direction.

The asphalt soon gave way to dirt. Father Paul downshifted, the van grinding through the gears as they bounced through the ruts in the pitch-tar blackness.

"Mofo! Bumpy as a whore in heat," Otis said. Another thought came to him and he whispered to Jonah that he was okay with what happened back at the cabin in Cazadero.

Jonah threw him a befuddled look.

"Between you and the altar boy is what I'm tryin' to say," Otis said to clarify. "Everyone finds pleasure in different ways. Know what I mean?"

Jonah laughed a silent laugh.

"Would've been nice to give the brother a heads up is all I'm sayin'."

Renée overheard enough to guess what the boys were talking about and turned around. She flipped up her top and exposed her breasts.

"Satisfied?" Renée said to Otis.

"Damn. Those real?" and Otis reached out as if to corroborate the evidence before him, but Renée slapped his hand away.

"You fooled the brother, that for sure."

A honk from the VW alerted the biker. Sonny made a U-turn and went back to the bus, which had stopped in the middle of the choppy road.

"What's the problem?" Sonny said to Father Paul.

"*Zut*!" Father Paul said in a frustrated tone. "Pardon my French, but I can't see a blessed thing in this fog. I am most certain that if we continue on this course, we will entertain calamity at a moment's notice."

Sonny couldn't argue the point, stating that they would make camp at a clearing up ahead. A few minutes later, they came to an opening in the redwoods where everyone began to unload.

Jonah tapped Sonny on the shoulder. "Got a second?"

They went to a quiet corner to sit on a fallen log. "What about Otis?" Jonah asked.

"Don't push it, kid."

"You're going to take him to your friend's place in Ukiah, aren't you?"

"What do you know 'bout that?" Sonny said with a tight look.

"Your operation back in the Haight holds quite a collection of loose tongues." Jonah paused, trying to recall a name. "George Wethern. Yeah, that's the guy. He's vice president of the Oakland chapter, right?"

Sonny knew where this was going and told the kid to shut up, but Jonah ignored the demand. "Sounds like this Wethern fellow is running a full time *underground operation*," he said, lingering onto the last words for emphasis.

Sonny understood Jonah's reference to the Angel's 156-acre ranch near Ukiah. Since the club had chipped in for half the cost of the property, Wethern was required to let the Hells Angels use it as an unofficial cemetery. It had become a handy dumping ground for undesirables and traitors to the brotherhood.

"You best cut your ties with your nigger friend," Sonny said.

"And if I don't?"

"That would be a shame, a real shame, but the choice is yours, kid."

⅄

The bonfire crackled as sparks floated on the night breeze. A chill settled over everyone while the fogbank continued to rise from the valley below. No one spoke as they huddled together in a circle around the flames. The quiet strangled the conversation.

"Someone tell a joke," Father Paul said.

But the uneasiness continued as each person harbored his own reasons for remaining somber. Complications were mounting while exits were dwindling.

"My ass is freezing," Sonny said, breaking the silence. "Altar boy, get some more firewood.

"The hell I will," Renée said.

"My dear," Father Paul said, "do as the man requests, *s'il vous plaĭt.*"

With a protest, Renée disappeared into the forest.

"My dear?" Otis repeated, scratching his head. "I'm still confused."

Since Jonah had come into possession of the entire truth, Father Paul saw no reason to hold back from Otis and explained that Renée was in fact his daughter, that his claim to be a priest may have been a bit of an exaggeration.

"No shit," Otis said.

"We are on a farewell tour, as it were," the priest said. "One last hoorah in honor of the old con game, but please do not cease from addressing me as Father Paul. I have grown quite fond of the title."

"Stop running your mouths," Sonny said to the group.

"Sir," Father Paul said, "I can see that you are in the deepest of thoughts, but if I may I would like to ask why in the name of Jesus are we on this mountain?"

"Have to stay off the main road," Sonny said.

"It ain't just 'cause of those crackers from Cazadero, right? Gotta account for the law as well," Otis said, showing off his street smarts. "And let's be real—you still need us. No way that Harley of yours can handle that shit-load of money all by itself."

⅄

Jonah sat by the campfire, gazing at the earthen floor with his thoughts. He longed for the days when life was breezy, when Sara and music drowned out the realities of his existence. Remembrances started to flood his mindscape.

The ladies in the brothel treated him as if he was family, coaxing him inside with the promise of hot chocolate or a soda or a vinyl forty-five. Jonah loved music more than anything or anyone. At eight years of age, he could list the top ten tunes of the month, detailing a complete biography of each singer.

The girls enjoyed the spirit that the kid brought to their doorstep. Most of them never had a child of their own, at least not one that they kept around for very long. Nineteen years the kid's senior, Sara coddled him with extra attention as might an older sister. She would have his favorite single on hand when he dropped by. Whether it was Percy Faith's "Theme From a Summer Place" or the Everly Brother's "Cathy's Clown," she knew which tune would bring a smile to his face. If that weren't enough, she'd purchase a store-bought sweater or a pair of pants for him, saying that the gifts were their little secret.

The two of them would sit in the drawing room of the brothel, singing off-key for the waiting customers. Smiles were easy…until they weren't. Jonah recalled the day over a year ago when Sara overdosed on a batch of bad heroin. She was interned at San Francisco General Hospital with a severe case of vomiting. Internal bleeding further depleted her protein levels, leaving her withering in silent consumption.

Everyone in the Fillmore knew who was pushing the tainted dope, but Papa Al proved untouchable. His connections with downtown were undeniable.

⅄

Renée dumped a load of wood and started to bark something at Jonah, but it went unnoticed.

"Hey," she repeated, "a little help would've been nice."

The others looked up from the campfire wondering if another tiff was in the making.

"Sorry," Jonah said as he came around.

"Is this how you treat all your lady friends, leave them in the wind to fend for themselves?" Renée said.

"Probably," Jonah said, the image of the sickly Sara still on his mind.

Renée noticed his downcast expression. "All right, what is it?"

"Don't know."

"Want to talk?"

"Someday," Jonah said before retreating into his thoughts.

Otis used the ensuing quiet to approach Sonny who was working on his Harley. "See you got the tabs out of the van."

"Phillips," Sonny said as he held out his hand without looking up.

Otis blinked before understanding his meaning and went to a toolbox. "Borrowed the acid from Piano Player at Morningstar Ranch," and he handed the screwdriver to Sonny. "I slipped in an extra fifty," Otis added. "Figured that ought to cover any interest involved."

"Wrench," Sonny said after he dropped the Phillips to the ground.

"We good?" Otis asked while passing over the instrument.

A disturbance from the darkness caused Sonny to lurch to his feet. He told Otis to shut up as voices and the snapping of twigs sounded an alarm through the forest. Crickets and bullfrogs ceased their singing.

Two figures approached with flashlights. They called out as they drew closer to the campfire. Without warning, a creepy-looking guy wearing a biker's outfit rose from the brush. The interlopers screamed and tried to run, but Sonny cuffed them by the collar.

"What're you two half-pints doing up here in the middle of the night?" Sonny asked as he hovered over the shaking frames.

The boys were about twelve years of age with bad haircuts and rags for clothes. "We're on a hunt," the towhead one confessed.

"What kind of hunt?" Sonny asked.

"Snipe hunt," the second boy said as he adjusted his eyepatch.

"What's a snipe?" Otis asked.

The towhead one turned away from the creepy guy to answer the Negro's question. "Uncle Leo didn't say other than it's some sort of critter," the towhead one said.

"How you hunt for somethin' without knowin' what it is?"

"Uncle Leo said that we would know when the time came. If we kept banging rocks together, the snipes would show themselves."

The boy with the eyepatch started to loosen up, saying that you had to get the cadence just right with the rocks. "It ain't easy."

"What're the hats for?" Otis asked pointing to the headgear, which were shaped like upside-down funnels and made of aluminum foil.

"They signal to the spirits of Devil's Backbone that we come in peace," Eyepatch said.

"Devil's Backbone?"

"That's where you're at," Towhead added. "Devil's Backbone Ridge."

"I don't care for the sound of that," Otis said.

"No reason you should."

Jonah felt relieved for the time being, knowing that Sonny wouldn't try anything foolish while so many witnesses were present. While ignoring Sonny's scowl, Jonah invited the boys to warm themselves by the fire.

Towhead and Eyepatch sat Indian-style around the blaze. They answered Otis's questions regarding snipe hunts and added a few details of their own. Everyone pretended to be interested, especially with regard to the part where spirits accompanied snipe hunters as protectors.

"Guess they don't care much for snipes either," Eyepatch said. "It gives us comfort knowing that we have such powerful escorts through these hills."

Towhead nodded in agreement. "No shortage of ghosts in this part of the country, that's for certain."

"Ain't no such thing," Otis said.

"They show themselves during the summertime," Towhead persisted. "I wouldn't be surprised if we saw one or two tonight."

"You're just makin' this up."

The boys expounded, telling how the Berkeley Music Camp was once known as "Truth Home". A woman by the name of Ollie had a divine vision that she was the chosen one and led her followers to this place of safety. Ollie kept her flock isolated, reinforcing a doomsday prophecy with negative news feeds.

"She just wanted those folks for her own selfish reasons," Towhead said, "to build her private haven."

"Bad luck and tough times came in bunches," Eyepatch added. "A few died of dysentery, others from food poisoning. One even croaked while milking a cow. That was enough for the rest and they hightailed it out of there. Some say that the dead have returned to seek revenge on the old woman."

"Where you from?" Jonah asked, keeping the conversation going.

"From just over the ridge," Towhead said, "from Lions Head Ranch."

"They got ghosts there too?" Otis asked with a serious expression.

"Oh, yeah," Eyepatch said with a bragging voice as he started telling the story of the previous owner. "Margaret Starbuck told a Jap woodcutter to give a little hell to some troublemakers who were behind on their rent. Well, he did more than scare 'em. He hacked them up and scattered their remains around the ranch."

"So the dead have returned?" Otis guessed. "To get satisfaction just like those ghosts from the music camp did?"

A nod.

"That's exactly what the brother would do. No way I'd let any lowlife, murdering coward get away with killing me."

Sonny returned to the campfire and ordered the boys home.

"Can't return without any snipes," Eyepatch said.

With the toe of his boot, Sonny kicked the boy across his backside.

Jonah asked the youngsters to hang around for a while longer, but they decided that perhaps this biker fellow had enough meanness in him to frighten away even the bravest of their spiritual guardians and they left.

Sonny set up his bedroll near the fire while the other four retired to the van. Murmurs filled the space as each in turn fell into a fitful sleep. Strange noises sounded from the forest. Fog crept up the ridge like an invading poltergeist while murderers, hatchet men and revengeful ghosts occupied dreams.

Otis heaved up sweating. The night wouldn't end. Disoriented from his battle with demons and other ethereal beings, he stumbled barefoot out of the van to gulp in the night air.

His heart began to return to a normal beat. An urge surfaced and he plodded toward the woods. On the perimeter of the encampment, he caught the sleeve of his ruffled shirt on a twig.

He gazed at the mishap, fingering the tear in disbelief. "Mofo!"

Without another word, he walked a few more feet down a little used trail and unzipped his pants when a growl emerged from the far side of the campground. He held back his needs and ventured away. Secure in the thought that he had put sufficient distance between himself and the creature, he streamed urine onto the trunk of a redwood. In the middle of his relief, the menacing sound rose again. Images of his earlier nightmares reemerged and he sprinted deeper into the forest.

With hands on knees, he took in loads of oxygen before bending an ear toward the path of his retreat. The music of crickets calmed him. He went to secure his fly when he noticed his soiled pants. Expletives filled the night air.

How far south could things go? He didn't have to wait long for an answer when he felt the sting of a hundred needles. An army of red ants covered his bare feet. He hopped on one leg swatting away the insects. The ground started to give way around him. An earthen slide took him partway down an embankment before he clutched onto an exposed tree root. The sound of rocks clanging together came from below. With each rhythmic thump, his fingers slipped further along his lifeline until he lost his grip altogether.

Chapter 19

Worries tugged at Jonah's psyche. He rolled over and bumped into Renée. A moan sent him in the opposite direction where he nudged up against the snoring cleric. Claustrophobic, Jonah made his way out of the van.

A growl beyond the tree line sent a warning not to stray from the campgrounds. He was stretching out his kinks when Sonny came into his line of vision. The biker appeared in the thralls of a deep sleep.

The image set Jonah to thinking of the evils this man was the master of. Even though Otis had repaid his debt of the stolen acid tabs, it might not be enough.

No reason to wait until George Wethern's ranch in Ukiah, Jonah thought. Sonny could do the dirty deed right here before they reached civilization, the last thing any decent outlaw desired. By the time the authorities discovered Otis's body, little of him would have survived the wilderness. With these fears nagging at him, Jonah retrieved a shovel from the vehicle.

The Hells Angel came and went within the flickers of the campfire. On the balls of his feet, Jonah approached. Each step drew him closer to an outcome of great magnitude. His resolve began to waver. It wasn't just anybody inside that bedroll—it was Sonny friggin' Barger—badest of the bad, champion of the bottom one-percenters in life and proud of it.

Unnerved, Jonah lost focus and stepped on a pile of leaves. The biker shifted under the sound of the rustling. Jonah balked. The shovel froze within his grasp until a series of snorts told Jonah that it was safe to continue.

With the tool raised above his head, Jonah braced himself for the thrust. The shovel began its descent when a familiar voice came from behind.

"S*tupide*," the person whispered in French.

Jonah pulled the weapon back. "What the hell?"

"Are you insane?" Renée responded. "You kill him, you kill all of us."

A head rose from the bedroll. "Who's there?"

Renée grabbed the shovel, tossed it into the brush and embraced Jonah with a full-throttle kiss.

Sonny wiped the moistness from his eyes before getting a clear view of the intruders. "Hey, take it someplace else."

Renée kept a lock on Jonah's lips and waved off the biker with a theatrical gesture as if to tell him to mind his own business. With enough sideshows for one evening, Sonny returned to his sleep.

The two slinked back to the van, Renée asking where Otis was.

"What? You're going to leave it like that?" Jonah said. "You can't get things started and expect me to turn it off without so much as a peck on the cheek. Guys don't work that way."

"No, I'm serious. Where's Otis?"

Jonah packed away his longings and submitted to her agenda. With no answer to her question, they searched the campground before finding a swatch of clothing dangling from a branch.

Jonah stripped the fabric from its lodging and showed it to Renée. She studied the piece of ruffled shirt before gazing back at him with a worried look.

"You think he's in trouble?" Jonah asked.

"Why would he venture into the woods in the middle of the night? Doesn't make sense."

"Maybe he just needed a moment to relieve himself. It's been known to happen," and he threw her a glare as if to suggest that they hang it up for the evening.

"Something's not right."

Not wanting to awake the biker, they exchanged opinions in quiet before heading down a trail. They walked for some distance within the fog until they came to an anthill. Human footprints danced every which way. Jonah knelt to one knee to exam the mystery when he spied the markings of a fresh slide. He glanced over the edge of an embankment and saw human activity below.

Jonah and Renée made their way along the bluff before discovering a switchback. While holding onto each other, they reached the bottom and followed the quivering flashes of light.

Two boys, one with blond hair and the other wearing an eyepatch, danced around a fire with a Negro, each clanging rocks to a hypnotic beat while wearing aluminum hats.

"Having fun?" Jonah said as he approached.

"Hey, dude," Otis said without breaking stride.

"Why are you out here?" Jonah asked.

"Went to take a leak and had a spill," Otis said. "Figured this might be the safest place to hang out for the rest of the night." Otis stopped his twirling when he noticed the befuddlement aboard his friend's face. "These boys"—and he gestured to Towhead and Eyepatch—"own the allegiance of the ghosts on Devil's Backbone. Shit ain't gonna fall on them. Thought I'd want to be a part of that, at least until the sun comes up."

"*Stupide*," Renée said and turned her back on the group.

"Let's get you back to camp," Jonah said to Otis.

"But we ain't caught a single snipe," Otis complained. "Captured a bunch of other critters, though," and he showed the contents of two burlap bags with a boastful grin. Squirrels, skunks, raccoons and fowl of various species rested in different stages of atrophy.

Renée pondered the absurdity of it all and threw out a line in French and then another, gesticulating with swipes of her hands. Jonah ignored her rant while convincing Otis that it was time to leave.

"You'll never find your way back," Eyepatch interjected. "Not in this soup," the youngster said while nodding to the thickening fog.

⅄

On their return trip to camp, a zephyr kicked up, pushing thunderheads along the mountain. The quarter moon vanished. Noises could be heard from the thicket as animals scurried about, agitated by the unknown.

Eyepatch pressed a moist finger to the breeze. "Storm's coming."

Jonah and Renée plodded forward trusting the instincts of their twelve-year-old guides. A hush descended until a clap of thunder sounded from the distance.

They came to the perimeter of the camp. Jonah held out his arm. Everyone ducked behind a ring of redwoods. Three pickups trained their beams upon two men who were tied together near the fire pit. The area appeared in a pool of light as if it was noon on a summer day.

A rube with stringy hair and wearing an outback leather coat stepped to one of the bound men and hit him across the face. "That's for back at the cabin, bitch."

"You punch like my grandmother," Sonny retorted.

Another slap and then another, each carrying more weight than the previous one. "Tough guy, huh?" The rube downed a beer, crushed the can and tossed it to the ground. "We're fixin' to have ourselves an old fashioned hoedown and you're gonna be the centerpiece. Might even let the good Father here give you a final blessing. How's that sound, bitch?" Mr. Sizzler said before popping open another beer.

Eyepatch turned to Jonah, whispering that the rube in the lead was the same guy who had been stealing their cattle. "Calls himself Mr. Sizzler. Likes to throw it in your face. White trash is all he is."

"Want to have a little fun with these yokels?" Jonah asked the boys.

"Gotta have something to show for the night, right?" Eyepatch said.

Jonah smiled before ordering Otis to hand over a couple of LSD tabs.

"Gave 'em all to Sonny," Otis said. "You know that."

Jonah didn't respond other than to gesture with his hand. Otis surrendered a dozen tabs, mumbling something about the fact that they knew each other too well.

"What else do you have?" Jonah asked.

Otis offered up a half-pint of whiskey and several condoms. He shrugged and said, "Took 'em from Dr. Smith's clinic back in the City. Thought I might get lucky."

Jonah asked Towhead and Eyepatch if they wouldn't mind donating their hats. They obliged, Eyepatch saying that it wasn't safe to wear them with the approaching storm anyway.

"We'd light up like Christmas trees," Towhead said before adding that there were three extra rolls of aluminum foil in their backpack. Jonah sifted through the carryall for other items that might be of use and collected fishing line before spotting a rifle.

"It's an air gun," Eyepatch explained. "Shoots pellets."

"Strong enough to kill squirrels and such," Towhead added.

"Are you good with this thing?" Jonah asked Eyepatch.

"Can shoot the whiskers off a rat at fifty paces."

⅄

Cases of Brown Derby sat in the bed of a pickup. Renée and Jonah slinked behind the beams of light, staying in the shadows. She climbed the tailgate and laced the lids of several beer cans with LSD while he connected the batteries of the three vehicles with handmade ropes of aluminum foil. Towhead climbed a redwood with the fishing line while Otis and Eyepatch filled the condoms with whiskey.

The rubes hollered and whooped as the party ramped up. The beers flowed freely. By the time they got to their third round, colors began to expand in everlasting beauty. The flames from the fire pit intertwined with the purple of a passing T-shirt, whizzing across the campground. Bolts of lightening hung in the night sky, refusing to let go.

With hands and ankles tied, Sonny and Father Paul looked at each other with quizzical gazes wondering what these yahoos were on and what dangers waited. Mr. Sizzler continued tormenting the Angel, burning his arm with a hot iron.

"You belong to me now, bitch," Mr. Sizzler said. "You got my brand on you for life," and then he admired his handiwork. "Looks good on you. I could smooth out the *S* a touch, I guess," and he went back to work.

Sonny winced. He breathed in spurts, heavy and long before examining the initials on the branding iron. "*MS*—that stand for Momma's Sissyboy?"

Another slap. Another beer.

Without warning, a squirrel flew across the area. Mr. Sizzler caught it out of the side of his eye, not sure what he was seeing. Next, a skunk danced on the air as if on a puppeteer's strings.

"Anyone see that?" Mr. Sizzler shouted to his cronies.

A raccoon soared above. The rubes stood silent, staggering in place. Eyes skimmed the redwoods. Nothing. Reassured that their minds were playing tricks on them, they went back to partying when a dead bird landed at the feet of Mr. Sizzler. Another critter hit him in the chest, accompanied by a stinging sensation. He put a hand over his wound and barked in an agitated voice, demanding to know who was out there.

No response except for the attack of different animal corpses, each strike followed by a silent shot to the body.

The rubes cowered in a cluster, scanning the shadows. Flames erupted from the campfire sending them in different directions.

"Whaddya want?" Mr. Sizzler shouted in the direction of the woods.

Otis lobbed another whiskey-filled condom onto the blaze while Eyepatch filled the rubes with pellets. Mr. Sizzler and his band of rogues began to flee to their pickups when a bolt of lightening traveled down an aluminum rope. Sparks radiated from one vehicle to the next. Beams flickered while car horns blared in uneven rhythm. Ethereal figures rose from the fog and chased after the rubes as they sped down the dirt road and out of sight.

⅄

The morning sun pushed its way through the mist. A crow cawed for a handout while a possum scurried into the forest. Jonah shook off the cold and started to gather some kindling.

Sonny batted the bundle to the ground. "We're leaving," he said as he kicked dirt onto the embers.

Otis yawned while exiting the van, stretching. "That was some night."

"Get the others up," Sonny ordered.

Otis spied the *MS* on the biker's arm. "That had to hurt."

No response as Sonny went to gather his bedroll and things.

"Guess you're glad we came to the rescue," Otis persisted.

No response.

"Maybe the scales have tipped," Otis said. "Maybe now you owe me."

Sonny ceased his packing and glared sideways at the black man.

With the idea that perhaps he had ventured too far, Otis returned to the encounter with the rubes. "Those boys pro'bly never seen these hills alive like that before. Pro'bly thought Devil's Backbone was livin' up to its name."

Jonah gave his friend the high sign to shut up, but Otis did what he does best and rambled on. "Gotta admit those condom fireballs added a nice touch. And those flying squirrels and skunks—classic. But my favorite was those spooks that swelled up from the fog and got after those rednecks… How'd you do that?" he asked Jonah.

"Do what?"

"The spooks," Otis said. "How'd you make them look so bona fide?"

"Never saw them," Jonah said in a matter of fact tone.

"Kiddin', right?" Otis said. When Jonah confirmed his reply with a shrug, Otis went to Sonny with the same question.

"Back off," Sonny said as he pushed him away with a tap to the chest.

Dumbfounded, Otis went to the van and woke up Father Paul and Renée, but they returned the same answer that Jonah had given earlier—no one else had witnessed the specters.

Everyone peeled off from Otis. He stood there with his thoughts. Images rushed back to him of Towhead and Eyepatch's stories of the revengeful ghosts of the Berkeley Music Camp and Lion's Head Ranch.

"The brother be damned."

⅄

Father Paul turned the ignition key. Nothing. Another try. The engine whined but wouldn't start. Complaints came from the four corners of the bus.

Renée sat in the passenger seat, shivering, promising eternal doom if the heater didn't come on. Otis stamped his feet, patted his knees with his palms, demanding that they leave the mountain.

"Is there any gas?" Jonah asked.

"I can't be sure," Father Paul said. "There seems to be no *juage d'essence*, no petrol indicator."

"We got no time for this," Sonny said as he approached. With a load of counterfeit money in the van and a paper bag of LSD tabs in a saddlebag of his Harley, the biker was wary of any further delays.

"I don't believe the VW bus came with a fuel gauge in sixty-three," Jonah explained.

"Well," Sonny said, "we sure as shit can't carry that money down the hill."

"That's what the brother's been tryin' to tell you," Otis said in the third person, but Sonny threw him that cold stare of his.

Jonah exited with Otis and Renée. The trio shook the van while Father Paul remained behind the wheel. The faint sound of fluid swishing inside the tank could be heard.

"I think there's a reserve," Jonah said as he started for the driver's side. He reached in and turned a handle under the seat. "Try it now," he said to Father Paul.

The vehicle backfired. The motor growled before settling into a purr while everyone hurried back aboard.

The caravan veered onto Old Cazadero Road. An hour later, they started to descend Devil's Backbone when the bus sputtered and coughed.

"I don't know if the good Lord will deliver us to our final destination," Father Paul said.

He put the van into neutral. They cruised down the hill, picking up speed, braking thru the turns. Sonny sped ahead. Renée barked at the Father to slow down. Otis bounced from one end of the backseat to the other.

The van caught up, crowding the Harley. Jonah started to will the vehicle on. A convenient accident might just do the trick, he thought. Then he remembered Renée's admonishment from last night and joined in the plea for Father Paul to use the brakes.

All arrived safely to the bottomland, which meandered alongside a creek. Calm returned as civilization began to show itself. Cabins became cottages. Cottages grew into homes. The bus chugged along, jerking between intakes of fuel and air, until with a final wheeze, it wrenched to a stop.

All disembarked and pushed the van another mile onto Highway 116. The town of Guerneville soon came into view where they rolled the vehicle into a Union 76 station.

Sonny parked his Harley out of sight. He scanned the nearby streets while an attendant arrived to service the van. The worker, wearing his blue overalls with the company logo stitched to his breast pocket, hand-washed the front windows before opening the hood in the rear and checking the oil.

⅄

They avoided Main Street and found their way to Armstrong Woods Road. Two miles north out of town, they hung a right onto Old Rio Nido Road. Lanes cut through the forest to create canyons of redwoods. Rows of dilapidated cabins sat with cockeyed windows. A patchwork of tarps covered rooftops while vehicles in different stages of disrepair scarred the landscape.

The hamlet at one time was a thriving getaway for Bay Area families, but it had lost its luster during recent years. Things were iffy at best, just the way a lot of its current inhabitants liked it.

The village center was buzzing with activity. Barefooted women in halter-tops and rainbow skirts scooted from one attraction to the next while the scent of Mary Jane rode the breeze. Sonny and the others swerved onto Willow Road and away from the action.

An isolated path caught the biker's interest. The lane wound its way up a twisty grade. The quiet swelled. Structures stood lonely and dreary. Moss and vines fought for space, clinging to the sides of weathered clapboards.

This is more like it, Sonny thought. He eased past Alta Canyon Four and came to a sharp bend in the road where a structure hung to the hillside. The place appeared abandoned. A widow-maker rested against its side. Redwood needles carpeted the roof and porch.

With the side of his boot, Sonny brought the kickstand forward. He dismounted and stepped to the bus.

"We'll stay here for a few nights," Sonny said to the others.

"But I got to report to the Marines next week," Otis complained.

"Out!" Sonny yelled.

After clearing a path, all arrived at a side door where Sonny took a nearby rock and broke off the padlock. Sun-kissed news articles with dog-eared edges decorated a refrigerator. Dates and headlines indicated that the items had been there for several years. Bold print read "Kennedy Assassinated"; another read "Dr. Martin Luther King Speaks at Lincoln Memorial"; and still another read "Dick Crest Retires".

"Who's Dick Crest?" Otis asked.

"He hosted the TV dance show, *Rock 'n' Rally*, in San Francisco," Jonah said. "On KPIX?"

"Don't watch that shit," Otis said. "White folks dance like they got a stick up their butt."

"Shut your black ass," Sonny said.

"Black ass is shut, yes, sir," Otis said. "Anything you say, Sonny."

Sonny didn't know if he could wait until George Wethern's place to bury this son of a bitch. Without an answer, the biker returned to the inspection of the shack.

The kitchen cupboards rested ajar, the insides bare. Cobwebs reached from one corner of the ceiling to the next.

Renée went to turn on the faucet. "No water," she said before stepping to a light switch. "Nothing here either." Next, she went to the refrigerator and opened it. "Found a hunting rifle and a box of cartridges."

"Can't eat that," Otis said, disappointed.

"Wouldn't bet against it," Sonny said.

They entered the living room where a woodstove's flue was bent to the floor. A nearby stack of wood rotted away while pyramids of sawdust harbored the unhinged wings of insects.

The place had been stripped of furniture—no chairs, tables or couches, not even a bed. Gloom was everywhere. Sonny added to the melancholy by drawing the shades closed. Jonah tried to console Renée, but she shook away his effort as if the state of things was his fault and his fault alone.

Women, Jonah thought, one minute they're showering you with hugs and kisses, the next they're chewing you up and spitting you out. An image came to him from TV's *Wild Kingdom* where a female praying mantis devoured its counterpart after mating. Jonah closed his eyes, trying to chase the snapshot from his head.

⅄

Jonah persuaded Renée to join him for a walk. She wasn't sure which was more depressing—their temporary quarters or their relationship, but she had to get out of there.

The distance between them mushroomed. Jonah knew what was on her mind. *Why can't she just let it go? One slipup and you're screwed.* Maybe he had it right the first time—bros before hoes. Who knows? He certainly didn't.

The stillness strangled the air between them.

"Where are you going next?" Jonah asked, trying to restart things.

No response.

"Still heading back home?" Jonah asked.

No response.

This is too much work, he thought. Maybe I should bite the bullet. Or, I could just let some gook do it for me.

They reached the bottom of Canyon Four where it leveled out onto Willow Rd. While walking up the redwood lane, they noticed longhairs sitting on stoops, passing around a doobie. Vans, clunkers and converted school buses clogged driveways. Women danced with each other to the sound of music blaring from a stereo.

"Yes," Renée said after another half block.

"Sorry?" Jonah asked having forgotten his original question.

"Yes, my father and I will be returning to Quebec after the weekend," Renée said

Relieved they were talking again, Jonah took a chance and asked, "Don't you have a change of clothes?"

"This is it," she said as she fluffed out her black cassock. "In the rush to leave Morningstar Ranch, I left with what I had on."

"It's getting a little creepy," he said as he scanned her altar boy outfit.

Laughter and boisterous conversation rose to them from across a creek. Rings of redwoods and the backside of several buildings blocked their view of the celebration. They circled around toward the noise, passing a two-story gabled Tudor along the way. The lodge appeared forgotten, left alone to survive whatever years it had remaining.

A nearby open space contained rows of benches laid out between a fire pit and an amphitheater. They sat and took in the scene as young folks pranced in small clumps from one building to the next.

"I had no idea all of this was here," Renée said as she scanned an outdoor bowling alley, pinball arcade, skating rink, soda fountain and more.

Upon a second glance, she saw the chipped facades, broken panes of glass and structures resting off-center. "Such a shame," she said.

Jonah pointed to a canvas winking-moon perched high in a redwood above the Rio Nido Bar and Grill. The whimsy touched her and she said, "This place must have been something at one time."

They sat there and people-watched. "Wouldn't be surprised if most of them are squatters, just drifters passing through," Jonah said.

"You mean like us?" Renée added.

"No one here to defend these properties," Jonah said. "Probably wouldn't fetch much anyways. Not worth the trouble, I guess. Heard someone say that owners were burning down their cabins rather than leave them to these outsiders."

"Let's get a malt," Renée said wanting to brighten the mood.

They meandered past the arcade and an ice cream store to the soda fountain. Renée entered when she noticed that Jonah had lingered behind. She waved him in but his attention was elsewhere.

"What is it?" she asked after she returned outside.

Without answering, he stepped to the front entrance of The Barn, the local dance hall. Yellow flyers read: *The Grateful Dead / Rio Nido / Labor Day Celebration, Sept. 3rd, 1967.*

Chapter 20

Residents armed themselves with placards that read R.I.P. CHARLES SULLIVAN. The tragic event in that dark alley one year ago to the day had never been resolved, at least not in the hearts and minds of the locals.

The Panthers, wearing black berets and leather jackets, formed an honor guard as the entire neighborhood marched down Fillmore Street. Bill Graham walked alongside Charles Sullivan's surviving brother, Marion. Jazz musicians Leola King, John Handy, Frank Fischer and Pony Poindexter shared the asphalt with rockers Steve Miller, Janis Joplin and Big Brother. A CLOSED sign hung outside the barbershop and the brothel. Employees and neighbors drifted into the street from the Booker T. Washington Hotel and Lee's Liquor store.

Men in blue flanked the procession while suits from city hall remained in the background. James McGinnis, head of the Redevelopment Agency, stood alongside Police Chief Cahill. Concern showed on their faces. The future of the Fillmore was at stake. If the leftwing *Chronicle* grabbed ahold of this and ran with it, perhaps downtown's plans for the area would go belly-up. Two thousand Victorians had been cleared and a "Fillmore Center" was already underway. No turning back now.

The mourners ballooned to five hundred strong. As the crowd grew, the police became agitated and started to move in, but Chief Cahill signaled them to stand down. The civil rights demonstrations and the riots from the previous year still stung. No way the chief was going to revisit that debacle.

The ladies from the brothel left the stoop to travel across the street. They remembered Charles Sullivan with fondness. The man had transformed the district into the Harlem of the West, bringing carloads of customers to their doorstep. But he wasn't all business. Several memories of his kindness lingered, including the time when he paid for the funeral expenses of their fallen Sara, the ill-fated whore who died of tainted heroin.

The Black Panthers formed a line at the curb of Graham's dance hall. The ground-floor businesses were closing their doors forever. Checks Cashed Here appeared as a ghost ship—its walls naked except for the dusty outlines where bulletins and decorative pieces once hung. The entrance to Bud's Bail Bonds listed a new address south of Market Street near the county jail.

Bill Graham stepped onto a bench, signaling for everyone's attention. Uncertainty thickened the air. Police waited the command to disperse the assembly. Civilians wore a defiant look.

"Thank you for coming today," Graham started. "Today marks the one year anniversary of the passing of Charles Sullivan, a man who had given his life for music."

Murmurs, chants and the fanning of memorial posters confirmed the sentiment. Bill Graham went on to render a brief account of Charles Sullivan, of how he had long been an advocate for his people, pushing boundaries.

"When WWII broke out, he tried to get a job at the Hunters Point Shipyard, but the union refused to hire blacks. Charles made such a stink that President Roosevelt himself intervened to change union practices."

Graham paused before adding, "Charles Sullivan was a feared man, as God is my witness."

Mourners welled up as one, repeating the chant as if it was a Sunday service—*"As God is my witness."*

"After the war," Graham continued, "Charles opened up the West Coast's most prominent jazz club, Bop City, right here in the Fillmore, but the City officials shut him down on trumped up health code violations. Charles Sullivan was a feared man, as God is my witness."

"As God is my witness."

"Downtown did not deter Charles. He went on to become the foremost black promoter of blues, delivering a bit of Harlem to us. Charles Sullivan was a feared man, as God is my witness."

"As God is my witness."

Bill Graham left his makeshift podium and went to the gaited entrance of his beloved auditorium. He ripped off an official-looking notice and retraced his steps.

"I have in my hand," he said to the throng, "a declaration from the Redevelopment Agency stating that the Fillmore Auditorium is to be closed to the public as of the first of next month."

Boos and fists penetrated the night breeze. Heads swiveled.

"Charles Sullivan first owned the dance permit to the Fillmore," Graham added. "He bequeathed its safekeeping to me so that his legacy should not be forsaken. It will not. Charles Sullivan is STILL a feared man, as God is my witness."

"As God is my witness."

Uneasiness worked the crowd. Snarls and glares made their way to the police.

Chief Cahill turned to the leader of the Redevelopment Agency. "I thought your man had these people under control."

James McGinnis said that his community liaison was out of town. "But as soon as Mr. Allan McCollum returns, we'll have a heart-to-heart."

⅄

With the heel of his boot, the sheriff pushed against his desk, tilting his chair back. He brought a bowl closer to fork a leaf of lettuce when the entrance moaned open ushering in the morning fog.

"Close the door," the sheriff ordered before putting his meal to his mouth.

"Nothing burns like the cold," a Negro said.

"How can I help you two," the sheriff said, including with his greeting a man in blue as well.

"Let me introduce myself. I am Allan Theodore McCollum the Third."

"That's quite a moniker," the sheriff said.

The policeman stepped in front of Papa Al to face the constable. "Are you Sheriff McGee of Guerneville?"

"Could be."

"I'm Sergeant Maloney, SFPD," and he produced a badge. "We met at the Nob Hill Theater in San Francisco six months ago."

"Don't recall," Sheriff McGee said.

"Nob Hill Theater," Sergeant Maloney repeated. "It's frequented by queers."

"That so?" the sheriff said.

"SFPD raided the joint on Sodom and Gomorrah Night," the sergeant said. "I pulled your country ass out of a stall with some other fruitcake. That sound familiar?"

Sheriff McGee put his bowl of greens down. "What is this?"

"When you showed me your credentials," Sergeant Maloney continued, "I let you zip up your pants and slip out the back."

From the uneasy expression on the sheriff's face, Maloney knew he had him. "You're going to help us track down a couple of punks we need to talk to," he said while placing photos of two teenagers next to the sheriff's meal.

Sheriff McGee leaned over and studied the images. "Don't recognize them."

Papa Al measured the local constable with his inspection. "Sheriff, these two interlopers are wanted for absconding with valuable pieces of evidence in an ongoing investigation."

The sheriff took another look at the photos. "Like I said, I don't..."

"How about this guy?" Sergeant Maloney interrupted, holding out a third photo of a tattooed man in a black T-shirt and leather vest.

"Yeah," the sheriff said, "I recognize him—Sonny Barger. He and a couple of Hells Angels got into some trouble over in Jenner. Had to escort the whole lot to the county limits."

"Any idea where they were headed?" Sergeant Maloney asked.

"I suspect they were joining up with George Wethern, another Angel. Lives in Ukiah."

"Could we bother you for the address?" Papa Al interjected.

"Sure but it wouldn't do you any good," the sheriff said.

"Why is that?" Papa Al asked.

"'Cause your Sonny Barger wasn't with the others. We suspect he might have been involved in some goings-on over in Cazadero the other night. People say there was a priest, an altar boy and a couple of teenagers with him."

"That would be the interested party in this police matter," Papa Al said.

"The Feds are looking for the bunch as well," the sheriff said. "Something to do with counterfeit money."

"That certainly is a very healthy meal you have there," Papa Al said, gesturing to the bowl of greens.

"The wife won't let me back in her bed unless I shed a few pounds," Sheriff McGee said.

"'Let food be thy medicine and medicine be thy food,'" Papa Al said. "Hippocrates uttered that in 460 B.C., and it is still true to this day, wouldn't you agree?"

"Well, I suppose so."

"What a pity it would be if you were not given the opportunity to conjoin with your wife once again." Before the sheriff could respond, Papa Al added, "Sergeant Maloney and I have all the confidence in the world that you will help us find our young hooligans."

"Gotta be a hundred miles of back roads up in these hills. They could be anywhere," the sheriff said.

"That is exactly why we are requesting your expertise," Papa Al said.

"Feds have roadblocks at all the major interchanges," the sheriff said. "Just need to wait your boys out is all."

"Patience is not only the ability to wait," Papa Al said. "It is *how* we behave while we are waiting that is of the utmost importance."

"Afraid I don't follow you," Sheriff McGee said.

"It is imperative that we locate our suspects before the Federal authorities do," Papa Al said.

"Well, that could be a little tricky," the sheriff said.

"It would dismay me greatly if your dear spouse were to discover your *other life*," Papa Al said. "Time may lie dormant as a blanket over a sleeping past, but in the end it will awaken to dictate what the future shall be...You best put your priorities in order, sir."

Chapter 21

The village center bubbled with activity. A couple of tykes in their dreadlocks kicked a can along the ground while nearby another in his buckskin vest placed a tab onto the tongue of a woman. She leaned her head back and swallowed before shaking her love beads.

Others in their tie-dye T-shirts braced themselves against the counter at the shooting gallery, widening their stances as they pulled the triggers on pump-action .22s. Cast-iron ducks and cats toppled over one by one.

A longhair jerked his rifle free of its chain, accidentally firing a round. The bullet ricocheted off a stanchion and embedded itself where a couple was sitting.

The longhair sauntered over and apologized. "Man, you okay?"

"Other than the death of my bench, there's no harm done," Jonah said. "Not to worry."

"No, man, that wouldn't be righteous," and the longhair offered Jonah a dozen tabs before hustling back to the arcade.

Jonah and Renée looked at each other with a carefree grin, shrugged their shoulders and downed the pills.

She tapped her toe on the ground, anxious to get started while Jonah stared off into the treetops.

His mouth fell open as a glazed look worked its way across his face. He began to lose himself in a parallel universe where objects appeared in a six-dimensional space. Humans, squirrels and birds materialized in various angular shapes as if robots on the wind.

They rose and walked past the bingo parlor where Jonah spied a historical marker. He peered closer, perused each word as if in slow motion, calling out his findings: "'*Harold Smith... of Harold's Club Reno...got his start in...Rio Nido along...the Russian River.*'"

"Steady there, sport," Renée said as she held onto him.

They glided further down the village, passing a dress shop where a one-piece bathing suit hung on a mannequin in the window alongside summer cotton frocks and parasols. A variety store came next with a potpourri of treasures. Inner tubes, beach towels and board games vied for space with Slinky and Chatty Cathy. G.I. Joe caught Jonah's eye and he leaned forward, the doll's uniform drawing him ever closer. He studied its face when, without warning, it transformed into his own likeness.

Jonah jumped back. "No, no. I won't go." He crouched behind Renée, putting up his arms in defense.

"Am I going to have to play the babysitter here?" she said. "You were supposed to wait for me before you started tripping. *Stupide.*"

They cruised in front of a grocery store with a one-chair barbershop upstairs before arriving at the post office near the western end of the village center. Pins stabbed various announcements to a bulletin board. One flyer beckoned all River Rats to a Labor Day party in Canyon Two to celebrate the fourth anniversary of Dick Crest's last concert in Rio Nido. Jonah fixed his eyes on the invitation as if stuck in a time warp.

The sun dipped below the tips of the redwoods. Stabs of light melded with patches of gold coating the branches above. He tiptoed along the carpet of needles underfoot. Fall had announced itself with dignity, and Jonah marveled at its beauty.

Renée shook him and raised her voice. He tried to decipher the sentences exiting from her lips, but only garbled sounds came to him.

"I think you are in need of a diversion, my friend," she said before leading him to a tunnel, which traveled under the main byway.

Arm in arm they entered the tube. Jonah smiled as his vision lingered on the graffiti. Names and drawings in different fonts moved toward him with their neon hues.

He extended his hand to touch the suspended colors. It was like traveling through a giant kaleidoscope. To put the experience into words, however, would have been beyond his capability.

"We're almost there," Renée said as she gestured to the daylight some thirty feet away.

"The walls speak," and he halted and cocked an ear toward the doodles.

Renée pulled on him but with no result. She thought that perhaps the tunnel was a bad idea, and she tugged harder.

Jonah looked down. His frame was clad in G.I. Joe's uniform. Then he spied a vision with crimson-colored wings at the end of the tube. A voice called out: "Do you want to go to war?" Jonah yelled back, "No!" The angel in red begged him on, saying, "Come with me then. There is no need for you to kill." Jonah hesitated, not sure if he could trust this phantom before him. "No, I won't come," he said. The jaws of the winged image opened to swallow him whole when musical notes interceded and pulled him into the daylight. Army fatigues fell from his frame, piece by piece, and he released a sigh of relief.

Renée guided him down a steep path to the river's edge where they crossed over a pedestrian bridge. With effort, she steered him along the boardwalk to a concession stand. She bought two ice cream cones, chocolate dipped. Jonah held onto his treat and started to walk toward the setting sun when Renée caught up with him.

"Come, my little acid boy," she said. "We're going on an adventure."

They boarded a boat, paid the fifteen-cent roundtrip fare and sat on a wooden bench. Words spilled from a handheld microphone.

"Good afternoon, ladies and gentlemen, I am Bid Green and I will be your captain for the short voyage to Guerneville. You should know that the River Queen will be adding on an extra run this evening, returning to Rio Nido after tonight's festivities."

Chocolate dripped down the arm of Jonah as he sat there in a comatose state. Renée licked on her cone enjoying the bucolic surroundings while listening to "Cruising Down the River" from the speakers.

They motored past egrets fishing for their dinner. A furry creature swam to a nearby bank and crawled onto the sand where a trio of naked sunbathers sat.

A wild-looking man with scruffy facial hair fed the critter while two ladies looked on. As the River Queen came closer, the unclothed man stood up and stepped forward into the water. He held up his hands as might a preacher and began spouting phrases in a biblical cadence.

The figure started to change from albino to tangerine to red. Jonah's pupils popped wide. The devil in angel's wings had reappeared. This time he wasn't sermonizing on the war in Vietnam but on the evils of the Negro race, of the impending racial strife between whites and blacks.

Jonah dropped his cone and slid up against Renée. She held onto him, not so much to lend him support as to anchor herself. Her head felt light, her brain breezy.

They stumbled as one off the River Queen and onto a rocky beach. The crowd carried them along like an incoming tide.

⅄

Hungry, Jonah and Renée checked out the menu at Murphy's Guest Ranch but alcohol wasn't offered. They walked east along Main Street and peeped inside both Pat's diner and Fry's Pancake House before passing a number of watering holes. People came and went in front of the Redwood Café, Stork Club and Louvre Saloon. While booze was needed, they felt trapped as if inside a pinball game, glancing off locals and tourists.

The couple broke free of the chaos and spotted the Guerneville Inn, which sat on a quiet side street. Not a single customer waited outside.

They crossed Armstrong Woods Road at the same moment a pickup rolled to the rear of the restaurant. A man with stringy hair and wearing an outback leather coat exited the driver's side. He and a couple of rubes pulled a dead cow from the bed of the truck. Jonah thought he detected the initials *MS* branded on the animal's hindquarter but couldn't be sure.

The place was empty with the exception of naked empresses hanging from the walls. Jonah studied the Roman nudes, which wore crowns of flowers, until feeling the swat of a hand across his head as Renée pushed him forward to a table decorated with candles and plastic grapes.

A waitress limped over with no menus in hand. She had flabby arms while sunspots dotted her face, which was framed by thin strands of orange hair.

"What don't you want?" she said.

"Pardon?" Jonah said, still fuzzy.

"What don't you want?" the waitress repeated. She could tell by their blank expressions that they weren't able to comprehend and explained, "We serve T-bone steaks with corn or peas. So, which don't you want—the corn or the peas?"

"But you advertise Italian food," Renée said with a struggle.

"Don't care if you are wearin' a religious outfit," the waitress said to the altar boy. "Haven't got all day to chit-chat. God knows I've got just so many words left in me to toss about. So make up your mind…or don't. No matter to me," and she hobbled off.

Renée and Jonah started to mumble to each other when a man with a three-day old stubble, wearing a veteran's cap, walked in with a woman who was sporting a floral evening dress. "I'll take a double bourbon on the rocks and the wife will have a gin and tonic," the man said.

"Mr. James T. Willett," the waitress said, "I eighty-sixed both of you last week…for good."

"Is that any way to treat a veteran?" James Willett said to the waitress before turning to his wife. "What do you think, Lauren?"

"Not patriotic at all," Lauren said. "A man fights for his country's freedom and can't even drink the fruits of his labor…Shameful."

"You're both lousy drunks," the waitress said. "Don't need your business or your attitude."

"Attitude?" the veteran said. "Everyone in town knows where your steaks come from. Ranchers are getting tired of seeing their cattle disappear. How's that for attitude, huh?"

"You know where the door is," the waitress said.

"Come on, Lauren," the veteran said. "This place doesn't deserve the pleasure of our company."

"But what about my drink?"

"I said let's go," and the veteran pulled his wife off her stool and they exited.

The waitress returned to Renée and Jonah. "Sorry about that," the waitress said. "You'd think that an ex-Marine like Willett would have more self-respect. No accounting for people, I guess."

"I guess," Jonah repeated.

The waitress asked the couple if they had made up their minds. They opted not to get the peas. With a pained expression, the waitress said that it was about time and left for the kitchen.

Toward the end of their meal, Renée noticed the man with the veteran's hat in the entranceway. The stone-faced figure marched forward and lifted a nude from the wall.

"No one's gonna speak to me like that," the veteran said aloud as he collected a second piece of art. "Nobody."

The waitress appeared from the kitchen holding a frying pan. "Mr. James T. Willett, just because you were some hotshot soldier once upon a time don't give you the right to come in here and act like a dumbass. Now put down those paintings," and she swatted him across the shoulder with the pan.

The scene sobered up Jonah and Renée. He threw a twenty-dollar bill down and they left. At the pedestrian crossing, Jonah spotted a roadblock near the Guerneville Bridge. Men in black manned the area alongside county deputies.

"What's all the fuss about?" Jonah asked a local.

"FBI is lookin' for a shitload of phony bills that have been showin' up."

"Must be terribly important to bring the Feds in," Renée added, urging the guy on.

"That Roy Cornett fella over in Cazadero," the local said, "left his house and everything to his neighbors before the Feds could get to it. Those FBI boys don't have a sense of humor. I imagine the whole thing rubbed them the wrong way. Anyways," the local said getting back on track, "turns out that a biker and his friends discovered the whereabouts of Cornett's counterfeit operation and took off with the loot."

"So the Feds think that this biker is still in the area?" Jonah guessed.

"What do I know?" and the local walked away.

Without warning, a ball of fire exploded forty feet into the sky from the Guerneville Inn. The lawmen at the bridge abandoned their posts and hurried across the intersection toward the inferno. Joining the taskforce was a square-jawed policeman and a Negro wearing aviator glasses.

Jonah turned his back to the scene and nudged Renée into the alcove of the mercantile. "We've got to get you out of those clothes."

"You wish," Renée said before she saw the fright in his expression and turned to see what the concern was.

"It's them, isn't it?" she said. "The ones you're fleeing from, right?"

Jonah talked on the run, saying, "I'm guessing that Papa Al suspects that you and Father Paul are with us. That altar boy costume has to go."

They entered a boutique store. A woman in her early forties, wearing a mod floral number, sauntered over and asked if she could be of assistance.

"My friend," Jonah said, "would like to try on a few things."

The employee said that the shop didn't carry men's apparel. "You should try across the street," the employee said in a highbrow tone. "Kings News and Tackle might have something for you gentlemen."

"Oh, we're just fine right here, thank you," Renée said.

Renée roamed the aisles while Jonah sat near the display window, peering up and down Main Street. Within a brief time, she picked a few items off the rack and disappeared into the changing room. The black cassock came off first before she unwrapped the ace bandage from her bosom.

With each new ensemble, she stepped to Jonah and modeled for him. The first one was a V-neck red tent dress trimmed with black ruffles. She spun around, fluffing out the fabric, but Jonah gave her a thumbs down, saying it would draw too much attention. Renée smacked her lips in disappointment and returned to the stall. The second dress was a sky-blue tube skirt, sleek and streamlined, ala Jackie Kennedy. Renée showed a pout and threw her head back in a regal pose.

"Too formal," Jonah said as the commotion down the corner took a backseat to the sight before him.

Renée slipped into another getup. Jonah sat ramrod. The miniskirt fit snug around her hips. His mouth grew dry. With renewed interest, he rose, walked to a mannequin and plucked off a tawny-colored wig and positioned it atop her head.

The employee returned with a stunned expression. "Incredible," she said as she surveyed the metamorphosis. On a second inspection, she told the customer not to move before vanishing to another corner of the shop.

"You look like Raquel Welch," Jonah said as he adjusted the hairpiece on Renée.

The employee reappeared and applied a touch of rouge, some lipstick and a bit of eyeliner. She stood back to admire the finished product and surrendered a single clap.

"Well done," the employee said. "Will there be anything else?"

"If it wouldn't be too much trouble," Renée said, "I'd like a bag for this," and she held up her droopy cassock.

"Are you sure?" the employee said, lifting the altar boy uniform with her fingers as if it carried every contagion known to mankind.

⅄

Fire hoses poured funnels of water onto the blaze. Tourists and locals gawked while deputies rerouted traffic. Employees of the Guerneville Inn milled around on the sidewalk. Sergeant Maloney and Papa Al moved toward an older woman wearing an apron. The policeman displayed a couple of photos to her, asking if she had seen either of the teenagers recently.

"Never seen the black one before," the waitress said.

"Are you positive?" the sergeant asked, leaning his hulk into her.

"I'd remember if I saw such a clown."

"What about the other one?" the sergeant asked, still bent into her, raising his voice over the arrival of additional emergency vehicles.

"Do you mind?" and the waitress tapped him on the forehead with a frying pan to push him back. With some breathing room, she studied the second photo, saying that the white kid reminded her of someone that was there just a short time ago.

"He was with an altar boy dressed in a black robe or something," she said. "Why? Is he in some kind of trouble?"

"Yes," the sergeant said.

"Can't be," the waitress retorted.

"Why do you say that, ma'am?" Papa Al interjected.

"'Cause he left me a nice tip."

"You wouldn't happen to have the money handy, would you?" Papa Al asked.

The waitress picked a Jackson from her apron pocket. Papa Al held the twenty up to the light and spied a smile on the hidden image of the seventh President of the United States.

Chapter 22

They strode down Main Street as if they had been girlfriend and boyfriend since puberty. He walked stiff with pride, nodding to passersby, showing her off.

"Wipe that smile from your face," Renée said.

"No can do," Jonah said before adding, "I have to agree with the employee at the boutique—you do indeed look *stunning*."

Renée lowered her head and said, "Thank you. It's been awhile."

The couple ambled past Gori's Tavern and the Bank Club where a tourist in his Bermuda shorts and knee-high socks came stumbling out. Revelry filled the entranceway until the door swung closed.

"The town's got more saloons than you can shake a stick at," Jonah said.

Renée threw him a curious look. "*Shake a stick at*?"

"It's an American thing."

"You're a curious lot."

They rounded the corner at the Associated Gas station and headed along Church Street toward the river where the sheriff's office stood. Jonah scooted to the far side of Renée, cocking his head downward, feigning a massage to his temple.

"Who are we hiding from now?" Renée asked.

"You have to ask?"

"I am no longer part of your sordid crime spree," she said. "The *gendarmerie* are searching for a pimple-faced altar boy not a sexy young lady in her new summer outfit," and she waved a hand over her miniskirt.

They reached Johnson's Beach where they strolled past campsites and one-room cabins. Recreational vehicles, station wagons and sedans fought for space along the tar-stained parking lot.

A boardwalk led them past a snack shack where a forty-year-old with a kind face sold them a couple of cheeseburgers and cherry snow cones. "You kids enjoy the show," and he threw out a man-in-the-moon grin.

"Show?" Renée asked the man, but Jonah whisked her away, saying that it was a surprise.

They walked with a lazy gait as if the worries that followed them had suddenly evaporated like the morning dew. Renée sucked on a straw, enjoying her snow cone while Jonah bit into a burger.

A voice interrupted, wailing out a warning over the outdoor loudspeakers: "Will the boy in canoe number seventy-one please sit down. I repeat—will the boy in…"

The words faded behind the sound of the breeze playing in the trees. They tightroped along a crooked path between blankets and towels and canvas chairs. At the far end near the summer dam, a spot of unoccupied beach showed itself.

They snatched it up and sat. Renée undid the black ribbon lacing from her shoes and let her toes play with the pebbles.

"You look a lot older than that altar boy I used to despise," Jonah said.

"I am," Renée answered, toying with him.

"Eighteen?" he guessed.

No response.

"Nineteen?"

"*Vingt*," she answered in French. "Twenty."

"So I'm dating an older woman?"

"We are not dating," Renée answered. "We are simply two strangers forced by circumstances to travel together."

"Anyway you put it, it still sounds sexy."

⅄

Attendants began to stow away beach umbrellas inside the equipment-rental shed. Canoes and paddleboats were chained together at the water's edge. The concession stand remained open. Parents corralled little ones, calling them from the river while others ignored the demands, making one last plunge down a slide.

The sun dipped behind the hills as a full moon soon took its place, casting sparkles of light upon the rippling stream. An otter swam to the distant shore where it vanished behind a thicket of blackberry bushes.

From the speakers, a squeal shrieked across the beach. "Testing, one, two, three." A tap on the microphone followed another screech.

"Folks, before we begin tonight's play, I would like to introduce ourselves. I am Clare Harris and this is my brother, Herbert."

Applause sounded from the locals. The Harris family was a familiar clan in the Russian River Valley as they had owned and operated the village center in nearby Rio Nido from the late 1920's until '53. It was the golden age of music featuring the Big Band sound with such luminaries as Ozzie Nelson, Woody Herman, Phil Harris and Harry James. But the sixties had not been kind. Squatters and counterculture types had forced their uncivil ways upon the area.

"Herbert and I are thankful to remain an active part of this community. As many of you know, this last summer we purchased Johnson's Beach Resort. Hopefully, we can do our part to bring the River back to its former glory. And now with great pride, we give you the 20th annual Pageant of Fire Mountain."

Full time residents and tourists alike put their hands together for this farewell to summer. The play would be the last lure by the chamber of commerce to fill up motel rooms and dance halls.

A parade of locals, carrying torches and dressed in not so traditional Native American outfits, walked single file across a temporary plank, which straddled the dam. The moon put a faint glow upon the string of silhouettes as the actors moved across the river to Parker's Resort.

Claire Harris narrated, announcing over the speaker that the Pomo natives were returning to their summer lodging. Flames rose from pits while shadows danced upon the walls of teepees. Princess White Fawn, wearing braids and a buckskin frock, addressed her father, the chief, worried about the rumors of a nearby warring tribe.

Jonah reached for Renée's hand. Fingers entwined in playful cadence with the dialogue. It was a hokum play, but emoted a welcoming innocence.

In a sudden spurt of theatrical energy, a surge of rival natives with painted faces swept down upon White Fawn and her fellow tribesmen. War cries reached across the river to the audience who added howls and whoops of their own. Eyes popped wide from the skulls of tykes who clutched onto their mothers. Dads rooted on the fight, wanting bloodshed. Renée and Jonah shared a laugh, unwinding.

A lusty brave stole White Fawn, and the band of renegades fled up the mountain along a switchback trail. Toward the end of the play, the rival warrior and the princess fell in love and were married.

Words pushed through the outdoor speakers—"Oh, Great Spirit, give us a sign so that these two may join hands in blissful matrimony."

With that signal, flares lit up the mountain. Five hundred feet of paths glowed while fireworks shot toward the stars. Pops with flashes of red, white and blue flooded the canyon. Trails of light drizzled down upon the beachgoers. In unison, Jonah and Renée sang out a chorus of "oohs" and "aahs", letting the last morsel of acid do its magic.

⅄

The throng filtered to the parking lot with their folding chairs and picnic baskets. Vehicles started to file out. Strands of "Cruising Down the River" washed over a thin line of tourists waiting to board the River Queen for the return trip to Rio Nido.

With her shoes in hand, Renée strolled barefoot along the beach toward the ferry. "That was nice," she said to Jonah.

"Yeah, it was, wasn't it?" he said with a grin.

"You're not so infuriating," Renée said, "when you're not talking."

"Less is more?"

They stepped closer to the river's edge where a scene brought reality back to them. Jonah spotted a man in blue standing next to the River Queen's captain. A Negro in a three-quarter-length coat, smoking a cigar, examined the line of waiting passengers.

Jonah pulled on Renée who sounded an objection. "Hey, the ferry is over there," and she gestured back toward the river.

"Eyes straight," Jonah ordered as he guided her in a different direction.

Without glancing backwards, she took his meaning and pressed on. They crossed under the Guerneville Bridge where the sounds of demanding voices and honking vehicles came to them from above.

A scattering of lodges and cabins dotted the way, but the distance kept their lights at a dim flicker. Fog started to rise from the river, shrouding the area. A flock of ravens scattered from a redwood, cawing a warning. He put his arm around her to ward off the cold as they trampled out of the bushes, returning to the pebbled waterfront.

A blaze showed up ahead beckoning them. They approached with caution, shivering within the mist.

"Mind if we share your fire?" Jonah said to a stranger.

"My pleasure," a scrawny, unshaven man said.

Jonah and Renée sat, warming their hands over the flames. Introductions were passed around. The man announced himself as Charles Manson while the girls on either side of him went by Tuffy and Squeaky. Fleshy ankles and feet poked out from beneath a single blanket.

Jonah thought he recognized the guy from somewhere—the wild eyes, the penetrating stare. *What the hell?*

"You folks from around here?" Manson asked the newcomers.

"Renée's from Quebec and I'm from San Francisco," Jonah said in a flat tone.

"Frisco—love that town," Manson said.

Only tourists and Hells Angels referred to San Francisco as *Frisco*, Jonah thought, but this guy was neither. A bad feeling invaded Jonah and he started to rise.

"Don't be like that," Manson said. "Here, have a sip," and he passed a bottle.

"Sorry," Jonah said, "but we have to..."

"Sit," Manson said with a scowl, his eyes bulging from his head. "Want you to hear a sad story."

Manson, after he took a toke on a joint, started to sermonize on the evaporation of their heritage. "The white man's culture is disappearing. Getting to the point where you can't walk down the street without seeing some Negro holding hands with a white woman. And you got this Stokley Carmichael guy creating havoc down in Mississippi with his black-power rants and such. Everything's helter-skelter."

"We really should be going," and Jonah tried to take a step forward when Tuffy and Squeaky, with nothing on except for love beads, caressed him, pressing him downward.

"Then they put this Thurgood Marshall guy on the Supreme Court," Manson continued before taking another drag on a joint. "But the Aryan race is rising up. Things are changing. We taught Malcom X a thing or two, blowing off his head a couple years ago. Best thing that could've happened. It got the white people to thinking that maybe they could retake their country, take back their culture."

A third woman appeared out of the fog in a drunken stupor. Renée thought the new arrival looked familiar but couldn't place her. She looked out of place, wearing a floral evening dress. Without any emotion, the woman sat behind Manson and put her arms around him, staring into the fire with dead eyes.

"People in Detroit woke up," Manson said. "Whites killed forty-three blacks. Same thing is happening in Tampa, Atlanta, Newark, Brunswick, Cincinnati...everywhere. A hundred and sixty-four race riots just over the summer and more on the way...The revolution is at our doorstep, my friend. All it needs is a little shove."

Manson took another swig of whiskey before passing it to one of his girls. Squeaky chugged a load before holding the bottle to the lips of Jonah.

"No thanks," Jonah said. "Sorry to bother you," and he rose to his feet again.

"Thought we might start something right here…in Guerneville," Manson said. "Good a place as any for a revolution. Whaddya say?"

Jonah had no idea what Manson was referring to nor did he care to know. He just wanted to get moving and said that while the overture was tempting, he was late for an important appointment.

"She can stay," Manson said, pointing to Renée.

"Don't think so," Renée answered. Another thought came to her and she motioned to the lifeless woman in the evening dress, thinking that perhaps she was in need of help.

"Would you like to come with us?" Renée asked her.

The woman's eyes peered upward before returning to the flames. Something wasn't right. With a sense of dread, Renée took hold of the woman and pulled her to the side.

"It'll be okay," Renée said to her before nodding to Jonah.

The three started walking away when beams of light showed from opposite ends of the beach. Jonah told Renée to stay with the woman.

"What about you?" Renée asked.

"Go," Jonah said before returning to the campfire.

Renée put her arm around the woman as they shuffled along the sand toward the advancing beacons. The bands of light soon caught her miniskirt.

"Thank goodness," Renée said to a man in uniform. "This lady needs assistance."

Sheriff McGee took the woman into his hold and studied her face. "Mrs. Willett, are you all right?"

He shook her shoulders, saying, "I need you to tell me where your husband is."

Mrs. Willett sagged within the sheriff's grasp before gazing up at him and planting a kiss on his cheek. "Is…it…true?" she started, stumbling out her words. "Is our town hero…a fruitcake?" and she slumped back into his arms.

"I need you to focus," and the sheriff shook her again. "Your husband blew up the Guerneville Inn and has disappeared. Do you know where he might be?"

"Is this the woman from the restaurant?" a Negro asked as he arrived with another.

"She's had too much to drink," the sheriff answered.

A third man in a policeman's uniform showed a photo to the woman. "Did you see this guy earlier tonight?"

Mrs. Willett lifted her head. "You're kinda cute. What's...your...name, sweetheart?" and she fingered his chin.

The man in blue waved her off and shifted his beam to the second female. A miniskirt fit snug upon her frame, which rested below a white high-collared blouse and a tawny hairpiece. The sergeant gave her a second examination before suggesting to his cohort that there was nothing here for them.

⅄

Sergeant Maloney placed his flashlight upon the bedraggled crew. Two men and two women huddled together under a blanket. Nipples, ankles, and other fleshy parts appeared from the folds of the covering.

"Any you punks seen this guy?" the man in blue said as he held up a black and white glossy.

"Officer," an unshaven one with wild eyes said, "why do you harbor the company of a Negro? Are you not aware of the impending holocaust?"

With the butt of his revolver, Sergeant Maloney thumped the stranger on the head. The wild-eyed one fell sideways to the ground. Papa Al surrendered a cursory glance at the others under the blanket before dismissing the bunch and marching on.

Jonah, after lawman and mobster disappeared into the night, rose and started to slip into his jeans. The girls complained, saying that he couldn't go, that the party was just about to start. Squeaky tried to undress him while Tuffy approached with a bottle of whiskey, but Jonah resisted and walked away.

"Say goodbye to your friend for me when he wakes up," Jonah said over his shoulder.

Another hundred yards down the beach, he caught up with Renée. He hugged her, thankful she was okay. Mindful of the surrounding danger, they pulled back and surveyed the area. Clear. They started up again when Renée observed an object protruding from the brush under a willow tree.

"It's nothing," Jonah said. "Let's go."

But something drew her in, something eerily familiar. She retrieved a discarded oil painting, blew off the debris and brought it closer. A naked lady with a crown of flowers filled out a gilded frame.

Chapter 23

Squad cars blocked River Road at the Rio Nido entrance. The fog settled over the asphalt with a quiet force. Even the hippie squatters had retired for the night. Traffic was nonexistent until a pair of headlights approached. A U-Haul eased to a stop near a flashing yellow light.

A bearded man wearing wire-rimmed glasses rolled down the window. "Evening, officer."

The deputy asked for ID and proof of registration while a man in a Sears & Roebuck suit looked on from behind. The driver plucked some paperwork from the glove compartment, saying that the vehicle was a rental.

"What's your business here?" the deputy asked in a matter of fact tone.

"We're The Grateful Dead," the driver said before elaborating. "I'm Jerry Garcia. Gonna play at the dance hall this Sunday. You know, at The Barn?"

"What's in the truck?" the deputy asked.

"Ah...gear, stuff like that."

The doubting tone in the driver's voice propelled the deputy to order the opening of the rear door.

"Seriously," Garcia said, "there's nothing back there."

The Fed in the suit stepped forward. "Open it."

Garcia released a pocket of air, exited from the U-Haul and stepped to the rear. "You don't have to do this," Garcia said.

The lawman gestured with his hand to raise the door. Garcia unlocked the metal entrance and pushed upward. A cloud of smoke spilled out.

The suit fanned away the haze, wheezing, before commanding everyone to get out. A trio of longhairs disembarked with their hands in the air. Possession of an ounce of grass was a felony and the boys didn't want to further piss off the law—the bust back at their place in the Haight was still fresh on their minds. While their attorney, Terrence Hallinan, had succeeded in having the charges dismissed, who knew what the FBI would do.

The Fed called for another who came with a loaded shotgun. With the barrel trained on the longhairs, the sheriff's deputy boarded and searched the truck. Amps, speakers, and electrical equipment came under inspection. The deputy unlatched one of the guitar cases and scanned the inside.

Frustrated, he climbed down from the rental and said to the Fed that he couldn't find anything of major concern, just the usual contraband and paraphernalia. The Fed returned a nod and walked away.

"You are free to go," the deputy said to the bearded one.

Garcia gazed at his fellow musicians with relief, but a curiosity filled his expression and he asked, "So what's all this about?"

"The Feds are looking for some counterfeiters," the deputy said, exhaling his cold breath. "These D.C. guys…they think they're hot shit. Be glad when I can go home to some warm sheets," and he rubbed his hands together.

One of the squad cars motored to the side of the road. Garcia shoved the rig into first gear. The U-Haul cruised through the roadblock and started to turn into Rio Nido as Garcia looked into the rearview mirror. Distracted, he never saw the object overhead. A thud greeted him. The truck shook.

Garcia exited to investigate. A twenty-foot-long sign reading RIO NIDO rested on the ground beside the entrance to the village.

A voice came from the roadblock asking if everything was all right. Garcia waved a thank you to the deputy and returned to the cab.

⅄

They trudged up the riverbank and walked through the underpass. Renée reminded Jonah of his last visit here when he had a bad trip, the tabs of acid taking him to "gookland" and beyond. He shook his head as if trying to discard the images from his brain.

Splashes of color greeted them as they exited the tunnel. Jonah studied the activity on River Road. Squad cars and black cutout figures blocked the main artery. This can't be good, he thought, and guided Renée toward the village center.

The couple hurried past the fountain when melodic notes rose from some hidden place. The shooting gallery, bingo parlor, arcade and skating rink were shuttered for the night. In front of one of the dilapidated buildings, a white U-Haul was parked.

Despite Renée's objections, Jonah marched toward the electric sounds as if lured by Muses, the Greek goddess of music. He swung open the entrance to The Barn. The Grateful Dead were on stage working out the kinks to a handful of fresh lyrics.

"Dark star crashes /
pouring its light /
into ashes /
Reason tatters."

Frustrated, Jerry Garcia swung to the other members of the band and complained. "Where's the four-four beat? Come on guys, let's get with it." He released a puff of air and suggested a twenty-minute break.

"New song?" Jonah asked as he stepped toward the stage.

Garcia leaned his Gibson against a speaker and stepped down from the stage and shook Jonah's hand. "Yeah, a buddy of mine wrote it last week while visiting the river. Let me introduce you," and he whistled to his friend.

"Robert Hunter, this is Jonah," Garcia said. "He writes many of our reviews for the *Chronicle.* Also helps peddle Owsley's LSD down in the Haight."

"Well, I'm not sure I'll be doing either for a while," Jonah said.

"Sure you will," Hunter said before going into a lengthy conversation about how he had hooked up with Owsley Stanley and Ken Kesey down at Stanford University.

"I got college credit and was paid by the CIA to take psychedelics," Hunter said. "Best gig I ever had."

Without warning, he delved into verse; his arms and hands gesticulating like a rhapsodist. "Sit back, picture yourself swooping up a purple shell while foam crests of crystal drops fall unto the sea of morning mist," he said before adding, "those were some righteous days."

"Robert's a poet as well as a songwriter," Garcia added.

"Cool," Jonah said before adding, "I liked what I heard on stage."

"'Dark Star'", Hunter said, "will be the Dead's signature piece. Mark my words."

"The lyrics," Garcia said, "speak to me. They talk about how this universe is truly far out, of how weird it could really get. Know what I mean?"

"Can't wait to hear the entire song," Jonah said.

Garcia turned to Jonah and asked, "How're you doing?"

"Good…sort of. You see I've got this issue with…" and he heard a theatrical cough from behind and stopped to introduce his friend. "Sorry, this is Renée Giguere. She and her father are scamming the countryside in the name of God, working their way back home to Quebec."

"Thank you for that," Renée said to Jonah with a smirk.

"Nice to meet you," Garcia said as he shook her hand. "Always nice to have another rebel in the crowd."

"Have you heard from Bill Graham?" Jonah asked Garcia.

"He's got a hot coal up his ass," Jerry said, "and rightly so."

Jonah furrowed his brow.

"You haven't heard?"

"What?"

"Downtown refused to renew his permit for the Fillmore Auditorium. City hall is trying to shut it down."

With this pronouncement, Jonah took a step backwards in stunned silence.

"The Redevelopment Agency is out to get Graham, want to put a wrecking ball to his place and put up a high-rise. They've already hung a 'Closed' sign on the entrance."

"But the music?"

"It's all about the dollar bill, my friend," Garcia said.

Jonah felt for the envelope inside his Pendleton. Still there. He had formed a plan days ago regarding the photos. It was bold, even for the likes of a street-smart kid like him, but it was all he had.

Another in a horseshoe mustache came over and said hello. "Hey, Jonah, mind if we talk?"

Jonah accompanied Owsley Stanley outside. "If this is about what happen over at Big Brother's place back in the City," Jonah said, "I take full responsibility, Mr. Stanley. That shipment of LSD was mine to..."

"Call me Bear," Owsley interrupted before adding, "Relax. That's not why I wanted to talk to you."

"Okay."

"Your employer, Mr. Sonny Barger, desires to purchase the distribution rights of my product for the Haight. I was told that you might know where he is."

"I do."

"Get a message to him," Bear said. "Tell him that he's got until the end of Labor Day to finalize the deal."

"That's coming up fast," Jonah said.

"Papa Al and his thugs are trying to muscle their way into the Free Clinic to set up their own drug outlet," Bear said. "Dr. Smith doesn't know how much longer he can hold on. Supposedly, a bounty has been put on the doc's head—a hundred dollars worth of speed to anyone who knocks him off. Papa Al is determined to beat the Hells Angels to the punch for the LSD market. I'd like to deal with Sonny...we owe him...providing free security at the Dead concerts and all...but business is business."

"I understand."

"Remember, the band performs tomorrow and leaves on Monday morning."

Another detail came to Jonah and he asked, "Are you going to see Bill Graham anytime soon?"

"Why?"

"Give this to him," and Jonah picked an envelope from under his shirt and gave it to Bear.

⅄

Fog settled in the redwood canyons while the cold gripped them like a vise. A faint glow from high in the trees signaled the last vestige of life for the night as the wink from the canvas moon took on a menacing sheen.

The darkness swallowed cabins whole while the last wisps of smoke spilled from chimneys. The slope of Canyon Four put them on their toes. Shacks came and went as they pushed up the hill. Most of these cabins had been left to fend for themselves, doomed to face a slow death at the hands of Mother Nature. Jonah took in the scene, thinking that perhaps his future held a similar fate.

Jonah offered his hand to Renée as they descended the needle-coated path where blackberry vines nipped at their heels. They walked through the side entrance, past the kitchen and into the living room. The woodstove's flue remained bent over. Jonah went to the duct and shoved a second envelope into it.

"It's freezing in here," Renée said, wrapping her arms around her chest.

"Is that you, my child?" another called out from a far corner.

"Yes, *papa*."

"Come here, my dear," Father Paul said as he spread out a blanket on the floor next to him.

Renée snuggled up against him as if she was a toddler once again. He started to drape a second blanket over her when he saw her outfit.

"You look *magnifique*," Father Paul said.

"I do, don't I?" and she showed a smile as she surveyed her white high-collared blouse and miniskirt.

"But do you think that it's the wise thing to do?" Father Paul asked.

"It was at the time, *papa*."

Jonah turned to Sonny and said, "I have a message for you."

"What is it?"

"Not here," Jonah said before leading the way to the kitchen.

Jonah explained that he ran into Owsley Stanley down at the dance hall. "Bear wants the money for the distribution rights before he leaves on Monday morning," Jonah said.

"What happened to the love?" Sonny said. "Back in the Haight we were all buddy-buddy."

"Seems as if Papa Al is applying pressure," Jonah said. "He's taken over the Free Clinic. Intends to sell Owsley's LSD out of there."

"Ain't gonna happen." Sonny said. "No one sells Owsley's product but the Angels."

"Is that what the phony money's for, to pay off Bear?" Jonah asked.

"In a manner of speaking," Sonny said. "I had a meeting set up with a fence to take the bills off my hands."

"So?" Jonah said.

"He won't be coming, not with the roadblocks," Sonny said. "Too risky."

⅄

Dawn arrived. The new day pushed through the forest. Streams of light leaked into the shack through the smallest of crevices. In a living room corner, Otis slept on a mattress, snoring.

"Get up, jerkwad," Jonah said as he threw the blankets off his friend.

"What you wanna wake up the brother for?" Otis said as he reached for the covers with his blind touch. "Gotta get my beauty sleep," and he rolled over into the fetal position, but Jonah gave him a swift kick.

With another complaint, Otis rose. "What?"

"You want to get out from under the fist of Sonny, right?" Jonah asked.

"How you gonna do that?" Otis said.

"Do you remember that story you told me where some locals from Cazadero were willing to buy the phony bills as keepsakes?"

"Yeah."

"I think it might work," Jonah said.

"What might work?" Otis asked.

"Just follow my lead…and try not to say anything."

"Yes, master," Otis said in play.

The pair approached Sonny. Jonah leaned over to the sleeping Sonny and poked him. The Angel rubbed his eyes and sat up.

"We can get you your cash for the counterfeit money," Jonah said.

"How?" Sonny asked, still groggy.

"Yeah," Otis said breaking his vow of silence, "how we suppose to do that?"

Jonah sent a warning to his friend before turning back to Sonny. "Not to worry…But if I do this, you'll forget your plans for Otis."

"Plans?" Otis interjected. "What plans?"

"Do we have a deal?" Jonah said, holding out his hand to Sonny.

"The brother don't care much for plans," Otis said. "Especially if they come with…"

"Shut your mouth," Sonny interrupted.

⅄

Sonny kept Otis at the cabin as insurance in case the others decided to do anything funny. Renée donned her altar boy wardrobe for the occasion, assisting Father Paul. Jonah followed, carrying duffle bags crammed with twenty-dollar bills.

The trio walked up the seven canyons of Rio Nido knocking on doors. Longhairs in their beads and tattoos greeted them with tokes, sharing the love. The squatters must have occupied five hundred of the shacks, everyone feeling the groove, waiting for the ticket office to open later in the day. The price to enjoy the Dead concert would be set at a premium. The band had come to the realization that Peter Coyote and the Diggers were soon to be buried in the great pantheon of the oblivious. Their moment had come and gone. Anarchy was the dream of the disenfranchised, of the broken and forgotten. Bills needed to be paid.

"Bless you, my son," Father Paul said to a young squatter who answered the door. "I bring you manna from heaven on this fine Sunday morning."

The braided-hair lad took a hit before offering the joint to the priest who accepted it with glad tidings. Between drags, Father Paul introduced his associates.

"We are here today to give you the opportunity to stick it to the bureaucracy," Jonah started before describing the contents of the duffle bags.

Word had circulated fast regarding the counterfeit money. Just as intriguing was the story behind the story: a little known local by the name of Roy Cornett from the backwater town of Cazadero had made a one-man stand against the Federal Bureau of Investigation. He had not only prevented the Feds from finding his cache but had stopped them from taking possession of his home, which he gladly surrendered to his neighbors. The man had become a legend within forty-eight hours.

"Right on, brother," the hippie said, raising a fist-salute. "Power to the people."

"And for just one sawbuck," Jonah continued, "you can own a piece of history." With that proclamation, Jonah plucked a twenty-dollar bill from the satchel.

The hippie yelled a "far out" before hailing his band of renegades. Fifteen longhairs lined the hallway waiting their turn. And so the day went, squatters answering the anti-establishment call, eager to support the folk hero from Cazadero.

Chapter 24

He emptied the duffle bags. The mattress disappeared under the faces of Washington, Lincoln and Hamilton. The money was counted and re-counted—forty-five thousand dollars.

"What the hell is this?" Sonny said.

"Who was Hamilton?" Otis interjected as he studied a sawbuck.

"Where's the rest?" Sonny asked.

"How the hell anyone get their mug on a bill without being President?" Otis asked.

"That's it," Jonah said to Sonny, ignoring his friend.

"My buyer was going to pay sixty cents on the dollar."

"Do you have enough for Bear?"

"Don't think so." Sonny paced the room, thinking. He stopped and fixed his stare on Otis. "He's gonna stay with me for a while longer. Just in case."

"In case of what?" Jonah asked.

"In case this all goes sideways."

"No one knows your involvement in today's exchange, I swear," Jonah said.

"That's right," Renée confirmed as she slipped off her altar boy outfit. "Your name was never mentioned on our door-to-door crusade."

"Besides, my son," Father Paul said, "think about to whom we have sold the counterfeit twenties to. They are a ragtag bunch of runaways with no permanent address who have arrived here from the four corners of the globe. How would your federal government track down two thousand drifters? It's fool proof," and the priest pushed out an outsized smile, proud of the con job.

"You idiots," Sonny retorted. "How many of the phony bills do you think will end up at the ticket window this evening? Not every one of your anti-establishment types are gonna save it to remember some small-time crook from Cazadero. They're gonna cash in the money for concert tickets."

"Damn, you're right," Jonah said. "How could I be so stupid?"

"What you talkin' 'bout?" Otis said. "We're all good here. Let's beat it," and he started for the exit.

Sonny latched onto Otis's arm and threw him back against the woodstove. Renée sensed the change in the Angel's mood. She sidestepped to the kitchen and retrieved the hunting rifle from the refrigerator.

Sonny turned back to Jonah, saying that none of the counterfeit money was meant to end up in Owsley's possession. "With a little fact-checking, the Bear will figure out where the bills came from. And when he does, there's no way he'll partner up with the Angels."

Renée slid a bullet into the chamber.

"Yes, well, I...huh," and Jonah continued to stumble over his words. "I can see your point, but with all due respect, I think you're..."

"Until I know there is no backflow from this," Sonny said, "your friend stays with me," and he motioned to Otis before retiring to the back room while Renée returned the rifle to the refrigerator.

⅄

The silhouette of a man with a salt-and-pepper goatee and a hawk nose appeared in the doorway at Pat's saloon in Guerneville. "Anyone in here seen a black guy with a San Francisco cop?" the stranger asked.

The bartender signaled toward the back. The stranger hurried past with neither a thank you nor a drink order. He went into a knotty pine room with no windows and stepped to a table where a man wearing a three-quarter-length coat, aviator glasses and cropped Afro was sitting with a burly Irishman in his street blues.

"I know where Jonah is," the man said between breaths.

"Have a seat, Mr. Berkowitz," Papa Al said.

Abraham Berkowitz slid into a chair, sitting on its edge, fingers tapping the table. "That bastard son of mine will be attending The Grateful Dead concert tonight over in Rio Nido," Berkowitz said.

Papa Al took a sip of coffee before saying, "I was under the impression that the Dead were opening up for Jefferson Airplane this weekend at the Fillmore."

"They were scheduled to," Berkowitz said, "but it looks like downtown will be denying Bill Graham his permit."

"Well, that is interesting news," Papa Al said as he put his mug down. "However, I don't imagine that Mr. Graham will lie down quietly."

"Forget about Graham," Maloney said. "We need to get those photos. I got five kids in parochial schools and now the wife wants to move into some fancy new digs over in the Marina District...Don't need any speed bumps along the way."

"What about the three thousand the boy stole from the pawnshop's safe?" Papa Al said. "Should we forget about that as well?"

"Can make that up in a week," Maloney said.

"A mountain is composed of tiny grains of earth, is it not?" Papa Al said.

"Don't need another one of your...,"

"And the ocean is made up of tiny drops of water," Papa Al continued. "Life is but an endless series of little details, of which the absence of even the least can be far-reaching."

⅄

A line weaved its way from the ticket booth past the soda fountain and arcade to the rows of benches, which were squeezed in between the amphitheater and a raging bonfire. Hordes of hippies waved twenty-dollar bills in the air as if celebrating the discovery of missing treasure. Mingling amidst the buckskin vests and headbands were a fair amount of block jackets and loafers.

The concert had beckoned kids from various neighborhoods of the City, not just the Haight. Jocks and straight shooters from the Sunset and Richmond wanted a piece of the action as well.

A curtain, stenciled with local merchant adds, rose. Applause and teamster-like whistles sounded. As was customary, the band would render a sampling of their musical talents at the amphitheater before leading all to the nearby dance hall for the remainder of the evening.

Phil Lesh and Bob Weir led the contingent, waving their guitars to the throng. Mickey Hart took a seat behind the drums while Pigpen McKernan escorted Jerry Garcia to the mic.

"Greetings, Rio Nido!" Garcia yelled over the chaos.

Hippies and jocks yelled as one, howling their allegiance to the Dead. Jerry raised his arms in a salute before returning to the mic. "Prepare yourselves for a special treat. During his stay here in Rio Nido, my good friend and lyricist Robert Hunter wrote a song just for you."

Garcia settled back in with the other members of the band. He and Weir started to strum on their Gibsons while Lesh played his Big Brown. A perfect sonic balance rose with a soft improvisational jazz riff. Acidheads bobbed to and fro, letting the weight of the earth fall from under them. The band slid seamlessly into a psychedelic refrain with Garcia's thirteen-minute solo.

A flower child, no older than fourteen, peaked on Orange Sunshine, her heart racing into a primal exploration of the universe. She rubbed up against one of the block jackets, smiling, looking into his eyes, saying, "Love yourself to know truth…Love yourself to know truth," and she stepped to the next jock, rolling her hips.

Garcia and Weir shared the vocals, dipping into the mic together:

"Dark star crashes /
pouring its light /
into ashes /
Reason tatters /
the forces tear loose /
from the axis."

The lyrics provided background music as Renée and Jonah slinked across the creek to the rear of the dance hall.

"We shouldn't be doing this," Renée said. "It's too dangerous."

"Papa Al and that cop didn't give you a second glance last night down at the beach. You'll be fine," and he slid his vision down her frame. "Besides, I like what I see," and he showed a smile as he gestured to her miniskirt.

"And you?" she asked. "You think that silly hat and coat will fool them?"

Jonah had borrowed Otis's feathered fedora and burgundy jacket. While it was a tight fit, it would have to do. They crept to the window of the ticket booth where Jonah began to inspect each transaction.

"Want to remind me why we're here?" Renée asked.

"We're counting," Jonah said.

"We are?" Renée asked.

Jonah nodded and explained to her that he had made a phone call earlier to Terence Hallinan.

"Who?"

"Terence Hallinan," Jonah repeated. "He's an attorney, works for The Grateful Dead. Bill Graham says he's a firecracker and a…" Jonah cut himself short when he saw the detachment in Renée's face and came straight to the point. "Anyways, he was able to give me some advice regarding the use of counterfeit money for the purchase of merchandise such as concert tickets."

"And what advice would that be?"

"To do nothing."

"Nothing? That's some hotshot lawyer all right," she said with a doubting expression.

Bored, she left without another word and walked to the grocery store where she gazed at the morning headlines: "MAN FOUND DEAD". Fright wormed its way inside her head. With a hurried stroke, she searched her pockets for change. Not a penny. She glanced sideways to the cashier before plucking the paper from the rack and scurrying back toward The Barn. Along the way, she skimmed thru the article, her fears confirmed.

"Read this," Renée said as she handed the periodical to Jonah.

"You made me lose count," and he steered his concentration back to the ticket booth.

"Read it," Renée commanded.

Jonah's expression tightened as he perused the article: "Marine veteran James T. Willett accidentally punctured a gas line with the frame of a stolen painting resulting in the destruction of the Guerneville Inn..." The piece went on to describe how Mr. Willett had been discovered later that night in a shallow grave beneath a willow tree along the banks of the Russian River. Foul play was suspected.

For a long minute, they looked into each other's blank expression before Jonah reread the headline. "Damn, we got lucky," and he let the newspaper fall from his hands.

Another sight, however, soon replaced their fears of the previous night. Men in black suits moved through the crowd asking questions. Feds walked up and down the ticket line. Hippies and jocks pulled out their wallets, displaying bills. One of the suits appeared to be holding up a twenty, inspecting both sides. Without warning, he marched to the ticket office and placed a piece of plywood into the cashier slot. A "Sold Out" sign appeared. A couple hundred Deadheads yelled their frustration, demanding satisfaction.

⅄

The band, after a lengthy rendition of "Dark Star", carted their instruments from the outdoor stage and approached the rear entrance to The Barn while Bear held open the door. Jonah gave him a thumbs up, which the soundman returned with a grin. In a few hours, Sonny would finalize the deal for the LSD distribution and Otis would be free. Or at least that was the plan.

Teenagers milled around, not knowing what to do. They hadn't come all this way just to smell the country air.

Inside the dance hall, the Dead started off with "Dancin' In the Streets". Jerry's guitar sang soft, weaving Indian and blues into rhythmic melodies before ratcheting up the tempo. When the dose got too heavy, he wrapped it up with an easy-going funky groove.

"Viola Lee Blues" began in grungy fashion with Weir and Lesh spinning their magical webs, flinging little strains all over the place while Garcia went into some bluegrass before switching over to sitar-like flavors. His dizzying notes between the verses were long and electric, winding out to where you thought the song would never return. Lesh and Weir strummed their way back in, relaxing the vibe once again while Pigpen locked onto his harmonica. Unable to track time, stoners swayed across the dance floor. After another fifteen minutes, the climax exploded with scorching Garcia licks, hanging onto the rhythm, Hart making love to the drums with soft staccato brushes.

"The Midnight Hour" rounded out the set in a half hour of glorious chaos with Pigpen rapping away. The screeching throng rocked out, riding bolts of lightning into pools of psychedelic bliss.

The melody drifted outside, catching up with Jonah and Renée. He started to explain the meaning of the song when she interrupted him.

"We aren't getting inside, are we?" Renée said.

"Not with the Feds hanging around," Jonah said.

Renée chortled. "I find it ironic that you are fifty feet from a Dead concert and can't attend."

"A first," Jonah said as he shrugged, pretending that it was no big deal.

⅄

The throng outside grew anxious. A few in their block sweaters and jackets started hammering through the wall with their feet. The Barn possessed no insulation or inner paneling as it was constructed for fair weather use only. Teens wormed their way through the manmade hole. More followed, eager to gain entrance anyway they could. One managed to wiggle his way down the bathroom vent. Another found access by crawling under the raised dance floor and entering through a trapdoor.

Others, however, took their anger out on each other. City kids paraded to the tennis courts. For several years, this had been the arena where toughs would defend the honor of their high school. A large circle formed around two combatants. An Irish lad from the Mission District rolled up his sleeves, ready to do battle with his opponent, a noted football player from Washington High.

Malt liquor made its way through the crowd as teens rooted for their respective champion. The challengers danced around the makeshift ring, warming up, pretending to be the next Muhammad Ali. An inebriated jock wanted a better view and shoved another into a tight cluster. Bodies spilled to the asphalt. A lad, wearing his gray and red jacket, rose and punched the nearest person. The skirmish soon matured into a brawl. Hippies, angered by the early closure of the dance hall, put aside their love beads and joined the melee.

⅄

Sirens sounded from miles away. Black-and-whites screamed past the roadblock to the village center. Clumps of jocks and squatters rushed from the tennis court. Deputies and CHP stepped from their cruisers, corralling youngsters on the fly.

A black Caddy pulled up near the water fountain. A Negro got out alongside a brute in a blue uniform and another wearing a salt-and-pepper goatee and a hawk nose.

"Stay close," Jonah said to Renée on the run.

They followed the pack of brawlers as it headed toward the tunnel. In Jonah's rush, the feathered fedora flew off his head. He went to recover it when Renée pulled on him, telling him to forget it. Jonah returned his expression to his pursuers. Papa Al's vision locked onto the teenager's.

The gang of kids sprinted through the tube and under the roadway. Jonah and Renée kept pace as they ran down the bank and across the pedestrian bridge to the beach on the far side of the Russian River.

The horde dismantled one end of the wooden bridge. The flimsy walkway collapsed into several pieces under the pressure of the current. Teenagers felt emboldened, dropping their pants with a greeting to the lawmen across the stream.

With the addition of time, jocks and hippies from different walks of life rallied together and rolled up the wooden boardwalk. A six-foot high pyre soon decorated the beach. A young woman in her braids and moccasins tossed a lighted match onto a trail of kerosene. Flames exploded into the night sky. Embers soared a hundred feet or more.

Jonah and Renée hid within the gathering near the blaze. Police and others began to clear the debris from the fallen bridge to ford the stream. Whistles blew. Warnings from a bullhorn echoed off the valley floor. Chaos took control again. Teens sprinted in every direction.

Jonah held Renée's hand and told her to flee.

"What about you?" she asked.

"I'm staying."

"You'll be arrested."

"I know. That's the idea."

"*Stupide*," she said in French and sped away.

⅄

Jonah stood rigid while others peeled off into the blackberry thicket or down a service road or further along the beach. The pack thinned out in a hurry until he was the lone figure beside the inferno.

Maloney spotted the kid from the Fillmore. "Over there," he said to Papa Al, pointing to Jonah.

A smile grew on Papa Al as he and his two comrades marched along the sand where a boardwalk once rested. They came to the burning pile of wood and Jonah.

"Jonah," Papa Al said, "your father has been worried sick regarding your sudden disappearance."

"Yeah, you little shit," Abraham Berkowitz added. "Had to close the shop to look for your ungrateful ass."

"Now that we have finished with the heartfelt-reunion-part of this exchange," Papa Al said to Jonah, "we would appreciate the photos," and he held out his hand in expectation.

"Don't have them with me," Jonah said stalling, looking back toward the pedestrian bridge to the charging file of deputies.

Sergeant Maloney patted down the kid before turning around and shaking his head to Papa Al.

Papa Al took his time, absorbing this information, before lighting a stogie. After a few puffs, he said to Jonah, "There is no need for you to play the hero for Mr. Graham. You are but a sullied pawn in his fight with downtown. There is nothing that you owe him...nothing," and he let the words hang in the air.

"What's going on here?" a deputy said as he arrived.

"So good to see you again, Sheriff McGee," Papa Al said. "We have found our fugitive," and he gestured to Jonah. "Remember? He was the one we told you about, the one who absconded with some very incriminating evidence in an investigation back in San Francisco."

Jonah looked on, waiting for the right opportunity.

"I told you boys before," the sheriff said, "that the Feds would be interested in this young man's association with Sonny Barger and those phony bills."

"I got three words for you," Sergeant Maloney said to the sheriff. "Nob... Hill...Theater."

A nervous tic ran up the sheriff's face. Jonah saw the man back peddle. Papa Al motioned for Maloney, but before the burly cop could cuff Jonah, the kid kicked Sheriff McGee in the shins.

"Damn!" the sheriff said as he massaged his leg. He rose to his full length, saying, "That's it. The kid is coming with me. Nobody assaults a lawman in these parts and leaves without so much as a how do you do."

"Would you prefer that we pay a visit to the missus?" Papa Al said.

"She ain't home," the sheriff said. "Went to visit her sister over in Santa Rosa for the night."

Chapter 25

Six patrol cars, with lights flashing, cruised into Guerneville along Highway 116. Even though the hour neared midnight, tourists and locals jammed the sidewalks, gawking at the parade of black-and-whites.

The Labor Day weekend had brought a plethora of excitement to the Russian River area. Besides the much talked about brawl at the Dead concert in Rio Nido, there was plenty of buzz over the counterfeit money as well as the recent homicide of a Marine veteran.

The patrol cars pulled into the parking lot of the sheriff's office. Handcuffs secured dozens of inebriated young men to various handle holds inside the vehicles. Sheriff McGee told Jonah to stay put, that the FBI was investigating a lead in Cazadero.

"When will the Feds return?" Jonah asked.

"Tomorrow some time," and the sheriff locked the car doors and went into his headquarters with the other deputies.

The jail possessed one cell, which on most occasions was sufficient to hold a night's catch of local miscreants, but this was no ordinary night. The patrol cars would serve as holding pens until morning.

For the next several hours, Jonah squirmed inside the patrol car, shifting his weight, trying to find a comfortable position. His four other "inmates" pulled and yanked and kicked to acquire more space. The scene replayed itself in the other four squad cars. Some twenty detainees shivered while waiting for the sun to show itself.

Being in the custody of the sheriff provided a safe haven for the time being. It also insured the well-being of Renée and the others from the long reach of Papa Al whose interest lay solely in the whereabouts of Jonah.

⅄

A homeless man cupped his eyes to ward off the rising sun's glare as he squinted into a patrol car. Bodies clothed in different outfits began to wiggle. Jonah sat up and stretched an arm before realizing that it was attached to another. The grogginess from Jonah's fitful sleep vanished as he steered his vision outside to a trio of men who stood behind the vagrant.

A burly frame in a blue uniform shoved the homeless man aside, telling him to beat it. Another with a salt-and-pepper goatee and a hawk nose rendered a second nudge to the defenseless person.

"Restrain yourselves," Papa Al said to his two companions before lighting a cigar. "Let us not import the war to our shores," and he handed the transient a dollar bill and said goodbye.

"You give gangsters a bad name," Sergeant Maloney said to Papa Al as Abraham Berkowitz nodded in agreement.

"There is no cause to be uncivil, gentlemen," Papa Al said before glancing into the patrol car where Jonah sat. "I'll be seeing you soon, my friend," and he blew a cloud of smoke into the windshield.

I'm counting on it, Jonah thought as he returned a grin to the mobster. Papa Al and the others entered the sheriff's office where a lawman sat behind a desk eating a salad.

"You boys still here, I see," Sheriff McGee said.

"We are not leaving without Mr. Jonah Berkowitz," Papa Al said.

"I told you, he's gotta do some time for assaulting me. "'Sides, the Feds wanna…"

"Want to talk with him," Papa Al interrupted, finishing the sheriff's sentence. "Yes, you've made the FBI's intentions very clear."

Papa Al gestured to Maloney who stepped to the phone and dialed a YUKON number. The sergeant greeted the person on the other end before handing the phone to the sheriff, saying that someone would like to have a word with him.

"Who's this?" the sheriff said into the receiver.

"Thomas Cahill, chief of police for the City and County of San Francisco."

The one-way conversation told of a disastrous outcome for Sheriff McGee if he did not comply with Papa Al's request regarding Jonah Berkowitz. "Besides a note of condemnation from the state attorney general, you can expect an official investigation into your...," and the chief paused to catch the right phrasing before continuing, "...an official investigation into your sexual indiscretions. All of which would become public record."

The pair concluded their conversation after which the sheriff returned the phone to its cradle. Without a word, he reached for a ring of keys and led all back to the parking lot. The patrol car was opened and Jonah was released. Cuffed teenagers complained, wanting freedom as well until the sheriff silenced all with a slam of the car door.

Abraham Berkowitz slapped his son across the face before Sergeant Maloney latched onto the boy's arm and escorted him to the backseat of a black Caddy.

"Where are the photos?" Papa Al asked the teenager.

The time had arrived. Jonah remained silent. Must be convincing, he thought.

"Answer him, you little shit," the old man said.

Jonah glared at his father, pausing for effect before saying, "The photos are back in Rio Nido."

⅄

The Caddy wound its way through the village center. The squatters had fled. The hamlet stood empty. Silence occupied the day as the vehicle eased up Canyon Four, the only sound being the crunching of redwood needles under the tires.

Around a sharp bend, Jonah told Maloney to pull over. All exited and walked down a steep path. Blackberry bushes crowded the walkway, which led to a dilapidated shack below. A widow-maker leaned against the side of the house near a window where a shower curtain was used as a shade.

Maloney drew his service revolver as he scanned the area from the back porch. Papa Al eased open the door and stepped into the kitchen. Cobwebs and ancient news articles decorated the confines.

"What a dump," old man Berkowitz said before spying a carving knife on the counter.

Papa Al's guard was up as he walked into the living room where a voice sounded from the shadows. "Hello, asshole."

Maloney quick-stepped beside Papa Al and pointed his gun in the direction of the inky figure. Abraham Berkowitz grabbed his son, putting a blade to his throat.

"Mr. Sonny Barger, is that you?" Papa Al said.

The biker came out from the darkness. "You better believe it is."

Maloney maneuvered for a better angle. Old man Berkowitz used Jonah as a shield.

"You should know," Sonny said, "that I've made a down payment for the distribution rights to the LSD trade in the Haight.

"So Mr. Owsley Stanley has taken favor with the neighborhood's guardian angel, has he?" Papa Al said. "What a pity."

Maloney thought he heard someone and pulled back the window shade and glimpsed outside. Nothing.

"A down payment you say," Papa Al said. "I would imagine that Mr. Stanley is a prudent businessman. One would think that such a person might prefer a complete accounting...upfront. Perhaps the negotiations are still open."

"That's not all," Sonny said. "Owsley has passed on some news, all bad for you."

"Do tell."

"He says that your thugs are holding Dr. Smith and the Free Clinic hostage."

"No harm will come to the good doctor, I assure you."

Sonny squared up to the Negro. "Not what I heard."

Maloney fixed his aim at the chest of the biker.

"I have a proposition for you," Papa Al said. "There is plenty of territory in the district for the both of us. What do you say to a sixty-forty split? Forty percent would make you a wealthy person. Not bad for a small-time outlaw from the East Bay."

No response.

Papa Al saw the resolve in Sonny's expression. "Okay, fifty-fifty."

"You and your boys are to clear out of the Haight," Sonny said.

"And if we don't?"

Sonny nodded to Jonah. "You're up, kid."

On the command from Papa Al, Abraham Berkowitz released his son. Jonah went to the woodstove and pinched out four photos from the cavity of the broken flue. He passed them to the mobster, saying that they were copies.

"I handed the originals to Owsley," Jonah said. "He and the Dead are probably back in San Francisco by now."

Papa Al reviewed the pics. The black and whites showed he and Sergeant Maloney in bed with several call girls at the Fillmore brothel.

"And I suppose that the originals of which you speak are presently in the possession of your Mr. Graham," Papa Al said.

"You suppose correctly," Jonah said.

"Then why the theatrics?" Papa Al asked as he held up the photos.

"You are to show those copies to your employers downtown."

"Why would I want to do that?"

"To insure that they will use their political influence to convince city hall to renew the dance hall permit for Bill Graham's Fillmore Auditorium. Otherwise, the pics will find their way to my friend Hal Hulbert at the *Chronicle*."

"And this would invariably lead to an examination of downtown's association with myself and others. Would that be a fair assumption?" Papa Al said.

"The findings of such an *examination*." Jonah said, "would no doubt leave a lasting stain upon the reputation of certain San Francisco officials, namely Police Chief Thomas Cahill as well as James McGinnis of the Redevelopment Agency."

Abraham Berkowitz saw the future of his money-laundering business going the way of his failing pawnshop. "You little shit," the father said to his son. "You're just like your mother, a self-centered good-for-nothing."

The old man stepped forward. He saw the surprise in his boy's face and showed a smirk. "Yeah, your old lady was a junky who worked up the street. I'm glad she OD'd. Good riddance."

"My mother worked up the street?"

"That's right. At the same shit-hole where those photos were taken," the old man said as he gestured to the black and whites with his knife.

"Sara?" Jonah guessed. "Was my mother's name Sara?"

"That was the one. A waste of humanity."

Memories flooded Jonah's head—the purchase of his favorite music records, the weekly allowance, the store-bought clothes. They weren't the actions of a friend. They were the actions of a mother.

Jonah felt rage and rushed his father. The old man raised the blade to strike, but Jonah plowed him into the broken flue. The old man's head bent backwards and caught the edge of the iron cast stove.

Jonah went to strike him again but there was no response. The boy kneeled to the limp body of his father. Fixed eyes stared back. Jonah dabbed his fingers across the pool of blood, bringing the gore closer in disbelief.

"All that lives must die," Papa Al said in a matter of fact tone.

With the blood of his father on his hands, Jonah couldn't respond.

"Best we move on," Papa Al said. "There's business to attend to."

"You can keep the Fillmore District," Sonny said. "Don't care 'bout no jungle bunnies. Pass out that bad heroin of yours to the entire neighborhood for all I care but don't ever step foot in the Haight again. Understand?"

"I say we kill 'em all," Maloney said, "including this pansy biker," and he pointed the barrel of his gun at the Hells Angel. "Got a wife and five kids to support. No way I'm gonna let this punk ruin everything."

Maloney took aim with his service revolver. The Angel started to backup when a trio banged through the kitchen to the living room. The cop wheeled around. Father Paul held a pickaxe in his hands. Renée raised a hunting rifle while Otis showed a Colt .45, going eyeball-to-eyeball with the cop.

With the distraction, Sonny reached into a duffle bag, seized a sawed-off shotgun and cocked it. The sound of the pump action caused Maloney to freeze.

"Drop the gun," Sonny said to Maloney.

Otis swung the butt of his .45 into the jaw of the cop who dropped to the floor. "That's for all the brothers in the Fillmo," Otis said over the unconscious man.

"God bless you, my son," Father Paul said to Otis.

"Are we about done here, gentlemen?" Papa Al asked.

"What about your friend?" Sonny asked, pointing to the senseless Maloney.

"Let sleeping dogs lie," Papa Al said as he walked over the body, puffing on his cigar. From the exit, he called back over his shoulder, "He'll find his way back to the City…eventually."

⅄

They gathered outside beside the VW bus where Sonny turned to Jonah. "Thanks, kid, for arranging the meeting with Papa Al."

"It was the least I could do," Jonah said knowing full well that the action was as much to save his own skin as anything else.

"I figured out what you were up to," Sonny said, "when your girlfriend returned and told us that you *wanted* to get caught. The warning gave us time to arrange a proper welcome."

Another thought came to the Angel and he said, "Owsley convinced me that everything was cool with any phony bills that might have showed up at the ticket window."

"Yeah?" Jonah said.

"He said you made a call to the Dead's lawyer, Terence Hallinan," Sonny said.

"I remembered what Garcia said one night at the Fillmore when the law impounded some of the band's gear," Jonah said. "Thought I'd take a chance and inquire. Turns out that the Dead's homeowner's policy covers the loss of revenue as well. In the short of things, the band won't be out any money."

Jonah shifted his weight before asking, "What about Otis?"

"He had my Colt .45 back there at the cabin, didn't he?" Sonny said.

"Nice to be standin'," Otis said before adding, "Roadblocks are down. Can we get? I got a date with a Marine."

"If the roads are clear," Jonah said, "the Feds have probably left."

"That means my boys can get back here to pick up the body," Sonny said to Jonah. "We'll take your old man to George Wethern's place in Ukiah."

"Promise me you'll give a decent burial for the *little shit*," Jonah said, stealing one of his old man's favorite lines.

"We'll use nothing but the finest dirt," Sonny said. "By the way, here's a little something for the road," and he tossed a saddlebag to Jonah.

Jonah unfastened the pouch. Rolls of cash met his examination. It was his get-away stash. He made a quick account and said, "There's only two thousand here. What happened to the other grand?"

"Call it a finder's fee. Good luck, kid," and Sonny retreated toward the cabin.

Jonah's vision tracked the biker's steps until he disappeared down the steep path and through the side door. The Angel had work to do. An image came to Jonah of his old man wrapped in a shower curtain—eyes stared back in a fixed trance above a hawk nose and a salt-and-pepper goatee.

The teenager felt as if fate had cheated him. His mother was taken from him far too soon while his dad was never a dad. That's life. Bullshit, that's *my* life, he thought, and he stepped away. His eyes welled up as he gazed at the distant ridge. Don't shed your tears on him, he thought. But they came, one by one.

Renée moved to his side and put an arm around him. "You okay?"

Jonah let the moistness linger on his cheek as if wanting something to remember the moment. "My old man told me once that he had ambitions for us to rule the Fillmore together. At the time it gave me hope that on some level we might find that place where fathers and sons grow alongside each other, if even for the wrong reasons."

Otis called out, telling his buddy to hurry. "We got just four hours to report for transport to basic."

With a tender touch, Renée led Jonah back to the van. The vehicle motored down Canyon Four and through the village center where a solitary figure swept debris into a pile. Gone were the hippie squatters and the jocks. The Barn, the outdoor stage, the lodge and other buildings were shuttered for the season.

They traveled west two miles to the bus depot in Guerneville. Otis exited the van and spotted an oncoming Greyhound.

"It's our bus," he said to Jonah. "Move it!"

Jonah stepped to him and straightened out the ruffles in his white shirt before a stench of body odor fouled the morning air. "If you're going to impress those Marines, you might want to shower."

"You're comin', right?"

"Like I've said before, Vietnam is not my fight."

"What about the pawnshop?" Otis suggested.

"Not interested," Jonah said. "Besides, the law may be waiting for me. There were plenty of witnesses to my old man's death."

"That was self-defense," Otis said.

"Maybe."

Otis glanced inside the van and saw Renée waving goodbye. He turned back to Jonah, saying, "You headin' north?"

"Thought I might figure out what all the fuss is with these French Canadians."

"The brother's still pissed at you for losing his hat," Otis said in the third person. "How's I suppose to hook up with the ladies without my hat?"

Jonah picked an object from the front pocket of his jeans. "This might help," and he pinned a Bronze Star onto the breast pocket of Otis's burgundy coat.

"My medal," Otis said with a stunned expression. "Thanks, dude," and he polished it with his sleeve. "How I look?"

"I have to admit, it fits you well." Jonah looked past Otis and saw the bus driver close the door. "You better get going."

"Right."

"*You and me, the world on its knee*," Jonah said before embracing Otis.

The Greyhound started to pull away from the curb when Otis rushed to its side and banged on the door. The bus jerked to a halt. Otis turned around to his friend, patting the Bronze Star with affection.

Jonah stared down Main Street as the coach motored out of town. Attachments that reached back to his birth seemed to fade as the vehicle vanished from sight. He remembered sitting with Sara in the lobby of the brothel entertaining prospective johns; running pickpocket scams on unsuspecting outsiders; sharing a moment with John Handy in the back room at Mario Sullivan's place; witnessing the underbelly of the Haight with his childhood buddy.

But what he would miss most of all was his association with Bill Graham and the Fillmore Auditorium where the threads of music connected him to life. Without it, he feared he would slide into the abyss of the mundane, paying homage to the rituals of everyday boredom.

He climbed aboard the van and slumped back into his seat. He closed his eyes…and there it was—his favorite song. Lyrics arrived from some deep place, loud and strong:

"Gonna wake up in the morning /
Gonna pack my bags, Lord /
I'm gonna beat it on down the line."

The music hadn't abandoned him. It was always there. It always will be. He exchanged a confident look with Renée as Father Paul called out to him from the driver's seat.

"Shall we go home, my son?"

Historical Notes

The San Francisco Scene:

Bill Graham (1931—1991) was a music promoter with a tough background. His mother and a sister were gassed by Nazis. At the tender age of nine he trekked across Europe, surviving off apples, eventually finding his way to Portugal where he boarded a ship to New York. After serving in Korea, he worked as a New York cab driver before coming to San Francisco where in 1965 he managed the S.F. Mime Troupe. Bill Graham credits Charles Sullivan with getting his start in the concert business. As manager of the Fillmore Auditorium, Graham's efforts to renew the dance hall permit were stonewalled by downtown until he blackmailed a crooked cop by taking pictures of him entering a brothel across the street. He went on to manage Fillmore East (East Village, N.Y.) and Fillmore West (10 South Van Ness Ave, S.F.) as well as Winterland Ballroom (Post & Steiner, S.F.). Musicians who signed with his Fillmore Records label included Rod Stewart, Elvin Bishop, Cold Blood, and Tower of Power. Graham was killed in a helicopter crash near Novato, California, on October 25, 1991 at the age of sixty.

Fillmore Auditorium was built in 1912, originally known as the Majestic Dance Hall & Academy. The name changed to the Ambassador Dance Hall, which hosted big bands in the 1930s and was operated as a roller rink from 1939 to 1952. Throughout the venue's lifespan, people of color were allowed to perform there but not permitted as customers until Charles Sullivan took over the lease. Ultimately, he changed the name to something more familiar to contemporary concertgoers, something that reflected the neighborhood: the Fillmore Auditorium. Since 2007 it has been retained as a music venue operated by Live Nation.

Charles Sullivan (1910—1966) was the top black music promoter west of the Mississippi during the fifties. He turned the Fillmore District of San Francisco into Harlem of the West. After-hours jazz clubs featured Miles Davis, John Handy, John Coltrane, Billie Holiday, Louis Armstrong, Thelonious Monk, Mastersounds with Wes Montgomery and Benny Barth, and so many more. Then one night in a dark alley in August, 1966, Charles Sullivan was found dead under very mysterious circumstances. The S.F.P.D. ruled it a suicide while the coroner said it was not. Homicide inspector Jack Cleary stuck with the suicide theory despite Diane Feinstein's attempts to convince him otherwise. Sometime later during a raid on Marion Sullivan's speakeasy, a participating police officer made the family connection and told Marion he knew who killed his brother. Marion, however, was too afraid to follow up on the claims.

Belva Davis (1932—) was the first African-American woman to become a television reporter on the West Coast. During her career, she won eight Emmy Awards. From 1961-1968, she was editor for the San Francisco *Sun Reporter Newspaper.* While employed there, she investigated Charles Sullivan's murder in 1966 and was told that powerful interests were behind his death. Belva Davis was pulled off the story and the *Sun Reporter* stopped covering it. Ms. Davis now lives in Petaluma, California.

The Grateful Dead was formed in 1965 amid the counterculture movement. They and Big Brother and Janis Joplin all lived in Marin County together near Lagunitas before renting separate quarters in the Haight-Ashbury District of San Francisco. Jerry Garcia was a scrappy kid who was born on August 1, 1942 in the Excelsior District of the City. He got in trouble for skipping classes at Balboa H.S. and in 1959 his mother moved the family to Cazadero in rural Sonoma County. He attended Analy H.S. in Sebastopol but did not graduate after stealing his mother's car. As punishment he was forced to join the U.S. Army. Accruing many counts of AWOL, he was given a general discharge on Dec. 14, 1960. Classically trained trumpeter Phil Lesh performed bass guitar. Bob Weir played rhythm guitar. Ron Pigpen McKernan played keyboards and harmonica until shortly before his death in 1973 at age 27. Bill Kreutzmann played drums along with Mickey Hart. Their devoted fan base, known as Deadheads, stayed faithful to the band's eclectic style, which fused country, folk, bluegrass, blues, jazz, and psychedelic rock. Their contracts stated that they had to be allowed a minimum of five hours on stage, which matched the length of an average acid trip. The band was a regular feature at the Fillmore Auditorium in San Francisco where they started as an intro group for Jefferson Airplane. Garcia died of a heart attack in 1995 in Marin County. Phil Lesh settled in San Rafael and runs Terrapin Crossroads Restaurant while Bob Weir lives in Mill Valley and tours with his band, RatDog. Drummer Mickey Hart went on to sink roots in Occidental where he continues to experiment with music created from radio waves and brain patterns.

Haight-Ashbury was the main scene in the late sixties of the counterculture movement. The youth believed in a society without the interference of government. A system of bartering took hold where food, clothing, housing, medical needs, music and even advice were freely distributed. This was at the heart of the tenets of the Diggers, a radical community-activist group. They were anarchists who had a close association with a guerrilla theater outfit known as the San Francisco Mime Troupe, led by Peter Coyote who later became a film star. The Diggers opened numerous Free Stores where you could find bell-bottoms, beads, eight track tapes, patchouli oil, or a red ribbon for your hair…at no charge. The Free Clinic was another example of community activism. Dr. Smith, from nearby UCSF, ran the medical facility, located at 409 Clayton on the corner of Haight. The clinic survived on donations and music concert benefits, which were often held at the Fillmore Auditorium.

The Switchboard on Fell Street would find shelter for homeless teens. The leather shop at Xanadu, the I/Thou Coffee Shop, the Psychedelic Shop and the Pacific Ocean Trading Company were just some of the other local hangouts.

Summer of Love: The Jefferson Airplane lived at 2400 Fulton Street while The Grateful Dead were just five blocks away at 710 Ashbury. Janis Joplin lived nearby at 635 Ashbury before moving to 122 Lyon Street. If that wasn't enough, other neighbors included Big Brother and the Holding Company who resided at 1090 Page Street. But the dream would fade quickly. One hundred thousand drifters (midwest teens, Vietnam Vets, college kids, and curiosity seekers) would invade the Haight during the Summer of Love in 1967, overwhelming the neighborhood's resources. Pimps, drug dealers and the greedy soon ravaged the district. By the fall the area had become a wasteland, ruled by opportunists. The dream was loved to death, decaying from within.

George Wethern (1939—) was vice president of the Oakland chapter of the Hells Angels. His 156-acre ranch located near Ukiah in northern California was bought with club money but placed in his name. It became a burial ground for interlopers and disloyal members. The law raided the ranch and found drugs, weapons and three bodies. George Wethern and his wife were arrested. He soon became a state witness in a deal where he and his wife received immunity in exchange for helping the police locate other bodies. Mr. and Mrs. Wethern are presently in the witness protection program.

Robert Hubert "Sonny" Barger (1938—) was the founding member (1957) of the Oakland chapter of the Hells Angels Motorcycle Club. He and his fellow bikers considered themselves caretakers of the Haight-Ashbury during the Summer of Love. They provided free security for music concerts, aided Huckleberry House with the corralling of wayward children, and assisted the Diggers with the distribution of free food, clothing and medical services. The Hells Angels and acid began their chaotic relationship in 1966 down at Ken Kesey's farm in La Honda along the San Francisco peninsula. Kesey was fresh off a commercial success with his novel, *One Flew Over the Cuckoo's Nest,* and celebrated by hosting Acid Test gatherings. There the Angels met Owsley Stanley, a.k.a. Bear, who was the sound manager for The Grateful Dead. Owsley was the first private individual to manufacture mass quantities of LSD, producing more than ten million doses between 1965-1967. Soon the Angels handled both wholesaling and retailing, enjoying a near monopoly of acid distribution in San Francisco. Sonny Barger lives in Modesto, California.

Papa Al was a successful speed dealer who lived in a Berkeley mansion. He began volunteering at the Free Clinic in the Haight-Ashbury, passing himself off as a Good Samaritan. It soon became clear, however, that he intended to use the clinic as a base for his drug operation. When Dr. Smith ordered him to leave, Papa Al put out a contract on the good doctor—anyone who knocked off Smith would get $100 worth of speed. Dr. Smith called Sonny Barger when push came to shove. The Hells Angel had a face-to-face meeting with Papa Al and supposedly told the thug never to set foot in the neighborhood again OR ELSE.

Terrence Hallinan (1936—) is an American lawyer and politician from San Francisco, California. Born to Progressive Party presidential candidate, Vincent Hallinan, Terrence enjoyed partaking in fisticuffs as a young man. Due to his criminal record, the California State Bar refused to admit him, which was later overturned by the state supreme court. He began his legal career during the 1960's counterculture, defending hundreds of drug charges including those against The Grateful Dead, Big Brother and other musicians. Janis Joplin's biographer alleges that Hallinan almost died after the singer shot him up with heroin at her apartment in the Haight-Ashbury District. David Talbot in his best selling novel, *Season of the Witch*, verifies this and adds that Janis made love to Peggy Caserta, Hallinan's girlfriend, while the attorney lay unconscious on the floor.

Charles Manson (1932—) is an American criminal and former cult leader. Manson borrowed the term "helter-skelter" from a Beatles' tune. He used the term to describe what he believed to be an impending apocalyptic race war, which he preached in the Haight District during the late sixties. Members of his quasi-commune also lived along the Russian River on Armstrong Woods Road. Several were suspected of murdering United States Marine veteran James T. Willett, but no arrests were made. At one time, Manson had aspirations of becoming a singer-songwriter. He lived with Dennis Wilson of the Beach Boys but could not convince the musician to produce his songs. In 1971 he was found guilty of conspiracy to murder seven people, including the actress Sharon Tate, a former friend of Dennis Wilson. Charles Manson is serving nine concurrent life sentences in Corcoran State Prison, California.

West Sonoma County Scene:

Occidental was settled by a criminal named Christopher Folkmann. He was a Danish sailor, who was hiding in the area after stealing a military boat from San Francisco Bay during the gold rush days. He changed his name to Bill Howard and settled in the hills of west Sonoma County in 1849. The town was named after Folkmann's assumed identity (Howard's Station) until 1876 when it became "Occidental." Italian immigrants arrived here in the 1880s to work as farmers, coal miners and loggers. The Gonnella (Union Hotel), Negri (Negri's Restaurant) and Fiori families (Fiori's Restaurant at the Altamont Hotel) are examples of Italian influence on the enclave.

Morningstar Commune (a.k.a. Morningstar Ranch, The Digger Farm) was an active open land counterculture commune in the late sixties located between Sebastopol and Occidental in rural Sonoma County. The thirty-acre ranch belonged to Lou Gottlieb (one of the original founders of the Limeliters). He coined the acronym LATWIDNO (Land Access To Which Is Denied No One). The commune of 30-50 hippies grew vegetables for the San Francisco Diggers. Gottlieb attempted to leave the land to God. A series of court appeals culminated in the 9th District Court ruling that God had no property rights in the state of California. As of 2013 the compound is up for sale by Gottlieb's heirs.

Jenner: Under Mexican rule, Muniz Rancho extended from Timber Cove to Duncans Mills. A 5,000 acre portion of this Rancho was purchased by John Rule in 1867. He built a sawmill at Russian Gulch with a capacity of 40,000 feet of lumber a day. The historical mill of Jenner was destroyed by fire on September 9, 1949. The town was also known for its boathouse, which crafted canoes and rowboats. Elijah K. Jenner, a dentist in Healdsburg, made Penny Island his own where he lived part-time. It is believed that when a name was needed for the new town, one of Penny Island's early owners was selected. The Hells Angels made a stop there in the late sixties. They were refused service at a local inn where an employee shot one of the bikers. Deputies escorted the batch to the Mendocino County line to avert further trouble. Some old timers say they have never seen so many bikers in one place.

Cazadero: George Simpson Montgomery, a wealthy businessman from San Francisco, purchased the town in January, 1888, naming it Cazadero ("The Hunting Place"). In 1890 he became a "Born Again" Christian and tried to make Cazadero a temperance town through the use of "restrictive covenants", but there were many clandestine bootleg stills hidden in the hills to counter his efforts.

Elim Grove is often stated to be "mile" spelled backwards (the grove of redwood trees along Austin Creek about a mile south of town). The name, however, comes from a passage in the Bible: Exodus 15:27 where scholars interpreted Elim as being "a refreshing place". The Bohemian Club made their summer encampments there from 1887-1891. These facilities were expanded for a number of organizations including the Salvation Army Church, the San Francisco YMCA, and the Boy Scouts of America. The city of Berkeley began leasing the fifty-acre camp in 1927 and advertised it as the *Cazadero Redwood Camp*. In 1957 it was known as the Berkeley Music Camp and in 1996 it became the Cazadero Performing Arts Camp.

Berry's Mill & Lumberyard: In 1877 the North Pacific Coast Railroad ran from Sausalito to the Cazadero sawmill. The narrow-gauge train carried redwood to S.F. and returned with weekenders until 1933 when it made its last run. Merrill Berry, son-in-law of George Montgomery, and his son Loren began a downtown mill in 1941 on the former NWP railroad depot site. The milling operations were moved to its current location on Highway 116 in 1983. In 1989 there was a tragic fire that destroyed the mill, but the community rallied. Six months later the buzz of saws could be heard once again. Bruce and Jim Berry currently manage the business.

Pole Mountain was established in 1898 as a U. S. signal station to triangulate map positions and elevations. The benchmark was pried from the ground and stolen and remains on Cazadero's *Ten Most Wanted List.*

Lions Head Ranch was formerly known as the Starbuck Ranch where Enoch and Eura Kendall and their son Tom were murdered on July 23, 1910. The Kendalls were in a lease partnership arrangement with Margaret Starbuck to run the ranch. Margaret wanted them to quit the lease early and after their refusal, she sent a Japanese woodcutter, Manjiro Yamaguchi, to "give 'em hell." Yamaguchi murdered the entire Kendall family and scattered their dismembered bodies throughout the ranch. He confessed his crime and then disappeared. Supposedly, the deceased haunt the ranch today seeking revenge.

Roy Cornett (1899-1969) was the ranch foreman for Helmuth Seefeldt who was bludgeoned to death in 1942. His body was soon discovered in a shallow grave on his Creighton Ridge sheep ranch. Cornett was arrested for his murder, but there wasn't enough evidence for a conviction. Later, he was sent to prison for forging checks and printing counterfeit money, but not before he told the locals to take his house in order to cheat the Feds of their share.

The Cazanoma Lodge (now the CazSonoma Inn) is located deep in the hills of Cazadero. At one time it was a hunting lodge serving German-American food. The stone mill building was built in 1941 along a tributary to Kidd Creek where you were able to fish for your dinner.

Guerneville Inn existed where the parking lot is today next to the Coffee Bazaar on Armstrong Woods Road in the town of Guerneville. It served Italian faire. Supposedly, the owners shot a cow near a fence line and brought it back to the restaurant for the menu. The building blew up in a fireball when thieves accidentally ruptured a propane line during their escape with stolen paintings.

Johnson's Beach was established nearly a century ago as a private resort by Gertie and Ernie Johnson. In 1967, brothers Clare and Herbert Harris purchased the complex. It consisted of thirty-five campsites, ten cabins, a lodge, and a five-bedroom bungalow. The eleven-acre site has served as a recreational hot spot with beach umbrellas, paddle boats, old-time music and soft-serve ice cream among its many standbys. After forty-eight years under his direct management, Clare and his family sold the resort in March of 2015 to Nick Moore and Dan Poirier.

Pageant of Fire Mountain was sponsored by the Guerneville Chamber of Commerce to honor Indian Summer on Labor Day weekend as well as to lure tourists one last time to fill the local lodges and dance floors. The play was held across the river from Johnson's Beach at Parker's Resort. Actors, dressed in Native American costumes, carried torches as they danced along switchback trails. The hillside would burst into flames as the pageant concluded with the marriage of an Indian maiden to a male warrior of a rival tribe.

The River Queen ferried sunbathers between Guerneville's Johnson's Beach and Rio Nido. Thomas Bidwell (Bid) Green and his wife, Amelia, operated the twelve-passenger boat. The charge was ten cents one-way, fifteen cents round trip. The voyage was accompanied by the strains of "Cruising Down the River", over and over. Bid Green died in Sebastopol, California on Oct. 2, 1978.

Rio Nido is an unincorporated community along the Russian River in northern California, dating back to 1908. Before that it was the site for Korbel's Eagle Nest Sawmill. Many famous Big Bands played in Rio Nido during the 1930's and 1940's. From 1953-1963, Dick Crest & His Musical Celeste was a favorite. In the sixties, a number of rock 'n' roll groups visited the area including The Grateful Dead, Moby Grape, Quicksilver, Big Brother, Morning Glory, and Overbrook Express. The dance hall was known as "The Barn" and was situated near an outdoor stage. In front of the amphitheater were rows of benches and a fire pit. Other buildings included the Rio Nido Lodge, roller skating rink, outdoor bowling lanes, arcade, soda fountain, bingo parlor and shooting gallery. With the addition of a variety shop, grocery store, barbershop, post office and a firehouse it became a self-contained village. Many of these buildings started shifting on their post-and-pier foundations, which extended over a creek. The 1954 flood mark was six feet over the highway, causing further damage. A bulldozer flattened much of the village center and by 1974 the beach had become overgrown with weeds. The tunnel under the county highway, which led to a pedestrian bridge, still exists.

The Grateful Dead played at Rio Nido on September 3rd, 1967. Upon entering the village center with their rig, they hit and brought down the hamlet's iconic road sign, which was commissioned by Harry Harris around 1939. Funds have been recently raised and the sign has been restored.

"Dark Star" was written by lyricist Robert Hunter during this Labor Day weekend at the river. "Alligator" was supposedly written nearby as well. *The Grateful Dead* album featured a live version of "Viola Lee Blues" from the above concert. Reliable sources state that Deadheads did indeed punch their way through the single wall construction to gain entrance while others slid down the bathroom vent of the dance hall.

Hard Times: With the advent of television, Highway 80, and affordable airline rates, the lure of the Russian River faded for many Bay Area vacationers. Cabins were abandoned becoming easy prey. The squatter problem grew to such an extent that many property owners burnt their cabins to the ground rather than have them soiled and defaced by outsiders. It is said that the tennis courts were removed and replaced with a pool specifically to discourage ruffians from using it as a boxing ring. During the late sixties, a standoff ensued between hundreds of squatters and the sheriff's office. The beach boardwalk was rolled up and set afire. The law arrested dozens of youth and detained them in patrol cars overnight since the local jailhouse in Guerneville could not accommodate all the juveniles. But all is not lost. Residents and neighborhood associations have worked hard to bring back the lingering memories from yesteryear.

Also by John McCarty

<u>A THOUSAND SLIPPERS</u>: *A Thousand Slippers*, a historical fiction novel, tells of the fear that paralyzed the West Coast after Pearl Harbor. Nobuo Akita, a Japanese aviator aboard the I-25 submarine, becomes the instrument for the first aerial attack upon North America when he drops his incendiary bombs near the fishing village of Brookings, Oregon. During a later mission, he fails to sink the U.S.S. *Lexington,* which is docked at Hunters Point Shipyard in San Francisco, and escapes through the back alleys of the city. Anne Klausen, a ballerina phenom, uncovers the foreigner and attempts to bring him to justice. In the meantime, her father and several of his vigilante pals go underground to finish a hidden agenda. Anne is forced into an uneasy alliance with Nobuo in order to save her father from his own kind.

"*A Thousand Slippers* is an ingenious and intriguing story with a counterpoint between a Japanese airman on a submarine in the early days of World War II and a colorful cast of characters in San Francisco…a delightful read."

San Francisco Museum and Historical Society

"The author's characters are painted with words in vivid color. You care. You are angry. You feel fear. You hate. You feel the heart-rending frustration of injustice. This is history. Character upon character gets introduced as the fabric of this story becomes more complex and emotionally as well as intellectually deep."

The Sonoma County Gazette

"Armed with a sharp wit, John McCarty weaves iconic characters through a historic maze with such ease and color that we simply shake our heads in a whaddya-know kind of wonderment."

Russian River Times

"I had a blast reading John McCarty's fun, historical novel about the early days of World War II in San Francisco."

Tom Gogola, news editor, *Bohemian*

MEMORIES THAT LINGER: *Memories That Linger* is a coming-of-age novel about fourteen-year-old Sean McGinnis who is torn between a religious calling and primal yearnings. While on vacation during the summer of 1953 along the banks of the Russian River in rural northern California, Sean confronts the aftermath of a family crisis. The resort hamlet of Rio Nido is also undergoing life-changing alterations as persistent rumors fly regarding the Big Band Era's last hurrah. The young lad must endure financial hardship, a wicked aunt, Bohemian Black Coats and country rascals in order to survive.

"In *Memories that Linger*, the author combines those bygone days with a sweet, coming-of-age tale of loss and renewal. A must read."

Robert Digitale, author of *Horse Stalker* and writer for *Press Democrat*

"*Memories* is a nostalgic trip back to the day when the Big Band sound did battle with Rock 'n' Roll. A grand accomplishment."

Benny Barth, drummer for Peggy Lee, Mel Torme, and The Mastersounds.

"John McCarty's novel, *Memories That Linger*, is set in a small pocket town along the banks of the Russian River, transporting the reader back to the fifties with delightful and colorful characters. The author has an uncanny talent for creating quirky but well-rounded characters. *Memories* is a great escape and a fast page turner."

Jeane Sloane, national award winning author of *She Flew Bombers*.

"John McCarty turns pop-culture and local antiquity into a fun and informative journey, a canny blend of lunatic farce and self-assured banter."
Russian River Times

"Mr. McCarty is emerging as one of our truly distinguished local treasures."
The Windsor Times

"The author's *Memories That Linger* renders a wonderful insight into the early 1950's and this intriguing part of the world known as the Russian River. Thank you, John McCarty, for your inspiration."
Johnny Venetti, music and film producer

IN THE ROUGH: *In the Rough* is a contemporary issues novel that revolves around the modern day concern of rural growth control. In 2008 Eddy Peters, a troubled military veteran flees to the backwater village of Monte Rio along the Russian River in northern California for solitude and recovery. However, he is soon swept up in a local political battle. The citizens are divided over a bond measure that would provide the tax revenue needed for the construction of a sewage treatment plant. Some fear the inevitable invasion of bureaucratic agencies and developers. Others agree with their chamber president and a deep-pocket Bohemian, hopeful for a financial facelift of their decaying town. Quirky twists, fate and greed intervene to propel everyone down a surprising conclusion.

"One of the fine accomplishments of Mr. McCarty's novels is his rendering of the tough and unsentimental way of talking you can find in these parts (Russian River Valley)."
Bob Jones, *Sonoma West Times and News*

"*In the Rough* is a little gem. Lots of local color and a fun read."
Sonoma County Gazette

"*In the Rough* is the best mix of eclectic characters since *On the Road.* John McCarty's wild ride through the anti-establishment denizens of the Russian River in Sonoma County is a throwback treat."

Mike Reilly, former county supervisor and president of the California Coastal Commission

"*In the Rough* captures the heart of local politics in its most basic and repugnant form. A must read."

Gil Loescher, professor of international politics at Oxford University, England.

STUMPTOWN DAZE: Set in the early 1960's, John McCarty's *Stumptown Daze* is a wild adventure of comedy and romance. Walt, a sixty-five-year-old San Franciscan with dementia, is bound to a young caretaker, Lani, from the South Pacific. With an uncanny ability to slip away from her, the old man creates havoc as he relives WWII. Haunted by Abigail, his conniving daughter and legal guardian, Lani and Walt manage to slip out of town for an unforgettable Memorial Day weekend in Guerneville in rural Sonoma County.

"From rednecks to prostitutes, sheriffs and politicians, the author vividly portrays the colorful history of the Russian River from yesteryear. Fans of John McCarty, as well as newcomers to his work, will be delighted and enriched by *Stumptown Daze*."

Sonoma County Gazette

"A nice intertwining with well-known names from the past. A fun read."

Russian River Historical Society

"For people who have done too much heavy reading recently, John McCarty's *Stumptown Daze* would serve as a charming antidote. The author shapes a variety of historic plot lines from San Francisco's beatnik North Beach to the Russian River's hokey-pokey."

Sonoma County Historical Society.

"*Stumptown Daze* is kind of a hoot with local history lurking behind it. Read it for the good times."

Sonoma West Times & News

"John McCarty's novel comes to a crescendo with the Stumptown Daze Parade of 1960, which features much that is wild, wonderful and a little off in the River scene. A wonderful experience."

The Upbeat Times

John Michael McCarty is a fourth-generation San Franciscan and retired educator. He was a history instructor on the secondary level as well as at Earl Shilton Community College in England and at St. Mary's College in Moraga, California. He is a member in good standing with the Russian River—, Sonoma County—, and San Francisco Historical Society as well as the Fulbright Association. John has written four previous novels. For more info, go to www.johnmccarty.org.